MELT

by

Robbi McCoy

Bella
BOOKS

2013

Bella Books, Inc.
P.O. Box 10543
Tallahassee, FL 32302

Printed in the United States of America on acid-free paper.

First Bella Books edition 2013

Editor: Katherine V. Forrest
Cover Designer: Judith Fellows

ISBN: 978-1-59493-353-0

EPILOGUE

To the whining disappointment of Gudny and Jaaku, Ortuq extricated himself from the rowdy game on the floor, standing and taking Asa's hand. "Come," he said. "Look outside. Just for a minute."

She wrapped a fur around her head and shoulders so she could follow him outside the hut. She crawled out into a blast of icy air that bit at her exposed skin. Ortuq stood behind her, his arms wrapped around her, and pointed her toward the horizon where colored lights danced against a black backdrop. Green, blue and yellow streamers glimmered like flames of cool fire, swirling up into the dark ceiling above where a million twinkling lights filled the sky. Snow blanketed everything in sight, blue in the darkness of the winter afternoon. Everything was still and silent. The only sound was Ortuq's breath, warm against her cheek.

"They're dancing tonight," he observed quietly.

To Ortuq and his relatives, the lights were souls of the children who had died during birth. He had told her this story after she told him about Torben, the child she had lost. The lights are the lost children dancing at the edge of creation, he had said, at the doors to heaven, happy and forever trouble-free.

The wind was so cold, Asa's nose started going numb almost immediately, but she stood there a while longer. He was right. The lights were especially beautiful today. As much as she longed for the warmth and light of summer, there was magic in a Greenland winter's day. There were other places in the world, she knew, that were completely different from this, that were easier to live in, but at this moment, she couldn't believe there was anyplace on earth more beautiful.

She tilted her head to glimpse her husband behind her, his gentle face tinted blue by the sky lights, and smiled her gratitude.

He smiled back. "The lights are the same color as your eyes today," he said. "So beautiful."

Other Books by Robbi McCcoy

For Me and My Gal
Not Every River
Something to Believe
Songs Without Words
Spring Tide
Two on the Aisle
Waltzing at Midnight

Dedication

To my sweetheart Dot for her inspiring spirit of adventure.

Acknowledgments

I want to express my gratitude to Grace J. Heindorf Nielsen of Nuuk, Greenland, for many things. First of all, for encouraging me to visit Greenland and taking time out to show us around Nuuk. Also for welcoming us into her home and cooking us a meal of traditional Greenlandic foods, an excellent introduction to the culture of the country. Finally, I want to thank her for giving her generous assistance with this story. Without Grace, I'm sure I never would have had the courage to make the trip to such an exotic land. I'm so glad I did. It was the trip of a lifetime.

Much appreciation to Angela Barlow, Joe McKay and David Wakefield for their help with ice climbing techniques. I've learned that no matter how careful a researcher you are, you won't sound like you know your subject unless you do.

I also want to thank my editor, Katherine V. Forrest for her keen perception of my weaknesses. Sorry about the comma explosion, Katherine.

CHAPTER ONE

"Make a wish and blow," her mother had said, hovering above her with a face beaming maternal pride, full of encouragement and expectation, waiting for her little darling to blow out four candles on a rabbit-shaped cake crouched on a white platter and coated in shredded coconut. Her mother had looked so happy she almost didn't want to look away, but there was the CAKE right in front of her, a whole plate of sweet yumminess with her name on it. Literally. It was written in white frosting on a fondant carrot resting across the rabbit's front paws: K-E-L-L-Y.

She had looked the bunny in the face—licorice whiskers, red gum drop nose and Junior Mint eyes—and blew!

What did I wish for? Kelly asked herself, trying to think back twenty-six years.

If she had known anything about how life would unfold, she would have wished for her mother to still be able to smile like that fifteen years later.

She walked swiftly over lichen-covered rock, her footfalls the only sound to reach her ears. There was a soft scuffing from the rubber-soled hiking boots, hardly a sound at all. Anywhere else, she wouldn't have heard even that, but the silence here was so complete that if she had been standing still, she might have heard her heartbeat.

The sun was high in the sky and a delicate breeze wafted in from the bay. *Everything is fine*, she reminded herself. There was no way to get lost, though miles of ubiquitous gray gneiss stretched behind and before her with nothing to mark her progress. No trees. No houses. No telephone poles. No sign of life at all. Not even a bird. In the bay, stretching away from the rocky shore, the same. No boats. Just that exquisitely beautiful expanse of still, shimmering water studded with slabs of ice, all sizes, shapes and textures, sparkling like enormous sugar cubes in the sunlight.

Further out, massive icebergs lined up along the horizon like the buildings of a city skyline, stark and silent, a parade of sculpted statues in a fascinating and infinite variety of profiles. They stood like majestic sentinels, seemingly motionless. But the forms changed day to day as new ones calved off the enormous Jakobshavn Glacier and floated indiscernibly slowly toward the open ocean.

People said that Ilulissat, meaning "icebergs" in Greenlandic, was the most beautiful place in all of Greenland. That was no small claim in a land this big…and this beautiful.

On any other day, she would have had her camera out, trying to catch the way the afternoon sun gave the purest white opacity to the ice. But not today. Her camera was in her backpack and would not be coming out. She couldn't afford the time.

As she hopped a narrow rivulet, her left foot slipped off the side of a rock into a spongy crevice, sinking through the mat of emerald groundcover into mud. She stumbled but avoided a fall.

Watch where you're going! she admonished herself sharply. *If you fall and break your leg, what will happen to Pippa?*

She sucked in a bracing breath, then opened her water bottle. The water was cool and welcome in her dry throat. She had stuffed her jacket into her pack and was comfortable in a short-sleeved T-shirt, walking fast enough to generate her own heat. It was a clear, mild summer day. Despite the warm sunshine and inspiring view, she could barely keep the sense of dread from overwhelming her. But there was no reason to panic as long as she kept moving and kept Disko Bay to her right. That meant she was heading south, and as long as she was heading south, she would reach Ilulissat, her home for the last two weeks. There she would get help for Pippa. *Wherever she was. Whatever had happened to her.*

Kelly felt a lump of emotion rising in her throat. She swallowed it down and screwed the cap on her water bottle. There was no point thinking about that. Any ideas she had about what had happened to Pippa were total guesses. It was as if she had simply vanished from the face of the earth.

After their snack break, Kelly had set up her tripod and gotten caught up in her photography. It had been no more than a half hour until she was ready to move on. That's when she had looked for Pippa. Her backpack lay on the ground nearby, but there was no other sign of her. Kelly had waited a half hour for her return, getting more and more worried. She had then gone searching for her, certain that with the clear air and long distance views she would easily spot that red jacket, even if for some reason Pippa was unable to answer her calls.

But there had been nothing. Just the indifferent rock and the eerie silence of this Arctic landscape. After two weeks in Greenland, the absence of sound still caught her off guard. It reminded her of the complete darkness every cave guide subjects you to. The lights go out and you see nothing but a solid field of black. It's a shock because you realize something that wasn't apparent before, that in the above ground world there's always some light, even in the middle of a cloudy night. It's never completely dark. Just as there is always some light, she had now learned, there is also always some noise. The hum of traffic in the distance, the rustling of leaves, insects chirping. But here there was no sound at all, even with the wind blowing. There was nothing for it to rustle. The only plants growing here were tucked into crevices between the rocks, most of them no more than an inch tall. One exception was the Arctic cottongrass, the delightful "flowers" Kelly had become so taken with. They grew a few inches off the ground on thin bare stems, soft white puff balls the size of a marshmallow. They bent and bobbed in the wind, but their fluffy heads made no sound.

Even in town the silence was almost complete. The other day, she had mentioned the remarkable silence to Pippa, who hadn't understood. She'd never been outside of Greenland. She had been born in Ilulissat and her experience of the rest of the world came from books, television and movies.

"What do you mean there are no sounds?" she'd asked. "I just now heard a dog barking."

"Yes, there are sounds, but in between those sounds, there's nothing. It's like a vacuum. There's no white noise. It's like if you had a fan running and it made a continuous hum. You wouldn't hear it at all after a while. But if it suddenly went off, you'd notice. You'd hear the lack of it. That's what I'm experiencing."

"Like a fan running all the time?" Pippa had screwed up her face, mystified. "Is that what it's like where you live? If I ever come to Colorado, I'll be sure to pack earplugs." She snorted at her joke.

Thinking about Pippa's pretty young face and her carefree snorting laugh reminded Kelly of her current situation, and a wave of despair threatened to swamp her. This morning when they'd set out on their hike, Kelly hadn't thought of it as dangerous at all. Just a little adventure. Lots of people did it. Pippa herself had done it several times. Walking over this same terrain this morning with Pippa leading the way, it hadn't been the least bit scary.

But now she was alone. Intensely alone. In a place she'd never been before, not knowing how urgently Pippa was depending on her to bring help. The decision to continue on her own had been tough. She had waited too long, hoping Pippa would return. She had wasted that hour, sixty minutes during which Pippa could have been bleeding to death for all she knew, and there she'd been, sitting on her butt doing nothing.

She shoved her water bottle into its elastic strap and continued walking, trying to get her mind off Pippa.

What did I wish for? she asked herself again, picturing the rabbit cake. She didn't know why she was thinking about that birthday. That was one of her earliest memories. Her fourth birthday and a bunny cake. It must have impressed her, since she remembered it in such vivid detail.

She decided she had probably wished for a bicycle like her older sister Jessica's, two wheels and almost too tall to get on the seat. She had tried to ride Jess's bike a couple of times, but Jess was fiercely possessive, especially after Kelly had taken a spill and bent the front fender. Their father had tried to bend it back into shape, but it always rubbed against the tire after that. And Jess never forgave her. Nope…that was an exaggeration. She did eventually forgive her when she got a new bike on her thirteenth birthday, a beautiful purple mountain bike. Kelly was so jealous of that bike she had fantasies for weeks about bending the fender on that one too. But she hadn't dared. Jess would have broken her arm.

Being the youngest of three girls, it seemed to her that her sisters always had better stuff than she did. But there were advantages to being the youngest too. You could get away with things. Jess, who was six years her senior, wouldn't have dared break her arm no matter what she'd done. She would have never been forgiven for such a vicious attack on the baby. The youngest child remains "the baby" all her life to parents and siblings. No matter her age, in their minds, she was the precious, adorable holy terror with the mad twinkle in her eyes, looking for the next opportunity to get away with some wickedness.

As recently as last month when she'd visited her sister Lee and offered to play Scrabble with her ten-year old nephew, Lee had said, "Okay, but you have to use real words with him. You can't just make up words like you do."

"I don't do that anymore!" Kelly had protested. "I only did that when I was a kid because you and Jess always beat me. You let me do it because it was the only way I could ever win."

Lee had given her one of those indulgent looks and said, "Well, I'd rather Trevor learn it correctly."

It was no use trying to overcome the image of herself in the minds of her family members. It was like they carried around a twenty-year-old photo of her in their brains. She would forever be a mischievous girl with ratty hair and knobby knees who broke everything she touched and whose only talent was the ability to suck milk into her nose through a straw and spit it out her mouth. Nothing she'd done since then had made much of an impression. Both sisters had become much more interested in their own lives as they hit puberty, dating boys and getting married. Neither of them seemed to have noticed that Kelly was the one who held the place together after all of the rest of them had gone, after Dad left, when Mom, debilitated by grief and regret, spent her afternoons drinking and her evenings passed out. Kelly had to take care of everything after that—make sure the bills were paid and clothes washed and meals prepared. There was nobody else to do it. She became the mother of the house during her teens, and her mother became the petulant child.

When Kelly was twenty, her mother, whose health was deteriorating, decided to sell the house and move to Portland where Jess lived. They found a nice condo for her only a few blocks away from their house. Jess came down to help her move and kept saying things like, "This is the best thing you could do, Mother. Now you'll get the care you need. I'll make sure you get to the doctor regularly and eat properly."

Nobody acknowledged the effort Kelly had made in the intervening years to try to cheer her mother up, to run her errands, to coax her to eat, and to try, unsuccessfully, to persuade her to quit drinking. Nobody except Jordan Westgate, her professor at Boulder, who was a patient and indulgent confidante, sympathetic and encouraging.

"The important thing is," Jordan had told her, "you did a remarkable job. You kept both you and your mother afloat through a rough time, and you can be proud of that. Your sister may grow to understand that once she has to deal with the same frustrations you've been facing."

It was a prophetic observation. A year later, Jess called in a state of desperation. "I don't know how you put up with this all those years!" By then, Kelly had been on her own for a year and was glad she no longer had the responsibility. Maybe if she'd been more of a complainer, Jess wouldn't have been so eager to adopt their mother in the first place. But she'd had an out-of-date image of Mom too, stuck in her head, an image of a rational, responsible woman involved in the lives of her children and husband, competently and contentedly taking care of all of their needs. It was possible Jess had even thought she was getting a free babysitter by moving their mother to Portland, but as it turned out, she didn't think it was safe to leave her kids alone with their grandmother.

Kelly had enthusiastically reported that phone call to Jordan, who had raised her hand high above her head and declared, "Vindication!"

She had met Jordan Westgate when, as a nineteen-year old sophomore, she had reluctantly walked into Introduction to Geology hoping to get one of her required science credits out of the way without too much agony. Science had never been Kelly's strong suit. She leaned toward the arts. For better or worse, it had been a fateful day. The brusque, wry, quick-witted woman at the front of the class had swept her off her feet, and the course of Kelly's life for the next two years had been established.

She wondered now if Jordan would be like her sisters, incapable of updating her mind's image of Kelly after nearly a decade. Would she still see her as a naïve child, more worthy of pity than friendship? She desperately hoped not.

She stopped walking and scanned the horizon. Somewhere out there in the vast wilderness of Greenland, perhaps within mere miles, Jordan was at work, unaware that she and Kelly were about to meet again. *After nine years, will she recognize me? Will she even remember me?*

She climbed a small rise, getting a better view of her surroundings. A hundred yards ahead was a ravine. She walked up to it and peered into a rocky crevasse littered with pools of reflective water. It was too steep and too deep to cross, continuing inland for several hundred feet before meandering to the right and out of view. On the bay side, the ravine gradually widened until it met open water. There was no way around it in that direction.

She had lost the actual trail almost immediately after her solo journey began. The trail hadn't been visible even this morning when they were actually on it. Bare rock doesn't allow for that, but there were occasional cairns marking the way, piles of rocks placed at intervals to guide hikers along the official path. The official path, Pippa had explained, was simply the easiest one, the most direct, most level and driest, generally following the contours of the coastline. They had passed several of those cairns this morning, but she had seen none for hours. That made Kelly nervous. She had begun to question her decision to head south into the unknown instead of turning back toward Rodebay, a route she had at least already experienced. At the time, it had seemed like a no-brainer. Mileage wise, they were closer to Ilulissat than Rodebay. But that was mileage according to her GPS receiver, and with the rugged nature of the ice-carved terrain, she was beginning to understand the fallibility of that logic. It was too late to second-guess herself now. She had already traveled too far.

She had to keep reminding herself she was doing okay. She knew how to navigate. Maybe she wasn't taking the most efficient route, but she was heading generally, steadily toward Ilulissat.

As she prepared to start off again, she heard a faint mechanical hum and turned to search the bay. She caught sight of a metallic glint far out on the water. Focusing on it, she saw a moving object and gradually recognized it as a small motorboat. There were two men in the boat. It disappeared for a couple of seconds behind an iceberg, then reappeared.

Thrilled, she jumped up and down and waved her arms, trying to get their attention. She let her pack drop off her shoulders and ran, stumbling over the uneven surface toward the shore. "Help! Help!" she yelled as loudly as she could, feeling the strain in her throat. But the boat continued unswervingly on its northerly course. She gradually gave up, recognizing they were too far away to hear her. The clarity of the view was deceptive. There had been no chance they would hear her, even though she had clearly heard their engine. Sound carried for long distances here, but she had been hollering against the wind. Watching the boat disappear from view, she let her arms fall slack at her sides in defeat.

She checked the GPS receiver to see how far she'd come. If she ever doubted the evidence of the bay and the position of the sun to tell her she was going in the right direction, this device would confirm it. The line showing her track was an irregular zigzag. She had gone only two miles toward her goal, a disappointing distance. She wasn't sure how far she still had to go. The GPS unit could only calculate her destination in a straight line and that was obviously not happening, not with this canyon blocking her path. And obstacles yet unknown. At the rate she was going, it could take all day to get to Ilulissat. At least she didn't have to worry about darkness. The sun would hang low on the horizon all night, creating perpetual twilight.

Heading inland, she walked alongside the canyon blocking her path, hoping it wouldn't take too long to circumvent. The official trail was probably further inland, routed in such a way as to avoid impediments like this. On maps of the west coast of Greenland, she had seen how irregular it was, cut up into deep gorges, fjords, lakes and islands. Looking at the map, it was hard to even imagine there was a path you could walk between Rodebay and Ilulissat without a lot of swimming and rock climbing. There was nothing gentle about this place. It was ruggedly beautiful and brutally unforgiving.

She was just one woman in the midst of all of this uncompromising land. If an observer could zoom out, Kelly imagined she would immediately disappear and in her place would be a thin strip of mountainous land, dark and barren. On the west side would be the frigid, endless sea. On the east, the massive solid ice sheet of the interior. On the tenuous fringe of bare land framing the island lived all the life possible in this country—human, animal and plant.

She felt small and humbled in a way she had never felt before. Trudging through this strange territory, so far away from everything she knew, she was completely immaterial.

Except to Pippa, she reminded herself. If she were alive, she would be hinging all her hopes on Kelly. *I'll make it*, she reassured herself. Of course she would make it, but the real question was, how long did Pippa have? Or was it already too late?

CHAPTER TWO

EIGHT HOURS EARLIER

"Sorry, Mrs. Arensen," Kelly said, sitting on the edge of her bed to pull on her hiking boots. "I don't have time for breakfast. I'll just grab a slice of that brown bread and butter on my way out."

Elsa Arensen stood in the doorway in a thin cotton dress that hit her pale legs midcalf. Her coarse hair, a homogenous mixture of gray and honey blonde, was pinned back from her face with pink plastic barrettes shaped like butterflies. Her somber, lined face, thin-lipped mouth and tiny gray eyes all contributed to the look of a no-nonsense woman in the crosshairs of late middle-age. She was tall and lean and sturdy, like a fence post. Her personality fit her appearance. Stern and unyielding, she was a paragon of stoic moral rectitude and she expected no less from her boarders. Among other things, the rules of the house explicitly forbade foul language and overnight guests. If there had ever been a Mr. Arensen, and one assumed there had, he had no doubt been a repressed and frustrated man. Sexual activity was not allowed in this house, not unless it was between a man and his wife. And even then, Kelly was certain, Mrs. Arensen did not approve.

"I have some fresh baked birkes to take along," she said in her singsong Danish accent. "It will make a nice snack, ja?"

"Yes, that would be great," Kelly agreed, remembering the buttery, flaky poppy seed rolls from last week. "We don't need many. We'll have a big lunch in Rodebay."

With a curt nod, Mrs. Arensen withdrew from the doorway. Kelly pulled on her jacket and slipped her arms through the straps of her backpack. She smoothed the bedspread carefully, knowing that boarders were expected to tidy their rooms, make their beds and put away their clothes. That rule had never been voiced, but Kelly had seen Mrs. Arensen in Chuck's room, shaking her head at his clutter with genuine pain on her face.

She gave a last glance around her room to make sure she wouldn't cause her landlady any heartaches today. Her bedroom was small, with one double-hung window facing the back of the building. From her window she could see a sliver of the bay and bare hills above it. The curtain and bedspread were made of lacy fabrics that reminded her of the yellowed doilies in her great-grandmother's house. Next to the twin bed was a narrow one-drawer nightstand, and in one corner a reading chair and lamp. A simple wooden table containing her laptop served as a desk. A straight-backed chair was tucked under it, softened with a faded floral cushion. The floor was bare wood polished to a high gloss, with a throw rug beside the bed and another by the door. The shared bathroom was down the hall.

Mrs. Arensen ran a clean and comfortable house that delivered all the necessities without providing any luxuries. Chuck had stayed here before and had assured Kelly that it was the best place available. The two hotels in town were far too expensive for anything over a couple nights, and some of the other houses that opened their doors to boarders were not sufficiently equipped for guests. She hadn't known what to expect in such a remote place, and was relieved to find the house so comfortable and so much like home. Chuck's description of "nice" had been too vague to imagine anything. For a guy who had spent plenty of nights sleeping in dusty trenches and blown-out buildings with no power or water, his definition of nice could be all sorts of things Kelly would recoil from. She had no complaints. Except maybe for the food. Mrs. Arensen was not a good cook. Combine her lack of imagination in the kitchen with the dearth of fresh fruit and vegetables and you were faced with what Kelly termed "perpetual plates of brown." Good beer and good bread and butter made it tolerable.

"Elsa!" Chuck's deep voice barreled down the hall. "Where the hell's my Van Halen T-shirt! I hope you didn't wash it! Nineteen eighty-four's not coming around again anytime soon, you know?"

He appeared in Kelly's doorway wearing sweatpants and a plain white T-shirt, his thick brown hair damp and uncombed. His chin was freshly shaved and his salt-and-pepper mustache trimmed. His forehead was deeply creased from one of his most common expressions, a skeptical frown. Chuck was a big man with a Scooby-Doo sort of charm. In his early fifties, he was physically strong and vigorous, the sort of man who dominated a room with his presence. In the two weeks they'd been working together Kelly had come to appreciate his skills as a journalist and respect his opinions. He was cool and cynical and knew his stuff. She liked him but he rubbed some people the wrong way. A lot of people, actually, because he pulled no punches. In his youth he had been a crack political correspondent on his way to glory, the kind of arrogant, foolhardy reporter who risked his life to get a story. He never made the big time. He had rubbed too many people the wrong way and eventually found himself outside the inner circle. Now he took fewer chances. Greenland was less of a risk than the beats of his younger days, but only because they weren't getting shot at or having grenades tossed at them. A lot of people would not consider this tame territory.

This was Kelly's first extended assignment with Chuck. Prior to this, she had only furnished him with a few photos for his articles back home. She found his style refreshing and intelligent, devoid of sentimentality. He didn't write fluff pieces. If you wanted to know the facts, he was your guy. An unapologetic carnivore, he wrote the way you'd expect him to write. He delved into the meat of a subject and presented it like a raw, bloody mass, untrimmed and unseasoned.

He wagged his head. "I know she washed that shirt again. And you know how she washes things. She may as well take it out and pound it with a fucking rock in the river."

"If she hears you talking like that, she'll be tossing you in the river next."

He rolled his eyes. "Naw, that old girl loves me. You know she does."

"She does seem to have a soft spot for you. You can get away with anything."

Chuck struggled constantly around Mrs. Arensen with his well-ingrained tendency toward crude language. He had complained to Kelly that every time he saw her wince at his speech, he was tossed into the abyss of Catholic guilt that had been his childhood. For reasons not too difficult to imagine, the landlady reminded him of ruler-wielding nuns.

"Maybe I can get it out of the machine before she washes all the character out of it." He dashed away.

Besides Chuck and herself there were two other boarders, another American named Trevor Waddell who was an oil company scout and a Greenlander named Annalise, a woman in her twenties from Nuuk who taught a summer accounting course to the locals, a government program designed to provide marketable skills to people who were no longer able to make a living at traditional fishing and hunting. Annalise spoke little English and kept to herself. Other than mealtimes, Kelly rarely saw her. The only other resident was Mrs. Arensen's twenty-one-year-old grandson, Jens, on summer break from his university in Denmark. He was a pre-med student who financed his education in part by taking tourists for helicopter tours. Altogether, there were six residents in the house and one cat, an old calico named Paluaq, a Greenlandic word meaning "butterfly." Cats were rare in this country. Greenlanders, especially in the northern cities, kept dogs, not cats, but Mrs. Arensen had brought the pet with her from Nuuk where she used to live.

Kelly went to the kitchen to pick up her bread and butter. Mrs. Arensen was cooking hot cereal in a pot at the stove. Muesli, no doubt. Kelly cut herself a thick slice of homemade bread from the loaf on the counter and smeared butter on it. The bread and the butter here were irresistible. She'd never tasted butter so good as this Danish stuff. *Børd og smør*, she practiced silently, reminding herself to work harder on her Danish.

"You will care for yourself out there," Mrs. Arensen cautioned, handing her the plastic bag of birkes.

"Nothing to worry about," Kelly replied breezily. "I hike all the time back home and Pippa's done this route lots of times. I don't expect to be back in time for supper, but any time after that."

Kelly ripped off a mouthful of bread as she emerged into the hallway, then went out the front door to find Chuck on the porch wringing out his sopping wet T-shirt.

"What'd I tell ya?" he groused, jerking his head toward the shirt. "That woman's OCD when it comes to cleaning. She's got some kind of dirt phobia. Do you know she actually scrubs the baseboards? I saw her doing it. Whoever heard of that?"

"Well, I—" Kelly began.

"This thing has to last me the rest of my life," he snarled. "The way it's made it this far is by being washed only once in a blue moon. So what if it's got a bit of a manly smell? What's wrong with that?" He held the shirt up by the shoulders, shaking it out. "Shit! It's already got some peeling here on the middle guitar."

The beloved shirt was a classic Van Halen design with a white VH in the center, scrollwork around that and three guitars underneath. In the background were the words *Rock 'n' Roll*.

"Chuck," Kelly said, "it's not going to last forever. If I were you, I'd look for another one on eBay or something. Besides, it's a little tight on you anyway. Thirty years has taken its toll on both of you."

He glared. "I got this shirt at a concert during the promotional tour of their 1984 album. That was the last time David Lee Roth performed with the group. They split right after this tour. If that isn't enough to make this a priceless one-of-a-kind memento, how about this? That was the night I scored with Janie Grosswaithe, the hottest sophomore at Penn State. We did it in the back of my classic 1979 Dodge van while an eight-track tape of Olivia Newton-John singing 'Let's Get Physical' serenaded our epic lovemaking. It was magical until a candle caught the shag carpet on fire and forced us out wrapped in faux leopard skin blankets. What a night!" He paused and regarded her with one half-closed eye. "If that was your memory, Sheffield, do you think you could replace this shirt with a soulless look-alike from eBay?"

"Olivia Newton-John?" Kelly asked. "'Let's Get Physical'?"

"On continuous play."

"To think, all of that was going on in your life before I was born. Amazing! And extremely vivid. I can almost picture it… but I don't want to. Besides, I have to go or I'll miss my boat."

"Where are you going?"

"Hiking. I told you."

"You did?" He wrinkled his forehead. Typical that her plans had zipped right through his consciousness without a pit stop.

"Yeah. I'm taking the tour boat to Rodebay and hiking back with Pippa."

"Pippa? Oh!" He nodded. "The little girl who's been hanging around here. The tour guide."

"Right. Sometimes I wonder how you can be a journalist with such a lousy attention span."

"I notice things that matter. No point cluttering up my mind with details about your extracurricular activities. When are you getting back?"

"This evening."

"Good. Don't be too late because we've got a morning appointment with that guy at the Jakobshavn Glacier. You're gonna love it. You've never seen a glacier this big. It'll blow your mind."

"Yeah, I'm stoked about that. By the way, when are we meeting with Jordan Westgate?"

"Don't know. I sent her an email last night. No answer yet."
He looked mildly puzzled. "Why?"

"Oh, no reason," Kelly said noncommittally. "Just trying to
keep track of our schedule." She hopped down the stairs and
called over her shoulder. "See you tonight."

Be careful, she warned herself. *I can't let him figure out the
truth about me and Jordan.* So far she had kept her many questions
about Jordan to herself, but the closer the time came to seeing
her, the more excited she had become. Chuck was a shrewd
investigator and could read people, an invaluable skill for a
reporter. But he didn't need to know anything about this. As far
as he was concerned, she and Jordan were complete strangers
who would be meeting for the first time in a few days. If it came
out later that they had known each other previously, that was
okay. It would just look like an interesting coincidence. But she
didn't want him to think Jordan had anything to do with her
being here. For that matter, she didn't want Jordan to think so
either.

When Chuck had sent her a rough itinerary of the trip,
asking her to come along, she had been shocked to see Jordan's
name on the list of scientists he would be meeting. Kelly hadn't
ever thought much about Greenland. She'd certainly never
thought about going, and she hadn't known about Jordan's work
here.

She had also never seriously expected to see Jordan again.
She'd gone on with her life, years had gone by, and the ache and
need had diminished.

But a few hours after seeing Jordan's name and realizing it was
possible to see her again, it became imperative that she *must* see
her again, if only to satisfy her curiosity. Sometimes opportunity
created its own need. Suddenly, there was no question that she
would go to Greenland. How could she pass up a chance to
see Jordan again? Under what better circumstances? They
would be meeting as two people working. It would all be very
businesslike, just the way Jordan liked things. No emotional
messiness. Jordan had never been comfortable with that. Kelly

was determined to present herself as a mature, professional woman, someone Jordan could respect and could regard, if not as her equal, then at least not as the foolish and immature adolescent she had once been.

No more questions about Jordan, she silently reiterated. It was only a few days now before Jordan would appear before her in the flesh and all of her questions would be answered.

CHAPTER THREE

When everyone was aboard the boat, the captain, Amaalik, doffed his cap and introduced himself and his eleven-year-old son Nuka in broken English. Both of them wore summer outfits of short sleeved shirts and lightweight pants.

"Titanic iceberg," he said, grinning cheerfully, "from here." He waved his hat toward the bay, then laughed and ducked inside the cabin. A second later, he appeared in the window above, ready at the helm.

"The iceberg that sunk the Titanic came from here?" asked an old woman with a British accent.

"Yes," Nuka confirmed. "From the Jakobshavn Glacier."

Kelly wasn't sure why a tour boat skipper thought that was funny or something to be proud of, but he had carted out the same piece of trivia the first time she'd been on this tour.

As the boat began to pull away from the dock, she leaned against the outer wall of the cabin and zipped up her coat. Next to her on a bench sat an American couple in their sixties, looking optimistically uncertain.

The boat inched its way through the harbor, dodging icebergs. Every time it hit a chunk of ice, the American woman stiffened and pressed her lips together in an expression of alarm. She and her husband sat close on their bench, swathed in layers of protective clothing, including parkas and gloves. Despite the chill breeze coming off the water, it was a nice day. Once they reached Rodebay and got off the boat, nobody would be complaining about the weather.

"No safety briefing," the woman whispered to her husband. "Do you think they even have life jackets on this thing?"

Before he had a chance to respond, they hit an iceberg on the starboard side that sent a substantial shudder through the craft. The jolt caused Kelly to pitch sideways. She moved to the railing and looked overboard to see the berg moving rapidly away from them, propelled by the impact. A chunk of ice like that wasn't big enough to damage "this thing," as the woman had called their boat. But she couldn't know that. What did this frightened American know of icebergs? Kelly knew Amaalik's joking reference to the Titanic didn't help.

Ilulissat Harbor changed from day to day. Sometimes it was nearly full of ice, mostly small chunks that boats could push aside. Yesterday boats had to squeeze past a monster berg at the mouth of the harbor. Today that one was gone. Some days the harbor was nearly ice free. Chuck had explained that it had to do with winds, mainly, and how much ice was coming off the glacier each day. He knew a lot about Greenland. He had been here many times before and was considered a Greenland expert among Associated Press reporters. There were a lot of scientists who spent their summers in Greenland, but not a lot of journalists did.

Their boat moved excruciatingly slowly toward the mouth of the harbor, finessing its way around the larger chunks of ice. Amaalik didn't even try to avoid the small ones, so the continual sound of the hull crashing against solid objects accompanied their journey, keeping the American couple's teeth visibly on edge.

Kelly glanced up at the helm to see Amaalik peering intently through the window, both hands on the wheel, carefully picking his course. For most of the year he was a fisherman, but for the short tourist season he conducted daily tours for travelers from around the world. In summer, if you had a boat, you could carry tour groups. If you had a car, you could be a taxi driver. If you had a big house, you could rent out rooms. Under circumstances like this, visitors couldn't be sure what they were getting into when they booked a tour.

Kelly recalled the dazed looks on the faces of the passengers as they had come aboard expecting something bigger and more accommodating, maybe a luxurious catamaran with a well-stocked bar and an indoor seating area surrounded by walls of windows. Instead they encountered a cramped fishing boat with no provisions for tourists. The boat had been retrofitted as a touring vessel only in the imagination of Amaalik and Pippa's employer, Arctic Explorer Expeditions.

Tourists to Greenland were mostly seasoned travelers and they quickly adapted, anxious to appear unruffled. As if they had expected this all along, the newbies gamely picked up a blanket and seat cushion and plunked themselves on any flat surface that could serve as a seat. But the American woman, peering out from the hood of her parka, seemed genuinely frightened that at any moment an iceberg would rip the hull open.

"The life jackets are inside the bench," Kelly told her. She didn't bother to add that a life jacket wouldn't be much help in this frigid water, not after the first few minutes.

"You're American!" the woman proclaimed, relief evident in her voice.

"That's right," she said. "I'm from the Denver area."

"We're the Coopers from Florida. Miami, Florida."

Kelly chatted with the Coopers for a few minutes, noticing how much calmer they had become. The presence of another American on board changed everything for them, made the whole experience somehow safer and more legitimate, adding something familiar in an otherwise tensely exotic setting. She understood that. Greenland was so far from anything she or the Coopers knew. It was the most different place she had ever been. Chances were they could say the same.

Kelly noticed the boat picking up speed. "We've cleared the harbor," she announced, excusing herself from the Coopers to join Pippa in the bow where she stood in a long-sleeved cotton shirt worn loose over khaki pants. Her straight chestnut-colored hair was pulled back into a ponytail and her narrow face and full mouth were uncluttered by makeup. She wore two tiny peridot studs in her ears, the extent of her adornment.

She turned to smile at Kelly, her clear blue eyes full of joyful enthusiasm. Those eyes were gorgeously incongruous against her bronze skin. She was the only Inuit Kelly had ever seen with eyes like that, here or in Alaska. *Five foot two, eyes of blue*, Kelly thought, recalling the words to an old song.

They had met several days ago when Kelly and Chuck had taken this boat tour to the tiny town of Rodebay. Eighteen-year-old Pipaluk Nannunniaq had been one of their tour guides, her summer job before her last year at school. She had welcomed them aboard with impressive English and barely a trace of an accent. Right away, Kelly had found her charming and likable. She was a spirited girl who'd led a sheltered life dreaming of the world beyond Greenland. Like America. She was nuts about American TV and movies. Which explained why her English was peppered with American idioms.

"It's an awesome day for a hike," Pippa said excitedly. "You're going to love it!"

"Can't wait." Kelly leaned against the railing and watched a seagull bobbing in the boat's wake.

In Disko Bay proper, there was lots of ice, mountains of it, but there was enough open water to maneuver, so the crashing thuds against the hull had ceased. The thing that had drawn Kelly's eye from the moment she had arrived in Greenland and the thing that continued to do so every day since was Disko Bay. From almost anywhere in Ilulissat, you had a view of it, a body of tranquil water stretching off to the horizon. The changing light throughout the day and night created a wide range of colors on the ice from the most brilliant white to pinkish golds and bluish purples. The entire scene was stunning. No photograph could have prepared her for this, the clarity and three-dimensional exquisiteness. Nevertheless she, like all visitors, took photo after photo trying to capture that elusive beauty.

Pippa scanned a document on her clipboard. "Seven today, plus you. Three Americans, a British couple, two Danes."

"Three Americans? I've only seen the Coopers."

"There's another woman, Sonja Holm. She's standing at the stern."

Kelly nodded. "What about the old woman? You don't have her on your list?"

"Old woman?"

"She's a Greenlander. I think she's in the cabin."

Before boarding, a woman wearing a man's cotton work shirt and sealskin pants had stood on the dock speaking to Amaalik. She had a perfectly round, weathered face, narrow eyes, a wide nose and yellowed teeth. Her black and silver hair was thin and straight, lying flat on her head, cut off unambiguously just under her jawline. The top of her head had been level with Amaalik's neck, and he wasn't a tall man. She had carried a bulky canvas bag over one arm like a purse.

"I'll go check," announced Pippa.

She walked back to the cabin and disappeared inside.

In the distance, the closely-packed wooden buildings of Ilulissat receded. The colorful little houses on the hills faced all different directions with no garages, no driveways, no roads leading to them. What became immediately apparent to a woman from Colorado were the odd-looking spaces between the houses. No grass. No trees or shrubbery. No fences. These cheerful little houses struck her as touchingly vulnerable, as if a strong wind could blow them away. But somehow they endured in the toughest inhabited climate on Earth.

Three or four short roads ran through the main section of town, the business district. No roads led out of town. Out here, there was nothing but wild, solid bedrock. No sign of agriculture or industry or anything to suggest a human had ever set foot on any of it.

The ice and extreme northern remoteness reminded Kelly of Alaska, but this place was also significantly different. It was harsher, less green and less populated. Ilulissat was the third largest city in Greenland, but back home it would be a small town. The entire population of Greenland would easily fit in one medium-sized American city. Most of the country was uninhabited and uninhabitable. The towns and villages that did exist were cut off from everything. Even in the middle of summer, Ilulissat seemed far from the rest of the world. She couldn't imagine what it was like in winter.

"Kaffe!" Nuka announced, standing in the middle of the deck, his golden brown face flashing a cheerful smile. The boy was the only crewmember on this vessel and his duties were to hand out cushions and blankets, to make coffee and to tie and untie the guide ropes whenever they docked.

The Coopers dashed toward the cabin. A hot cup of coffee was the extent of amenities on this ship, but it was a welcome one. Kelly was ready for a cup herself, her ears and nose partly numb from the freezing wind.

Pippa returned with two cups and handed one to her. "I added hot water to yours."

"Thanks!"

"The old woman isn't a tourist," Pippa reported. "Her name is Nivi. She lives between Ilulissat and Rodebay. She's hitching a ride home."

"Oh. I didn't realize this was a ferry service."

Pippa shrugged. "Not exactly. Amaalik's just giving her a lift. Somebody else apparently took her into town. She had some seal pelts to sell. So we'll be making a stop along the way to let her off."

Kelly held the coffee under her nose, letting the steam thaw it before she drank. Mr. Stewart, the elderly Englishman, wobbled toward his bench, both hands around his coffee cup in an unlikely attempt to make it back without a spill. Pippa ran to his aid, taking the cup from him until he was seated.

A young woman appeared from the back of the boat and slid her sunglasses onto the top of her head before peeking into the cabin. Sonja Holm, Kelly surmised. Someone put a cup of coffee in her hand, then she walked toward the bow, giving Kelly a brief smile before tasting the brew. She was attractive, in her mid-twenties with long legs, a lanky frame and short platinum blonde hair full of sharp edges. She wore a dark blue turtleneck sweater, blue jeans, and well-used hiking boots. A point-and-shoot digital camera hung on a cord from her neck. After taking several gulps of coffee, she regarded Kelly more directly, her hazel eyes lingering familiarly. Her wide mouth turned up slightly into a subtle, ironic smile.

"Hej," she said. "Jeg er Sonja." Her pronunciation was marginal but understandable.

"Hi, Sonja. I'm Kelly. Sorry, I don't speak Danish. It'd be easier if we stuck to English."

"Oh!" She laughed. "You're American. You must know some Danish. You understood me just now."

"I know a few words. Very few."

"Me too. About all I can manage in Danish is to order a cup of coffee and say thank you for it. What do you think about this Danish coffee anyway?"

"It's impossibly strong for me. I usually water it down about halfway."

"How long have you been in Greenland?" asked Sonja.

"Two weeks. A business trip. I'm a photographer."

"That's awesome. What a place to take pictures!"

"What about you?"

"It's business for me too. I'm working at a science base a few miles from Ilulissat. For the entire summer. I'm a graduate student."

"Where at?"

"University of Colorado in Boulder."

"What?" Kelly was stunned. "CU? That's my school! I mean, my alma mater. I still live in Broomfield."

"Weird coincidence. So we have something in common." She regarded Kelly with undisguised interest. "Speaking of coffee, there's this place near campus called the Jumping Bean. Do you know it? The barista there is a genius."

"I do know the Jumping Bean! I used to go there years ago. Back then, they'd just hired this tattooed feminista who could write your name in the froth on your latte."

"That's her! She's still there. She goes by the name Absinthe. People come in just to watch her make coffee."

"Absinthe," Kelly said, remembering the spiky hair, black eye shadow, nose ring. "She was an interesting character. I should stop by there some time."

"You should, if just to see Absinthe again. If she didn't already have a girlfriend, I'd make a move on that. God, she's sexy!"

"You're gay?" Kelly asked incredulously.

Sonja nodded matter-of-factly.

"Me too!"

"Shit!" Sonja shook her head in disbelief. "We're like twins separated at birth!"

Kelly laughed, marveling at the coincidence of meeting someone from home way up here in the Arctic. "Is this your day off? Or is this a working trip?"

"Just sightseeing today. I haven't seen much of this country yet, so I thought I should get out and take a look. A couple of my team members took a tour to the Eqi Glacier to watch the calving but I've been camped beside a glacier for three weeks now, so I wanted to see something other than ice."

"You'll like it. Rodebay is a very cool place. Let me give you a little advice, though. At lunch they give you samples of local specialties like fresh fish and shrimp. Most of it's terrific, but don't try the dried halibut, the stuff they call ræklinger." Kelly laughed and shook her head. "You'll be sorry."

"You've been on this tour before?"

"Yeah, but I'm not here for the tour this time. Pippa and I... that's one of our guides." She pointed Pippa out. "We're hiking back."

"Hiking? How far is that?"

"About twenty kilometers. Twelve and a half miles."

"That sounds like fun. I might try that myself on my next day off." She held Kelly's gaze briefly, then drained her coffee cup. "Greenland is such a remarkable place, isn't it?"

"It's fascinating," Kelly agreed.

Sonja's eyes lit up as she caught sight of a beautifully sculpted iceberg approaching on the port side. It had a smooth-sided hole through the center with a halo of soft blue framing it. "I have to get this."

She stepped to the side to take photos. Though the midday glare off the ice wasn't ideal for photography, Kelly unpacked her own camera. Removing the lens cap, she got momentarily distracted by Sonja leaning over the railing, her sweater riding up to reveal the bare skin of her lower back, her jeans stretched tight across her shapely rear end. Kelly pressed her lips together to suppress an inappropriate smile, admiring the view.

CHAPTER FOUR

By the time they'd reached the halfway point of their journey, most of the passengers had lost their initial sense of excitement and were seated quietly, huddling together under blankets. Kelly and Pippa stood on deck talking to the young Danish couple, Christian and Brita, who were both fluent in English, both tall, thin, blond and blue-eyed.

"This is our first trip to Greenland," Brita said. "We've just come up from Narsaq. We were there for three days."

"Did you see Brattahlid?" Pippa asked.

"We saw it," Christian said, nodding. "We love the old Viking sites. We have seen most of them in Denmark."

"What's Brattahlid?" Kelly asked.

"It was a Viking village," Pippa answered. "Established by Eric the Red in the tenth century. It's called the Eastern Settlement and there are some ruins and a reconstructed chapel and longhouse."

"Is there anything to see of the Western Settlement?" Christian asked.

"Not really. There's been excavation, but it isn't a site for tourists. Same for the Middle Settlement."

"Middle Settlement?" Brita asked. "We have not heard of it."

"It was smaller than the other two. There are no written records of its existence so we don't know who lived there, but ruins have been uncovered that show about twenty farms. The site was occupied for a few hundred years until the fourteenth century like the other two."

"What happened to them?" Kelly asked.

"Nobody knows for sure. There are a lot of unknowns regarding the Greenland Vikings. All we know is that when the Little Ice Age was over in the eighteenth century, missionaries came back looking for the colonists and didn't find any. The settlements had been abandoned for a long time by then."

"They all died," Christian said confidently. "They couldn't make it here without supplies from back home. Once they were cut off, they died."

"Most of them probably did die," Pippa agreed soberly. "But some of them might have survived."

"If they had," he reasoned, "they would have still been here when the ships came back to find them, wouldn't they?"

Pippa shook her head. "Not necessarily. They could have survived by assimilating into the native population. The Thule were here at the time. They were well adapted and did survive. As you can see all around you. The Thule were the ancestors of the Greenland Inuits. Like me. It could explain why I have blue eyes when nobody else in my family does." She flashed Christian her playful smile. "So maybe the Greenland Vikings didn't die out completely. Maybe they're still here in their blue-eyed descendants."

Christian looked intrigued, gazing into Pippa's light eyes. He smiled warmly and nodded, then the two of them wandered off.

"Is that true?" Kelly asked. "Are there no other blue-eyed people in your family?"

"Nobody knows of any as far back as anyone remembers, so the blue-eyed gene has to go way back, back before the modern Danes arrived."

"How do you know there's been no mixing with the Danes?"

Pippa shrugged. "I can't be a hundred percent sure, but my family comes from a village where no white people ever lived. My grandmother says she never even saw a white man until she was nineteen. There are a lot of them in Nuuk, but not so many in the rest of the country, and definitely not then."

"But why the Vikings?"

"It's the only explanation that makes sense. There had to be a bunch of people with blue eyes who got it started. And the most likely place, the only place we know of, to find a pool of blue-eyed people was in the Viking colonies."

Pippa looked satisfied, her smooth, golden-hued face creating the perfect canvas for her richly sculpted lips and those incredible eyes.

"Why do you like that idea?" Kelly asked.

She shrugged. "Otherwise it's just so sad. Those poor people and their totally crappy lives—barely surviving for centuries and then just gone. All for nothing. We don't even know most of their names. They were born and suffered and died and there's no evidence they ever existed."

Kelly nodded sympathetically. Pippa was right. It was a sad idea, and her romantic young imagination wanted to turn it into a happy ending.

"If I could do anything at all with my life," she said sincerely, "I'd want to study genetics and unravel the mystery of my blue eyes."

"Do you think that's possible?"

Pippa nodded. "Oh, sure! Everything we've ever been is coded in our DNA. If we could understand it all, we would know the story of life on earth. Not just how humans evolved, but the evolutionary history of everything that lives or ever has lived on this planet."

Pippa had clearly spent a lot of time thinking about the mystery of her blue eyes.

Kelly raised her camera and focused on Pippa's face. She thrust out a hip and smiled coquettishly as her photo was snapped, then darted off to help Mr. Stewart who had lifted off from the safety of his bench again.

The old woman, Nivi, emerged from the cabin and approached the Coopers, producing a pair of butter yellow boots that she held out for their inspection. The boots were decorated with tan fur.

"Kamik," she announced proudly.

"This is very soft," Mrs. Cooper said, feeling the leather. "Did you make these?"

Nivi smiled, but said nothing.

"Let's get the guide to translate," suggested Mr. Cooper.

They called Pippa, who took one look at the boots and became visibly alarmed. She addressed Nivi in Greenlandic and sent her away. The only word Kelly recognized was "American."

"What's wrong?" Mr. Cooper asked.

"She can't sell you those," Pippa explained. "They're made of seal skin."

Mrs. Cooper's eyes widened. Mr. Cooper nodded his understanding. "It's illegal," he said.

"It's illegal to import any marine mammal product into the US." Pippa clarified. "It's not illegal here. Or in Denmark, so I sent her to the Danes."

"Did she make those?" Mrs. Cooper asked.

"Yes."

"From a seal?"

"It's how she makes money," Pippa explained. "She sells most of her pelts to a tannery. But she makes a few traditional pieces like the kamik to sell to tourists."

"So she kills seals," Mrs. Cooper persisted. "With a club?"

"With a rifle. Like you would shoot a deer." Pippa smiled cheerfully, unfazed by Mrs. Cooper's distress. "Seal hunting is a way of life here."

Mr. Cooper put his hand over his wife's. Kelly took that as a silent request not to make a scene. She apparently got the message, as she said no more about it.

As the boat slowed and turned toward land, Kelly stepped over to Pippa and asked, "Is this where Nivi gets off?"

Pippa nodded, then pointed. Kelly followed her finger to locate a bright yellow house on shore, a sheer wall of rock behind it. The house was a typical Greenland-style wooden structure, square with a steep roof. With its bright paint, it stood out in sharp relief from the gray landscape beyond it. There were no other houses in sight. Kelly heard dogs barking. As they got closer, she saw them, several huskies chained just out of reach of one another among a cluster of doghouses.

"There's no village?" Kelly asked, searching the shore for other houses.

"Just this house. She lives here with her son and daughter-in-law. They're hunters."

"It seems awfully scary to be so isolated."

"Don't you have people who live outside of towns in Colorado?"

"Sure. But they can get on a road and drive to town if they need to."

Pippa laughed. "It's all in what you're used to."

They edged up to a weathered dock and Nuka clambered onto it, taking one of the guidelines in both hands and easing the boat into position. He wrapped the rope around a post and Amaalik cut the engine. Pippa rushed over to the side to unfold the stairs, then she reached for Nivi's hand. Nivi gripped it firmly and stared intently into Pippa's face. She spoke to her in Greenlandic, gesturing emphatically, then stepped up on the stair and transferred her grip from Pippa to Nuka, who helped her make the final stretch to the dock. When she had steadied herself, she turned and waved up at Amaalik with a toothy grin.

When they were underway again, Kelly joined Pippa in the cabin for another cup of coffee.

"What did she say to you?" Kelly asked.

"Nivi? Oh, nothing. Just talking about my eyes. I get that a lot. The old-timers have their stories." Pippa held her mug between both hands.

"Stories? Like what?"

"Legends, you know. Like light-eyed people have special sight. In English, you would say seer or shaman."

"She thinks you're a shaman?"

Pippa snorted. "Yeah, sure. Traditionally, Greenlanders gave special status to people with blue eyes because they were so rare. They believed we could see into the future and the past and talk to spirits. Some of them still believe that. Like Nivi." Pippa shrugged. "Anyway, she was just telling me I was special."

Kelly smiled. "You *are* special, Pippa. Even if you can't see into the future."

CHAPTER FIVE

When at last the time came to send the boat back to Ilulissat, Pippa helped the Stewarts aboard while Sonja Holm stood beside Kelly on the dock. She wrote her name and email address in a small notebook, then tore out the page and handed it over.

"Send me a note when we're both back home," she said. "we can meet at the Jumping Bean for coffee." She leered, holding her bangs back from her face. "Or something."

"Thanks," Kelly replied, tucking the note in her camera bag.

"Maybe we'll run into each other again here in Greenland."

"Maybe. We'll be around the area for a few more weeks."

"If that's an invitation to visit," Sonja purred, "I may just make an effort."

Kelly smiled at her teasing hazel eyes and the liquid movement of her body, so obviously offering to pour itself onto Kelly's.

Pippa waved her arm impatiently to urge Sonja to get onboard.

"Have fun on your hike," she said, grasping Kelly's hand briefly, then she ran to the boarding ramp.

Pippa and Kelly waved goodbye as the boat eased away from the dock. A few moments later the sound of its engine faded as it moved further into Disko Bay and disappeared around a bend. Almost as soon as the boat was out of sight, two little boys came running across the rocks, a puppy scampering awkwardly after them. A woman appeared from one of the houses with a basket of laundry, walking toward the community building, the only building with running water. The ordinary life of this village went unobserved by the tourists. You would hardly know there were people living here when the boat was at the dock. But now, as the visitors made their way back to town, the villagers emerged to resume their daily lives.

From the dock the whole town was visible. A couple dozen houses framed a small, sheltered harbor where the only vessels in sight were a few kayaks. The houses were painted in the colors seen all over Greenland—brick red, mustardy yellow, bright green and sky blue, each one built in the same style, steeply slanted roof, a square attic window above a white front door with two small windows on either side of that. Each roof had an identical chimney and all the buildings were trimmed in white. The only difference between the dwellings was the color of paint.

Drying on wooden and twine racks throughout the village was the staple food for the sled dogs, halibut. The couple dozen adult dogs were chained in a cluster on a small hill and several thick-furred puppies frolicked loose. Next to one of the houses a red snowmobile was parked, useless until autumn.

Kelly and Pippa stood in front of the post office and general store, the Pilersuisoq. The only other commercial building in town was a restaurant, a brick-red building across the harbor that survived by serving lunches to tourists and the occasional group of hikers.

"Was she flirting with you?" Pippa asked, sounding slightly annoyed.

"Sonja? A little."

"Do you like her?"

"No idea. I just met her. She seems okay."

Pippa was curious about the lesbian dating game, Kelly decided. Though she hadn't come right out and said it, she had thrown out a few timid remarks that suggested she might be gay. Or at least wondering if she was. Without a community of lesbians around, she naturally had questions about how women get together.

"Are you going to see her again?" she persisted.

"I don't know, Pippa. Flirting is just harmless fun. It doesn't have to mean anything." She put a hand on Pippa's shoulder. "Come on, let's get going."

"In a minute. I want to get some ræklinger first." Pippa nodded toward the little store.

"Oh, crap! Are you going to eat that stuff on the trail?"

"You don't have to eat it."

"I won't, believe me!" Kelly wrinkled up her face in disgust. Remembering the one bite she'd had of the stuff the last time she was here, even the thought of the dried halibut made her cringe.

"You don't have to kiss me either," Pippa said cheekily, casting a sideways glance at her before sauntering toward the store.

Kelly stood where she was, taken off guard by Pippa's joking comment, then roused herself to follow. For such a small space, Pilersuisoq had a remarkable array of goods, like an old-fashioned general store—food, fishing equipment, clothing, CDs and DVDs, small appliances, tools. There wasn't much choice of any one thing, but there were lots of things. Since this was the only place to shop for twenty kilometers around, the inventory had to be diverse.

Pippa found her ræklinger, sold in a small package, which surprised Kelly, considering the racks and racks of dried halibut throughout town. She decided these packages were for the tourists looking for a fitting souvenir. Fitting, maybe, but not edible for anyone who wasn't raised on it. She was sure of that. It was the worst thing she'd ever tasted. Dry and sponge-like, unsalted, with an intense rotten fish flavor that lingered on your tongue long after you'd spit it out. Pippa, like other Greenlanders, loved the stuff and ate it as a snack.

After leaving the store, they put on their packs and started on their journey, heading south along a rocky ridge. Rodebay remained clearly visible behind them for the first kilometer before they dropped down over the ridge and lost sight of both the town and the bay. Now there was no sign of human habitation. Wilderness in all directions. Ahead of them was nothing but essential Greenland terrain—bare rock, mats of green ground cover and ruddy-colored lichen. Above them was a cloudless pale blue sky.

Pippa led the way in her baseball cap and bright red jacket, her thin but sturdy legs striding confidently onward. Kelly followed, feeling happy and energetic with the onset of a new adventure.

"Do you think we'll see anyone on the way?" Kelly asked.

"Maybe. But I won't be surprised if we don't. There's a group hike once a week for tourists, but that's on Wednesdays, so we won't run into them. You don't usually see locals doing this." She laughed. "Greenlanders aren't big on hiking."

"I appreciate your doing it for me."

"No problem. I love it! I'm not your typical Greenlander." Pippa flashed a joyful grin over her shoulder.

Without slowing, Kelly removed her hat to wipe the sweat off her forehead. "How far are we from the ice cap?"

"About forty kilometers."

Kelly did a quick conversion in her mind to come up with twenty-five miles.

"It's closer in some places," Pippa explained, "but the only ice you'll see this close to the shore in summer are the tongues of glaciers."

They walked over uneven terrain, dropping into gullies and rising up to expansive views of the sparkling bay, following trail cairns placed at irregular intervals on bare ridges. They traveled steadily, covering mile after mile, stopping only when Kelly took an occasional photo. After a few hours on the trail, her stomach started grumbling in earnest.

"How much longer until snack time?" she asked. "Lunch has apparently worn off."

"Just a few minutes."

The spot Pippa chose to stop was a long flat slab of rock with an incredible view in three directions, sheltered by a low wall against the wind. They sat down and unpacked their snacks.

Pippa opened the bag of dried halibut and popped a piece in her mouth. An odor of rotten fish wafted past Kelly's nose.

"I brought some birkes," Kelly said, "if you want some."

"Sure. I'll share my ræklinger too." Pippa grinned impishly and bumped up against Kelly's arm.

"You can stuff your ræklinger up your butt for all I care," Kelly joked.

Pippa chewed on her snack like a cow on its cud, calmly and contentedly. "I guess you really don't like it," she noted.

"Are you kidding? I hate it! It's the worst thing I ever ate. Hands down!"

"For reals?" Pippa looked surprised.

"For reals."

"Maybe it's an acquired taste."

Kelly wrinkled up her face. "In fact, you should quit eating it around me. I can smell it. I might just barf."

Pippa folded the top of the bag over and stuck it in her backpack. "Sorry. I could eat that stuff all day." She squinted in that way she did when she was apologetically happy, which she often was. It made her small nose look even smaller. In the short time Kelly had known her, she had observed Pippa to be happy most of the time. She was a naturally happy person, despite the narrow scope of her life and the brutally cold and dark winters. People simply are who they are, Kelly reflected, independent from their surroundings. Her mother, for instance, would be unhappy whatever was going on in her life. To justify it, she would emphasize every negative thing she could latch onto. Pippa, on the other hand, would always bounce back from adversity. She was cheerful, open and affectionate, and easy to like.

They ate the poppy seed rolls, sitting side by side on their rocky perch. Kelly wiped her hands together to brush off the crumbs, then wrapped her arms around her knees and sat contently gazing at the peaceful floating ice.

Pippa popped the last of her roll into her mouth. "Have you ever been in love?" she asked.

Kelly turned to see a serious, questioning look on her face. It was a personal question but she decided it wouldn't hurt to answer. "Yes," she replied. "I was in love with my last girlfriend, Megan...at first. We were together six years. It's been almost two years since we split up."

"Was that the only time?"

Kelly hesitated. "No. I was in love one other time, but she didn't want me."

"Was she straight?"

"No. But she was older. I had nothing to offer her. Except adoration. It was ridiculous, really."

"Why ridiculous?"

"Because I was too young for her. She saw me as a child. It wasn't possible for her to love me like that. I was naïve and immature and completely inappropriate in every way. It was a classic crush. I absolutely adored her."

"She must have been something!"

Kelly gazed into Pippa's sincere face, encouraged to elaborate. "She was. She was a fascinating woman. Like nobody I'd ever known. She was a professor at my school. She taught geology, meteorology, physical sciences."

"I didn't even know you studied science."

Kelly laughed shortly. "It was never my thing, but sometimes, you know, you find a teacher who sparks an interest."

"You mean an interest in the teacher?" Pippa snorted, then grinned.

Kelly nodded indulgently.

"What happened?" Pippa asked, clearly enthralled with the subject.

"Nothing happened. She transferred to a school in California when I was a junior and that was the end of it."

"And then you met Megan."

"Yes."

"Did you ever see your teacher again?"

"No. But I've often thought about her."

Kelly looked away. That was an understatement. She had forgotten almost nothing about the two years she had been obsessed with Jordan Westgate. After that initial geology class, she had taken every undergraduate class Jordan taught. Kelly still saw her clearly in her mind, the intelligent, ironic look in her eye, the tilt of her head when she considered a student's bizarre statement, as absurd perhaps as two plus two equals six. Without revealing surprise, she would invariably give that unruffled look and say, "Hmm. Perhaps not." Kelly got so she would start giggling before it even came out, in anticipation of it. When Jordan was in a more sarcastic mood, the response would be the less neutral, "Not in this universe!"

In the beginning, when Kelly was nineteen and going through the first phase of falling in love, it was sweet and happy, but by the end, just as she turned twenty-one, it was merely painful. The day they said goodbye, as Jordan prepared to take a position at UCLA, was an episode of sheer agony seared into Kelly's heart. Yet it was a moment of sublime happiness as well. Shockingly, Jordan had kissed her on the lips, a few seconds of bliss that would live eternally in her mind. One kiss was as close as she had come to realizing her dream of forever-after happiness in Jordan's arms. And then she was gone, leaving the echo of her voice and touch like a flickering spark Kelly had nurtured for years against the chill of time and space.

Now, with the anticipation of seeing her again, the spark had been fanned into a full-blown bonfire. Kelly worried that she would be unable to retain her cool when she met Jordan again face-to-face, standing in the midst of that inferno. But that was her goal, to come off with extreme grace and composure, to emulate as much as possible Jordan's own example of elegant poise, to be the sort of woman, in short, that Jordan would find appealing.

In her mind, she endlessly rehearsed the moment of their meeting. When their eyes met, she would utter a nearly inaudible gasp of astonishment at seeing Jordan again after nearly a decade. Then she would say, with restrained pleasure, "Jordan! What a delightful surprise to see you again." For her part, Jordan would be equally surprised and, Kelly hoped, glad, as someone might be at a chance meeting with an old friend. Or maybe she would forgo the feigned surprised and merely say, "Hello, Jordan. Nice to see you again. How've you been?" In a businesslike manner, she would shake her hand and look her in the eye with confidence. Jordan would say, "Kelly Sheffield, for Christ's sake! I thought I got rid of you years ago. Now here you are following me to the top of the world, hoping that nine years could have changed the laws of physics and created a reality in which I could return your wretched love. Not in this universe!"

Kelly shook the image from her mind. She'd never been any good at fantasies. They invariably betrayed her insecurities and were so much worse than reality would ever be. Same with dreams. Her dreams and fantasies played out like they were written by a sadistic puppeteer. There was no way Jordan would be that brutal. But her response to seeing Kelly again could very well be a gentler equivalent.

"What about you?" she asked Pippa. "Have you ever been in love?"

She snorted a short laugh. "I've never even been kissed. Not kissed for real. A dorky boy took me out once and kissed me goodnight so fast he almost missed my mouth. Then he ran away like he was being chased by a chainsaw murderer." She rolled her eyes. "There's not a lot to choose from here. Not the kind that interest me, anyway."

"You mean women?" Kelly ventured.

"Yeah." Pippa smiled self-consciously, then averted her eyes. "Specifically lesbians."

Kelly laughed. "That's what I meant. No other lesbians in Ilulissat?"

"As if! I barely know of any gay people," Pippa explained. "I don't expect to meet anybody here. This is how I figure it. In all of Greenland, there are only twenty-eight thousand females. In Ilulissat, there are two thousand females and a hundred and sixty girls in my age group. Over half of those are married, so that leaves about eighty. Nobody really knows what percent of the population is gay, really gay and not just experimenting, but I've heard it's about three percent."

"That's conservative," Kelly pointed out.

"This is a conservative place."

"Okay. You have a point."

"Mathematically speaking, that means there are two single lesbians, at most three, in my age group in this town. And I'm one of them." She sighed fatalistically. "I've had my eye out for the other one, but so far, nothing."

"Those aren't very good odds. But when you go away to college, everything will be different."

"If I ever do. Even if I do get to go to college, it could be two, three or four years from now before I even know another lesbian." She grimaced. "Can you imagine staying celibate until you're in your mid twenties?"

Kelly sputtered. "Uh, that's not a death sentence. A lot of people aren't sexually active until their twenties. It's really not that unusual, especially in a situation like yours where there isn't anyone appropriate to date. There's no urgency about sex. You don't have to feel pressured about it."

Pippa shook her head, looking mournful. "It's not just sex. It's the whole thing. Going steady. Holding hands. Kissing."

"It would be nice if you had that." Kelly patted Pippa on the back sympathetically. "I guess it's kind of lonely here for girls like us, isn't it?"

Pippa brightened at the suggestion that she and Kelly were in the same club.

Kelly stood and stretched. "Do you mind if I set up my camera and take a few shots here before we go on?"

"No problem! Take as long as you want. We're making good time. We're over halfway there now."

Kelly walked out to a point with a particularly fine view of the bay and set up her tripod, her mind still occupied with thoughts of Jordan.

She wanted to find out, after all this time, if the sight of Jordan still tugged at her heart, if the nearness of her still made her knees weak. Or if, as Jordan had predicted, she had merely had a crush and had outgrown it in the intervening years.

But she already knew she hadn't outgrown it. She had never believed Jordan's assertion that her love was a transitory infatuation. Jordan thought of her as a child, full of heady dreams and illusions. Even as a teenager, Kelly had been more grounded than that. Some might say more cynical, but she liked to think of herself as merely realistic. She hadn't been a romantic idealist like many girls her age, prone to flights of fancy, but neither was she a pessimist like her mother. What she had found in Jordan was a woman whose spirit resonated deeply with her own, someone she would even dare to call her soul mate.

She had never loved Megan as deeply as she had loved Jordan. She had tried to be happy with Megan, but her heart knew there was something more profound and satisfying available, if not with Jordan, then with someone else. In the end, that was why she and Megan couldn't make it. She had always felt a little like she was settling for second best. She couldn't forget the exquisite joy of all-consuming love, of wanting to give herself wholly and selflessly to someone else. She wanted to find out if that joy was still possible or if her heart had hardened. Even if Jordan was still unavailable to her, she yearned to feel that old emotional intensity, just to know it was still a part of her.

There was also a chance that Jordan would see her in a different light now that she was older and more experienced. They weren't that far apart in age, less than ten years. The age disparity wouldn't seem so great now. It wouldn't be out of the question for Jordan to see her as more of an equal. She might even be able to love her. But she hardly dared think that for fear of wounding her carefully guarded hope.

These were the thoughts Kelly had been carrying around since signing on for this trip, all the while having no clue if Jordan was even available. None of the information she had found about Jordan's many recent accomplishments had anything to do with her personal life. That didn't surprise her. Jordan could be married with five kids and none of her students or colleagues would know it. Unless she had changed.

She attached her camera to the tripod and turned it down snug. Out of the corner of her eye she saw Pippa's bright red jacket moving along a nearby ridgetop. Poor kid, she thought, with her wild, romantic heart and no place for it to run free. Was that better or worse than having a wild, romantic heart that fixed itself on a hopeless pursuit?

She was soon immersed in her work, transfixed by the beauty and solitude all around her. She forgot all about Pippa... and even Jordan.

CHAPTER SIX

Pippa's head throbbed like thunder. She opened her eyes and tried to comprehend her situation, gradually realizing she was lying on the cold ground in the dark. Why was it dark? It was summer, the middle of summer. It never gets this dark in the middle of summer. She saw a circle of light above and her eyes finally made sense of it. She was looking at an opening to the outside. Through it, the blue of the sky was unblemished by any detail. She was in a cave, she reasoned. That was weird. There are no caves in Greenland. Startled by a whistling sound, she listened more carefully and recognized it as the wind passing over the opening above.

She tried to raise her head to look around, but everything swam violently, so she closed her eyes and lay still until it was calm again. Then she tentatively rolled onto her side, feeling a sharp pain in her ankle. She must have fallen. She looked up again at the opening ten feet above. Her head hurt. She felt around until she located a sticky mass of hair at the back of her head. She realized she was bleeding…or had been bleeding.

The blood was nearly dry. Maybe it wasn't too bad. But what about the ankle? She tried to move her foot, then winced at the sharp pain.

Peering into the dimness around her, she could see the outlines of large boulders, but only barely. God, she thought, I hope there's no polar bear in this cave! Then she remembered again that there are no caves in Greenland and wondered where she was. *What country is this?* I hope it's America, she thought with sudden excitement. Or France or England. Or Africa. Maybe she'd fallen into a diamond mine!

She remembered the penlight on her key chain and reached into her front pocket to fish it out. Its beam exposed the space around her: rock walls and a dusty floor containing smooth, featureless boulders. Against one wall was a pile of soccer ball-sized rocks about two feet high that looked like they'd been arranged there purposely like a stack of cannon balls. They looked like a cairn, but a cairn inside a cave would be a strange trail marker. Maybe not so strange a marker for something else, she reasoned, like a buried treasure. A buried treasure inside a cave, now that idea had potential. Her mind raced off with visions of gold doubloons.

Beside her on the floor were the few scattered cottongrass flowers she'd dropped on her way down. She'd been picking them, she recalled. That was her last memory, stepping toward a patch of fluffy blooms with the intention of presenting a bouquet to Kelly as a cheery gift. Kelly was so taken with them. She'd never seen anything like them, she'd said, and had taken dozens of photos of them on her first trip to Rodebay.

"They grow all over," Pippa had informed her. "Very common, like weeds."

"What seems common has to do with your frame of reference," Kelly had said. "I think they're darling!"

Kelly took a lot of photos. Not just for the articles Mr. Lance was writing, but of whatever caught her eye. She even took pictures of Pippa. *Does she think I'm darling too?*

She decided to sit up again, but her head spun wildly as before. In the split second before her thumb released the penlight button and the cave went black, she thought she saw someone on the other side of the chamber. Adrenaline flashed through her body and her blood went cold as she lay perfectly still holding her breath, listening. It had been a face only, a pale face framed by light-colored hair. It was a woman. Maybe not a human woman. Maybe a ghost or a witch or a vampire, but whatever it was, it was a female one, for sure.

Hearing nothing for two, three, four seconds, she fumbled to turn the light back on, but the room spun around her so fast, she grabbed at the floor, feeling like she would fall off. She squeezed her eyes shut again and curled into a ball, waiting for the spinning to stop.

Flashes of light shot across the black field of her vision as she lay still and quiet. Then there were indistinct, flickering yellow flames as the world gradually slowed and came into focus. Though her eyes were still shut, a scene was forming. Bit by bit, the flames solidified into a small, cool fire in a stone fireplace with a stone mantel. Above that an intricately carved wooden cross hung on the wall, its design a fascinating network of curving tendrils like vines or snakes.

An iron pot sat on a flat stone in the fire, its oily contents simmering.

She reached into the fire with a cloth wrapped around her hand and lifted the pot out, setting it on the hearth. She stirred through it with a metal spoon to check that all the seal blubber was melted. This would be enough oil to fill their lamps for a couple of weeks, she estimated.

Confused, she stared into the oily pot to catch her hazy reflection, seeing long, light-colored hair pulled back from her face. She reached up and pushed an errant strand back, noting the coarse texture, noting also how large and strangely colored her hand was. It was pale and marked by a network of ruddy freckles. This was not her hand...and yet it was. She felt oddly within and without her body at the same time.

She glanced around the room. Like her hand, it looked familiar and strange all at once. It was no more than twelve feet across, with a hand-hewn wooden table and chairs and a cramped workspace along the wall adjacent to the hearth. An oil lamp stood on the table, cold. Next to a heavy wooden door there was one window with open shutters letting in a feeble light. On the worktable stood a pitcher, some cups, a pot, utensils and a basin of water. On a peg by the door hung her overcoat, and beside the door was the wooden bucket she used to milk the goats.

The confusion sifted out of her mind as all of these familiar objects reminded her who and where she was. She was Asa, daughter of Torvald, wife of Bjarni, and she was home.

As she stood upright, she felt the kick of her child in her belly. She recalled Bjarni's cold gray eyes when she had told him about this one, another child on the way. He was not happy. Not like the first time, when his firstborn Alrik arrived. He had cried with joy at the sight of his son. That was twelve years ago. So much had changed since then. Bjarni was unhappy most of the time now. Their crops had failed again and many of the villagers had died from the winter sickness. Others had left on a desperate overland journey to reach Brattahlid, hoping that their brethren to the south were better off. That was last year. Nobody knew if they had made it or what they had found if they did. They had promised to send help, but so far there had been only silence.

No help was coming from any source, Asa had concluded. There were never any ships, not anymore, but the sagas told of a time when there were. The ships used to come every summer, bringing grain, timber, livestock, cloth, tools and even new settlers. They were huge, beautiful ships that could hold many people and travel great distances. Asa had never seen such a sight. She had been born here in Greenland in this village. Her husband Bjarni had been born here too. And this child, son or daughter of Bjarni and Asa, would also be born here.

She glanced at the cross hanging above the hearth and wondered again if God had forgotten about His tiny flock freezing on this rock, that He had brought them another short, cold summer with poor crops, poor hunting and no food for their animals. As always, she felt ashamed of the thought. God never abandons any of us; that's what she'd been told. If He doesn't hear you, you're the one at fault. You need to pray harder or work harder or be better.

That cross was one of her few possessions that had come from Norway. It had been in her family for several generations and had gone to Iceland with them. It had made the journey here with her grandparents. Now that her grandparents and parents were gone, it was hers. Like the blue crockery she used for their table. The table itself had been made by Bjarni from scraps of lumber scavenged from an abandoned farm. He wasn't a very good carpenter. The table, like most things he made, was rough and ill-proportioned, but it served its function. The luxury of beauty belonged to the past. Or some other world, as she had heard stories of.

She sighed as her daughter Gudny pushed open the door and burst in from outside, bundled in her wool jacket patched in many places, her little face peeking out from her hood with a carefree smile, her blue eyes shining. She ran up and flung her arms around Asa's legs. Asa embraced her, lifted her up and kissed her cheek, pushing the hood off her beautiful blonde curls. Gudny was always happy. She seemed not to know all the reasons not to be. Oh, what a foolish child to be so happy in the face of so much hopelessness! Asa laughed and gave Gudny a squeeze.

"Do you want some milk?" she asked, setting Gudny on the floor.

Gudny nodded eagerly. Asa removed the child's coat, then gave her a cup of goat's milk in a chipped blue cup. They had two goats left. It would have been none, but Bjarni's brother had died of the sickness and Bjarni took his animals and furniture. There was almost nothing left for the goats to eat, though, so they wouldn't last much longer. Once the snow covered the ground, the goats would starve. Then her family would eat the goats like they had the sheep and cows before them. Then what? No milk. No cheese. They would eat fish, Bjarni said. And seal meat. They already ate fish and seal meat. But without any milk to cook the dried fish in, it would be nearly intolerable. You can live on fish and seal meat, Bjarni insisted to his family. The Skrælings do it. When he had mentioned the wild, dark people, his mother Hild had protested, saying, "We are not Skrælings!

We are Norsemen. We must have bread and milk. Have faith. God will provide."

They could survive on fish and seal meat like the Skrælings, but even the fishing and hunting didn't seem as good as they used to be. In days past, according to the elders, there were so many seals and walruses, they could take as many as they could carry back to the village. And no trouble either with the Skrælings. They lived further north. They were hardly ever seen. But now they were seen more often, parties of hunters in their long narrow boats gliding past in the ocean beyond the ice. When they appeared, a ripple of fear and loathing ran through the village and all the men became alert and watchful. There had been recent violence between the two groups. Several months before, a party of men had brought down a walrus. As they butchered it, they were attacked by a half dozen Skrælings who stole the walrus and left two men injured.

Asa had never seen a Skræling except from a great distance. All she knew about them was that they were brown-skinned savages to be abhorred and avoided.

Her mother-in-law Hild was bitter and unhappy. Since Bjarni was the only male left of her family, she blamed him for everything that was wrong. Her husband had died years ago. Her other son and his entire family had been taken by the sickness last winter. Her youngest child, a daughter, died in childbirth. Bjarni sometimes got angry at his mother and told her she should have gone with the others, the ones who left last year for Brattahlid.

"How could I leave my family?" she had answered. At that time, Bjarni's brother and his family had still been alive. "Besides, you know they never made it."

Most of the villagers had assumed the party couldn't make it. The weather was rarely mild long enough to allow such a journey on foot. It would have taken a miracle, more than one person had declared, for that party to have made its goal. Even some among those who left expected to die. They gave their possessions to those who remained and wished them well, saying farewell with a grim resignation. If they had had dogs and sleds like the Skrælings, Asa reflected, they might have made it.

But the villagers weren't past hope. They still hoped for a good summer each year, for healthy crops and animals, for good fishing and hunting. And, most importantly, they were still alive.

Asa smiled at her daughter with her milky upper lip.

The sound of excited voices outside drew her attention. She pulled on her coat and opened the door, seeing a group of men nearby. Bjarni saw her and walked rapidly toward her, his towering frame bulky in his layers of clothing. He grinned and pointed toward the shore.

"We got a whale!" he said triumphantly. "We'll have a feast!"

He brushed the hood off his head, letting his ginger hair fall loose. His lined face was rugged, his jaw hard and square, his chin broad. His thin lips were stretched into a seldom seen exultant smile.

"A whale!" she exclaimed.

"Big enough to feed everyone for weeks."

As the thankful villagers butchered the whale, the story of the hunt was told and retold by each of the hunters to his friends and family members. They had spotted it close to shore and had gone after it in two boats. Halvard had been first to land a clean hit with his harpoon. The wounded animal had put up a fight, but was overwhelmed by several weapons. While they were battling the whale, three Skrælings had appeared in one of their narrow boats. The men had vowed that they would not lose another catch to Skrælings, so while one boat finished off the whale and lumbered toward shore with it, the other boat put itself between the Skrælings and the whale. They shadowed each other into shore where all three vessels were pulled onto the rocks and the whale was secured. The Skrælings ran toward them, brandishing spears and yelling. There were only three, so five of the men ran out to meet them. A hand-to-hand fight took place with knives and clubs. One of the Skrælings was killed by a stab wound to the chest. The other two then ran back to their boat and paddled away.

"They ran away!" the men boasted, proud that they had defended themselves and their catch successfully this time. "And left their dead brother to be eaten by bears."

"Heathen dogs," Bjarni chuckled. He was still excited by the day's events.

During the course of harvesting the whale flesh, they were surprised at the discovery of a broken-off harpoon tip embedded in the whale's side. It was a Skræling harpoon made of bone, not iron like their own. The hunters grew less boastful after that, understanding that the first blow landed on this whale had not been Halvard's after all.

The villagers went to their chapel and gave thanks to God for providing food and asked for protection from the Skræling devils.

Asa said a special prayer for her unborn child, that he or she would not live in suffering. What she meant by that, she didn't allow her imagination to pursue.

CHAPTER SEVEN

Kelly stumbled again and went down, landing on two hands and a knee. She lowered herself to rest on the rock she'd tripped on. Her legs were wearing out. The few miles between their break spot and town belied the difficulty of the journey. Without finding the official trail, she was left to scramble over loose rocks, climb steep hills and skirt dozens of lakes. She had ended up having to backtrack for an entire mile at one point because the route she had chosen dead-ended at an impassable fjord. Now she was a quarter mile into crossing a low area that had seemed like an easy path when she'd chosen it. But it had been a mistake. It was a bog. Her boots were soaked through. Her legs were splattered with mud up to her knees.

If it was winter, she thought, *my feet would freeze and fall off.* But it wasn't winter. What would she be doing here in winter anyway? She shook her head, realizing she was having trouble staying focused.

She again conjured up the image of the coconut bunny cake and tried to remember if she had gotten her first bicycle for that birthday. Or was it Christmas? Her memories from that early age were too sketchy. She began to realize that she couldn't really even remember the bunny cake itself. The clear memory she had of it wasn't a memory of the actual cake at all. It was the memory of a photograph taken that day. In the photo, she sat on a booster seat at the kitchen table, wearing a pastel yellow dress with a yellow ribbon in her hair, her eyes wide with the prospect of the amazing cake. Her mother faced the camera, standing beside her with the most wonderfully happy expression on her face. That was why she loved that photograph so much. It was because of her mother's beaming smile. That sort of happiness had gone out of reach for her later, in times Kelly remembered much better. But the photo proved it had once been possible.

Photography was a kind of magic. Some aboriginals wouldn't allow themselves to be photographed because they thought the image would steal their souls. Remembering that photo of her mother, Kelly could see how one could imagine it had stolen something from her. Because there it was in the photo, a joyful vitality in her eyes that had gone out in later years. But the magic of a photo wasn't that it stole your soul. It was that it stopped time.

In those days, her mother had dutifully put the photos in albums in chronological order. Like everyone's albums, the pictures were of special occasions—holidays, birthdays, vacations. The albums ended by the time Kelly reached her teens. That was when everything fell apart and happy family occasions no longer took place. Pretend happy took place for a while. Then even that ended. Dad left and their house became a place of mourning.

Some people grow stronger from defeat. Wiser and more determined, they take life's lessons into the future with them. Some people let disappointment break them. That's what her mother had done. Her disillusionment turned to despair and she remained stuck there, full of bitter regret, to the present day. When anybody asked her if she would ever remarry, she would answer, "Why? So I can be tossed on the trash heap again?" She was afraid to risk her heart. But one thing Kelly knew was that you can't win if you don't throw the dice.

No, Kelly didn't remember that birthday. She couldn't have said who else was around that table or whether or not she got a bicycle or who took the photo. It was her mother's happy memory, not hers. Funny how you think you remember something when there's a photo. It begs a philosophical question: what was the difference between a memory of an event and the memory of a photo of the event?

In a way, those ever-joyful photos could seem ironic, and that's how her mother saw them. Her mother looked at them and thought, *It was all an illusion.* But it wasn't like that for Kelly. The photos were her proof that for many years they were all happy. At the time, life was wonderful, and the fact that the happy period ended didn't change that. It had still happened. It was her childhood. She thought it was a mistake to turn bitter about the good times just because they didn't last forever. The way to avoid regret over the past and fear of the future was to live in the moment. For Kelly, a photograph was a symbol of that philosophy. It was a true, unchanging glimpse of a moment in time.

Rousing herself from her thoughts, she contemplated her surroundings, trying to decide how to proceed. Ahead of her was more of the same terrain, ground soaked with the water from melted snow and ice. Spotty patches of dense green plants marked the danger zones. She had to try harder to keep out of them. Unfortunately, that meant slowing down.

She felt like crying or screaming. *I should have stayed and waited*, she thought. Pippa would have come back, eventually. She had probably come back right after she left, found her note and cursed her for leaving. She had probably walked back to town already on her own, on the proper trail, and was in the midst of arranging a search party to look for the stupid American woman who had gotten herself lost on a simple hike from point A to point B.

I am not lost, she assured herself. She knew exactly where she was. All she had to do was look at her GPS receiver to see that she was sitting on the west coast of Greenland beside Disko Bay just a few miles north of a little dot labeled "Ilulissat."

She was struck with the oddity that a place so alien just two weeks ago, a place she had never even heard of, had now become her symbol of refuge. Ilulissat represented everything that home ever did to anyone: safety, comfort, people who cared.

Yes, Kelly sighed, Ilulissat and the cozy boarding house with its hazardous balconies and dour-faced landlady was the only place she wanted to be right now. She checked her phone again just in case she had wandered into a pocket of reception. "No service" flashed across the screen, just as it had every other time she'd checked. Not a lot of demand for cell phone coverage out here in the unpopulated Arctic, she mused.

How easy all of this would be if I could just dial 911. She shook her head mournfully, realizing that even if she could make a call, she didn't know the emergency number in Greenland. The day was full of ironies.

She took the last birke out of her pocket and ate it, wishing they had brought more food.

Trying to entice her to come to Greenland, Chuck had promised her "the adventure of a lifetime." Of course that had piqued Kelly's interest. She wasn't someone who would turn down *the adventure of a lifetime*. She looked around at the vast, hostile wilderness she was trapped in. *You were right, you son of a bitch!*

She wondered how long it would be before he would miss her. If he even would. He probably wouldn't notice her absence until tomorrow morning when she didn't turn up for breakfast. No, she reminded herself, she would be there for breakfast. It was only a few more miles. Chuck would remain cheerfully oblivious to her ordeal and walk into the dining room tomorrow morning, failing to notice her scratches, bruises and haggard appearance and say, "*God morgen, alle!*" Then he'd tell them how well he had slept once he found that horrid little pea under his mattress that had kept him tossing and turning until midnight.

Then Kelly would strangle him.

She uncapped her water bottle and drained the last of it. The standing water everywhere around her was probably safe to drink. It wasn't like there was a herd of cows grazing anywhere nearby. But there were musk oxen, she understood, and reindeer. Still, it didn't seem likely there was anything to worry about. She hadn't seen a single animal other than sled dogs since she'd set foot in Greenland.

All she had seen so far of marine mammals were a couple of black dots in the water reputed to be seals and a whale carcass on the shore. Just the skeleton, left there by hunters after they harvested the meat. In ancient times, the bones wouldn't have been left behind. They were valuable, like every part of every animal. According to Chuck, the Greenland Inuit used to make their winter houses out of whale bones, using them like other people use framing lumber, then layering on animal skins and turf to create a cozy den. They knew all the tricks for survival here in the Arctic. Goes without saying, she thought. Otherwise, they wouldn't have been around very long. Like the doomed Vikings.

A mosquito buzzed near her ear and lit on her cheek. She slapped at it and got up. Sitting still was a sure way to get eaten up by mosquitoes. She glanced at her phone to see the time. It was just past five o'clock. The "No Service" message persisted. She had wasted so much time. She began to worry that she wouldn't make it before the sun fell low on the horizon and gave no warmth. She worried that Pippa might be lying somewhere exposed to the elements. Summer nights in Greenland could get very cold. No more breaks, she told herself, hoping she had the strength to keep moving until she reached her destination.

Aiming hopefully toward what she thought was a trail cairn, she slogged slowly through the muck, thinking that if she could just regain the official trail, she would make much faster progress. It wasn't a cairn after all, just a jumble of rocks. She was hot, tired and increasingly frustrated. Mosquitoes swarmed around her. The repellent was surely saving her life, but a few intrepid insects had their way with her anyway.

Her only goal now was to get out of the bog. She aimed for a passage up ahead that would lift her out of this mire and onto a higher path. Her pace had slowed to a miserable crawl since she'd entered this valley. She climbed upslope and finally onto solid rock. She kept climbing and emerged at a point where the bay came into view a mere quarter mile away. She stopped walking just long enough to congratulate herself on surviving the bog ordeal.

With the sun low on the horizon, the light had a golden hue, casting long shadows and changing the appearance of the sea ice. The icebergs were yellowed, the color of old newspaper and glowing in an entirely different way than at mid day, with a soft aura. The air had gotten noticeably cooler, so she took her jacket out of her pack and put it on. The bay was as beautiful as ever, but she wasn't as charmed by it as she had been before today. Everything seemed cold and sinister now.

She continued walking, her feet wet and her boots heavy. Then she caught a flash of color further along, near the shore. She stopped and focused on the spot. There was something orange in the distance, solid bright orange, like fabric or plastic. It wasn't a natural looking color or shape, but it was too far away to identify. Whatever it was, it was likely a rare sign of human habitation. What if it *was* a piece of fabric or plastic? It was probably some debris that had washed up on shore. Some careless person's trash, likely nothing of interest to her.

She let her gaze wander in that direction as she dipped and climbed along a ridge. The orange object went in and out of view, coming gradually closer.

On the other hand, she thought, it might not be trash. It might be a sign of a campsite or even a homestead. She stopped walking again, trying to decide what to do. If she went to investigate the mysterious orange blob, she'd take up a lot of extra time on the detour. She'd have to find a way to get down there and, if it turned out to be nothing, get back up again. After her march through the bog, she was in no hurry to leave the comfort of the ridge. But if there was someone there, if she could get help... If there was any chance at all that there was someone there, how could she pass up the possibility?

She reluctantly altered her plan, looking for a navigable path down to shore and keeping the orange blob in view, hoping it would reveal itself in more detail before she had wasted a trip down to investigate. Unfortunately, she lost sight of it completely while she forged a nonlinear path through the rugged landscape.

It seemed to take forever to get down to sea level and by the time she was almost there, she was afraid she'd overshot Orange Blob. She looked north and south, trying to get a glimpse of it. Instead, she saw something wonderful up ahead. On the sloping gravel shore stood a house! A yellow house! Wood siding, pitched roof, white-framed windows. Like the houses in Ilulissat. Like the houses in Rodebay. She closed her eyes and reopened them, urgently hoping she wasn't hallucinating. The house was still there. The sound of barking dogs reached her ears, sounding like the most beautiful music she had ever heard.

She knew she was nowhere near Ilulissat, that this was merely one isolated dwelling and that many such houses and even towns stood abandoned on the Greenland coast, but the fact of the dogs meant this house was inhabited. Her pulse raced with excitement as she scrambled down the last stretch of rocky slope, feeling a huge sense of relief that she had finally found help for Pippa.

CHAPTER EIGHT

Everything had happened so fast: a blur of bodies, blood spattering, screams, a jumble of horrific images that Asa could make only partial sense of. She had seen Bjarni go down, felled by a powerful blow to the head from one of the Skrælings. But she hadn't been able to get to him before she herself was caught up in the rough arms of one of the attackers. She was flung over a broad shoulder and held fast. She struggled, but made no impression on the mute savage who ran with her to the frozen bay, his feet silent, his breath labored, the musky smell of him flooding her nostrils. She screamed to attract the attention of her friends, but they were in the midst of their own battle and unable to assist.

The buildings of her village sank behind a hill until she saw nothing but the black smoke rising from the burning chapel. Her kidnapper tied her to the back of his sled with leather straps, then covered her with a heavy bearskin, blocking her view. Amid his yells and the terrifying barking of dogs, the sled jerked and took off across the ice as Asa lay silent and petrified in the womb of her bearskin.

That had been two days ago. She and her abductor had eventually arrived at a Skræling village where she had been put in a dark and stuffy tent. There was a cold fire pit in the center of the floor, a smoke hole at the top, and an opening in the side to crawl in and out of. She wasn't bound, but she'd already discovered the doorway was guarded. When she had tried to crawl out, a savage with a spear hollered at her and threatened to poke her. He had a round, brown face, dark brown eyes and straight black hair. He had opened his mouth wide and laughed at her in a thick, mocking tone. She had immediately withdrawn into the tent.

She sat huddled against a wall on a musk ox skin, wondering what had happened to the rest of her family and kinsmen. She could hear the voices of the Skrælings throughout the day. Their language was gibberish to her. It barely sounded human. She heard the barking of the sled dogs and smelled food cooking. Hours went by during which nothing happened. She was hungry and thirsty and had no idea how long she had been sitting there.

Finally she lay down on the thick fur and fell asleep. She woke to the sound of scuffling at the tent entrance. She bolted to a sitting position. The flap opened and a woman came in holding a bowl. She looked like a female version of the man Asa had encountered guarding the tent, brown-skinned and black-haired. She moved cautiously toward Asa, as if she were afraid of her, her dark eyes wary, and put the bowl down just out of reach. Then she grinned nervously and backed out.

Famished, Asa reached out and took the bowl, sniffing. She tasted it. Boiled whale meat. Was this the whale they had stolen from her village? She hesitated before taking a piece of the oily meat between her fingers and putting it on her tongue. She thought maybe she shouldn't eat. Maybe she should let herself starve to death. She didn't know what these horrible savages had in mind for her, but she knew there were limited possibilities. She would either be killed, enslaved or be forced to be some brute's mistress. That would be worse than death.

She had been taken as a prize of battle, she assumed, like the whale and whatever else they had found interesting. It was the way of war, as she had heard in tales of Viking raids on other lands. They raped the women, killed the men, enslaved some of the survivors, took their possessions and burned their villages, leaving total destruction behind. Had the Skrælings done the same to her village, she wondered, remembering the smoke from the burning chapel.

When she had first been led through the camp to her prison, everyone had stared in amazement, men and women alike. She had shrunk back ineffectually when a brash young man approached and touched her hair as if he had no idea what it was. Then he had jumped back, whooping like he had felt something wondrous. This had been her first close-up look at these people. She wasn't sure they were people. They were not people of God, that much was certain. For the first time in a long time, Asa prayed with a sincerity she had forgotten.

She hoped she would be killed quickly. That's what she prayed for. But if they were going to kill her, what were they waiting for? And why were they feeding her? For that matter, why had they brought her here at all? They could have killed her back in her village. More likely they were going to torment her in unspeakable ways. She would have to kill herself, she decided.

Movement at the tent entrance drew her attention. The same woman, crawling in on her hands and knees, peered in, pushing a ball of fur through the opening ahead of her. The ball rolled over and revealed a face. Asa sat up and gasped, transfixed by the familiar bright blue eyes and blonde curls. That little pink face was the most beautiful thing she had ever seen.

"Mama!" Gudny cried.

They clung to one another with tears and kisses while the brown-faced woman rocked on her ankles across the room, smiling benignly.

"My baby! My baby!" Asa said over and over, holding Gudny tight against her chest.

They must have taken her from the house and understood she belonged to Asa, and now they were giving her back. Asa was confused and scared, but she was overjoyed to have her daughter with her, safe, at least for the moment. When the Skræling woman withdrew, leaving them together, Asa reasoned that there seemed even less chance now that they would kill her.

And now that she had been reunited with Gudny, she no longer wanted to be killed.

"I want to go home," Gudny implored.

"So do I," Asa told her.

"Where's Papa?"

"Maybe he's looking for us," she suggested hopefully, but she doubted it.

Bjarni, she feared, was dead. He wouldn't rescue them. Perhaps nobody would. It would be dangerous. It would be hard to find them. And who would enter into a quest like that other than Bjarni? No, she decided grimly, nobody would come for them. If they were to be rescued, Asa would have to do it herself.

For one week she obediently did what she was told as the women tried to teach her their chores. Through gestures and demonstrations, she understood what to do, but she was unskilled. They shook their heads in dismay and laughed at her, as if she were the best entertainment they had had in a long time. She failed at sewing. The stitches they made with animal sinew were so fine, she couldn't replicate them. A shoddy job was unacceptable, she understood, because everything had to be waterproof. They gave her and Gudny a pair of their sealskin boots and caribou skin pants and parkas. Though they felt strange, she admired these garments. They were warm, lightweight and weatherproof.

There were five women in the camp, three mature adults and two younger women. There were three children also, two boys and a girl. Altogether there were eleven Skrælings in this group. Asa saw others come and go, so she knew there were other groups nearby.

The men watched her and made her nervous. There were three adult men. One of them, Ragnoq, was the man who had taken her away. He seemed to be the leader. There was another man, Ortuq, who may have been Ragnoq's younger brother. His smile, Asa noticed, was neither mocking nor smug. She thought she detected a hint of sympathy in his eyes when he looked her way, but she wasn't sure she could read his face. One day when she was struggling to lift a too-large vessel of water to the fire, he came to her aid and did it for her. Other than this one gesture of help, none of the men had bothered her or even seemed to notice her. But the boy who had touched her hair the first day seemed fascinated by her. He greeted her by pointing to his dark eyes, then to hers and laughing. After a few days, she decided he was harmless.

Asa was surprised the men left her alone. She had expected to be ravaged immediately, perhaps by all of them. She didn't know their laws of female possession or what superstitions guided them. Perhaps, she thought, they avoided her because she was carrying a child. She knew they had pagan gods and heathen ways, so the laws of her God didn't apply to them. Their pagan gods were different from the old gods of the Norse countries, so there was nothing she could know about their strange beliefs. Because they did not know God, it was generally understood that they were governed by no moral laws.

Though they hadn't yet touched her, she knew it was merely a matter of time. She didn't intend to stay around and wait. She planned her escape, assembling a store of food and supplies by surreptitiously hiding them under her garments and caching them in the tent she and Gudny slept in. She was so cooperative with the chores, her captors didn't seem to be concerned about her posing any danger to them or running away. After the second day, their tent was left unguarded. Possibly they didn't think she dared run away, having nowhere to go, no idea where they had taken her and being too far from home. She herself wasn't sure she could do it. Making her way home on foot would be difficult. Judging by the time it had taken to bring her here, she guessed she had a three-day journey back, but it was just a guess. Another possibility troubled her deeply, that they knew she had nothing to go back to. If they had left her village destroyed, burned to the ground, no one could survive there. With no timber, they couldn't rebuild, and with no shelter, they were doomed. Asa carried a tremendous burden of doubt about her plan. There was no question in her mind, though, that she had to try, if only for the sake of her daughter.

Gudny was nearly silent all the time. Asa hadn't seen a smile on her face the entire time they'd been in captivity. Her daughter, whose irrepressible joy had cheered her gloomy days, now wore an expression of fear and confusion. She was inconsolable. Every time a Skræling looked her way, she cried. Asa didn't blame her. They were so unfamiliar looking and acting. Asa, too, was afraid. But she didn't cry. She hadn't cried for a long time. Nor had she laughed very often. There was something about enduring hardship over time that deadens the sharp edges of one's emotions. Gudny was still capable of tears and of joy. Her emotions were not yet dulled by adversity. Asa wanted to preserve that trait as long as possible.

On the night she had chosen for escape, she waited until long after the camp was silent, her heart pounding furiously with fear as she picked up Gudny and wrapped her in a caribou skin. Her eyes opened briefly, but she settled back into sleep with her head on Asa's shoulder. Asa then picked up her bundle of supplies and slung it silently onto her other shoulder. It was heavy, but contained only essentials: skins, tools and food. She pushed aside the flap of the tent and stepped into the cold night air. Everyone else would be in their own tents, asleep, she hoped. The real problem was the dogs. They were tied up just outside of camp. She needed to go south, but didn't dare. Instead, she slipped silently behind her tent and walked north, making sure there was always something blocking her from the dogs' view, first her tent, then the rocks she ducked behind. Wearing the Skræling boots, she chose her path with precision. Her footsteps made no sound on bare rock.

She realized she had been holding her breath and silently released it, continuing north. There was light to guide her, though the sun wasn't visible. Clouds in the west obscured it. That was good. On a cloudless summer night, she would be more easily seen.

She continued north for a while before heading west and making a wide arc, keeping the Skræling camp a good distance away, out of sight and hearing. She didn't think she needed as much distance as she allowed, but didn't want to take a chance. She didn't know anything about dogs, how far they could see or hear or smell. She also didn't know where the other camps were and was worried about coming too close. She decided to walk on the frozen ice of the bay, keeping clear of any Skræling villages on shore.

She dropped down from the rocky coastal hills to the flat expanse of ice, then headed south, knowing that each footstep brought her closer to home.

When Gudny awoke, Asa put her down and allowed her to walk. Her arms were already tired from carrying the girl and the supplies. She knew they would travel more slowly this way, but she also knew she couldn't carry Gudny all the way home.

"Where are we going?" Gudny asked.

"Home," Asa replied.

They held hands as they walked. The landscape was unfamiliar to Asa. There were no landmarks she recognized… yet. She had seen maps of this coast and had heard the men talk often enough about hunting expeditions up and down it, so she knew roughly where she was. She was surely near where the hunting parties went for seal and walrus. That was why the Skrælings were here, she realized. They had pitched their summer camp where the hunting was good. She had heard the men complaining that the Skrælings had invaded their hunting grounds.

The ice was solid and smooth underfoot, allowing them to make rapid progress. People said there used to be no ice in summer other than floating icebergs. That was how the ships used to come into this bay. But she had never seen such a thing. Now there was solid ice on the water year round.

She kept gauging the time by the path of the sun across the horizon. She could see its halo behind the clouds as it traversed the horizontal line toward morning when her captors would awaken and find her gone. She feared for morning. They would have no trouble catching up to her with their sleds. She knew she would have no chance against several strong men and their ferocious dogs. Her only chance of eluding them would be to hide.

When Gudny became too weary, she lifted her up and carried her. At least they were warm. The Skræling clothes, so much lighter and thinner than wool, were remarkably effective.

"I'm hungry," Gudny whined.

Asa put her off until she too felt the clawing of hunger in her stomach. They didn't have a lot of food. They would have to use it carefully. She stopped for a short rest. She cut reindeer meat with a knife made of stone she had taken from the Skrælings. It was finely made, fashioned into a thin blade that could easily pierce the skin of an animal...or a man. It was sharper but more fragile than the metal knives she was used to. Knives and other metal tools were becoming more and more valuable, as there was no iron to make new ones. There were things she had seen in the Skræling camp, like this knife and the boots she wore, that made her wonder if her people could learn something useful from them. They had brought in fish every day she was there. She didn't know how they caught it, but they clearly had a good method.

As the sun moved higher and freed itself of the low clouds, the light of morning changed the color of the ice to bright white. By now her captors would be awake and would have discovered her gone. She wondered for a moment if they might let her go. Maybe they wouldn't think she was worth the trouble to track down.

Later that afternoon, Asa came to an area of thin ice and reluctantly walked inland, climbing the coastal hills to continue on solid land. A short time later she heard the distant barking of dogs and her heart leapt to her throat. She stopped to listen, to make sure she had really heard it. Yes, it was dogs, the sound that always alerted her village to nearby Skrælings. She gathered Gudny roughly into her arms. Her panic alarmed the child, who started to cry.

"Shhh!" she warned. "You must be quiet or they'll find us."

She ran, looking for a place to hide. The barking seemed to be coming from the south, causing her to stop in confusion. They were coming from ahead of her? Not behind? There was a ravine nearby. They wouldn't see her there. But the dogs... would the dogs smell them? There was nothing else she could try. There was nowhere to go.

She ran with Gudny in her arms to the edge of the ravine, then put her down and said, "You can climb down here. Follow me."

Gudny nodded, her bright blue eyes wide and full of fear.

Asa started down, scrambling hurriedly as the barking got louder. She lifted Gudny over the larger boulders as they made their way down the steep incline, loose rocks dislodging and sliding ahead of them. Her heart pounded furiously as she leapt over a crevice. She landed awkwardly on a rock that gave way, knocking her off her feet. She fell and rolled, striking her body hard against an immovable boulder below. It knocked the wind out of her and she lay there for a moment in a daze, cold stone against her cheek, the terrible barking of dogs insistent in her ears.

"Mama!" Gudny cried, appearing at her side.

Asa looked up at the top of the ravine and slipped an arm around Gudny, pulling her close. She put her finger to her lips to caution the girl to be silent. They hadn't made it as far down as she had planned, but they were out of sight…until the dogs caught their scent and followed. Asa lay beside the boulder that had stopped her, still and silent except for her breathing, and looked straight up at the clear blue sky, waiting to be recaptured.

The barks and howls of the dogs came closer and seemed to be all around them. Asa fixed her eyes on the top of the ravine, expecting any second to see the menacing head of a dog appear at its edge. But she saw nothing, and within moments, as if the sled had never even slowed down, the fearful noises began to subside. Inexplicably, they were moving away.

Asa roused herself. "Stay here," she instructed Gudny, then scrambled back to the top of the ravine where she peeked over. She saw a single sled on the frozen bay, heading away to the north. A man drove and a young boy rode on the back, bundled up in his fur clothing so only a small brown round of his face showed. They were too far away for Asa to see the boy's face clearly and the man was facing the other direction, but this was obviously not a tracking party. These two appeared to be alone. The sled and the sound of dogs barking faded into the distance, eventually becoming just a dark spot on the white expanse of ice.

Relieved they were safe, Asa rubbed her nose with her gloved hand. The chill coming off the icy bay left her exposed skin numb.

She started back down to where Gudny waited. Halfway along, she was struck by a sharp pain in her abdomen, so sharp it stopped her cold. She waited for it to pass, then took the rest of the slope more cautiously. As she skirted the rift she had tried to jump earlier, she noticed a dark opening between the rocks. She peered into it and felt a current rising up from below, slightly warmer than the air around her. She motioned to Gudny to come to her while she investigated the fissure. A jumble of boulders was piled into the ravine, solidly stacked. She walked around them, noting one or two places where there was a narrow opening. It appeared this jumble wasn't a solid mass. The rocks had fallen and arranged themselves in such a way that they had created a sheltered cave. She was able to enlarge one of the fissures by removing some dirt, gravel and smaller stones, opening a tight passage into the blackness beyond.

What was inside and how big a space it was, she couldn't tell, but judging from the exterior, it couldn't be very large.

She was taken by surprise by another deep and severe attack of pain and allowed herself to collapse to the ground. Her earlier fall, she reasoned, must have done more damage than she'd realized. Gudny was cold and hungry and night was coming. Asa would have liked to walk until twilight at least, but now she reconsidered. They had possibly found some rare and precious shelter and she was worried about her own physical condition. She put a hand on her swollen stomach, then tried to smile at Gudny.

"No more walking today," she said. "You know how a little fox lives in a burrow in the ground? She keeps herself and her babies warm all bundled up in a cozy earth house. We can do that too." She pointed at the opening she had created in the rocks. "I'll go in first and make sure there are no foxes in there."

Gudny nodded worriedly and Asa smiled to reassure her before crawling through.

CHAPTER NINE

Still not believing her luck, Kelly scrambled down to shore, then hurried toward the yellow house while the dogs barked frantically to warn the homeowner of the intruder.

Before she reached the house, the door opened and a squat old woman stepped out. She waited, her arms slack at her sides, her graying hair pulled tightly back behind her head. As Kelly neared, she recognized the woman as Nivi, their boat passenger from that morning. Startled, she observed the house more closely. All of the houses in Greenland looked alike to her, but it must be the same house.

She came to a stop, out of breath. "Nivi!" she blurted, as if they were old friends. "It's you! Nivi!"

The woman pointed to herself and smiled, deeply creasing her face. "Nivi." She nodded good-humoredly and seemed perfectly at ease, as if it was customary for people to drop by for a visit.

"I'm Kelly. Do you remember me? From the tour boat? You remember Pippa, don't you? Pippa?" The woman showed no comprehension. "Pipaluk? My friend Pipaluk?"

"Pipaluk?" Nivi said, pointing to her own sable eyes.

"Right! Pipaluk, the one with the blue eyes."

Nivi shook her head. She pointed at Kelly and said something that Kelly interpreted as, "You're not Pipaluk."

"No, no. I'm not Pipaluk. I'm Kelly." She pointed to herself again as she said her name. "Pipaluk is in trouble. I have to call for help. Look, it doesn't matter. Do you have a phone? A radio? A computer? Any way to get a message to somebody?"

Nivi answered in Greenlandic. Exasperated, Kelly took her phone out of her jacket pocket and held it up, noting it still had no signal. With this visual aid and hand gestures, she hoped she communicated her message when she said, "Telephone? Computer?" She made typing gestures with both hands to simulate keyboarding.

Nivi shook her head. Kelly wasn't certain she was being understood, so she pointed past Nivi into the interior of the house and said, "Can I look around?"

Seeming to understand, Nivi stood aside and allowed Kelly into the house. It was musty, dim and cramped inside. Old furniture filled up the room and there was no sign of anything modern. No electronics, no television. After a few minutes, Kelly realized there wasn't even electricity. A couple of oil lamps provided light. There was a wood-burning stove in the kitchen and no running water. What had she expected from a family living above the Arctic Circle miles from anyone else? She realized it had been stupid to think there was a computer here. It was possible, of course, to have a satellite connection, but if that was something of value to Nivi's family, they wouldn't be living like this in the first place.

She gazed into Nivi's calm brown eyes and sighed. Why did they live like this? she wondered. A few miles north was Rodebay with electricity, a Laundromat, people to talk to. A few miles south was the modern city of Ilulissat.

Then she remembered why she was here and felt herself succumb to despair. As tears fell on her cheeks, Nivi clucked at her and looked concerned.

"I wish you could understand me," she said. "But even if you could, what can you do with no way to call for help?"

Nivi looked solemnly at Kelly as if she were trying to read her mind, then she disappeared into another room. While she was gone, the small head of a child peered out from the doorframe, his eyes fixed on Kelly with curiosity. He must be Nivi's grandson, Kelly assumed. She waved a greeting at him and he pulled back and disappeared from view.

When Nivi returned, she wore an overcoat and carried a rifle. Alarmed, Kelly stepped backward, wondering if she should run for her life.

Nivi spoke to her rapidly and motioned toward the door. Kelly passed through it into the daylight beyond. The old woman followed and gestured as she walked toward shore. Kelly hesitated, so Nivi gestured even more emphatically.

"What?" Kelly cried. "I don't know what you're saying. I have to get to Ilulissat."

She turned and started walking away, deciding she had no other option than to continue with her original plan. Nivi caught up with her and grabbed her arm roughly, pulling her back. Kelly resisted, shaking her off, despite the rifle. She was determined not to be intimidated. She had been through hell already today and was in no mood to be messed with.

"Pipaluk!" Nivi growled, frowning intensely.

Kelly pointed north. "Pipaluk." Then she pointed south. "I'm going that way." She pointed at herself.

Nivi nodded as if she understood, but Kelly was sure she didn't. Then she took hold of Kelly's arm again and led her down to the shore. Kelly decided to let herself be manipulated until she at least knew what Nivi had in mind.

An orange tandem kayak lay on the gravel beach. Orange Blob! Kelly realized. Nivi placed her rifle in it and pushed it into the water. Then she pointed to it, urging Kelly to get in. There was no doubt about what she wanted, but there were too many ways this wasn't a good move. Did she think the two of them should return to rescue Pippa? Was she planning on paddling all the way to Ilulissat? Not a terrible idea, Kelly realized, though Nivi was an old woman and may not have the strength for it. Maybe between them they could manage. It would be quicker and easier than walking, that was certain. Or was she just taking Kelly out on a fishing trip? In view of the rifle, Kelly reconsidered that last thought. More likely a seal hunting trip.

Hoping to persuade the kayak toward Ilulissat, Kelly tucked her backpack into the bow and got in, taking the forward seat. Nivi got in behind her and they pushed off. Nivi offered no resistance as Kelly turned the craft south. Feeling chilled, she zipped her jacket up to her neck and cinched her hood tight around her head.

They paddled smoothly over the glassy water and Kelly began to relax. This would work. In no time they would be there and a rescue team could be sent out.

But they had only been on the water ten minutes when Nivi pointed inland, into a deep, sheer-cliffed fjord and attempted to turn the kayak toward it. Kelly resisted, paddling the other way and saying, "Ilulissat!"

"No, no!" Nivi argued, shaking her head. The rest of her argument was in Greenlandic.

"What the hell!" Kelly said to herself. Then she faced Nivi and said, "Pipaluk!" She drew her index finger across her throat and made what she figured was a universal sound for a last gasp.

Nivi nodded as if she understood perfectly, then pointed into the fjord again.

They fought each other until the kayak turned uselessly in a circle and Kelly felt her arms losing strength. She stopped trying to overpower Nivi, as they were clearly going nowhere. Defeated, she sat with her paddle resting across the boat.

Nivi seemed to take that as agreement and turned them into the mouth of the fjord. It curved up ahead, so Kelly couldn't see how far back it went. Apparently they were on a seal hunt after all. She decided she would have to get out and start walking again as soon as she could get off the water. Nivi obviously had no idea what she was trying to do and she didn't know how to make her understand.

As they traveled deeper into the fjord, the walls on either side grew higher and closed them into a narrow and dramatic channel. The water had changed color. It was now murky, a milky greenish gray. Kelly knew what that meant. This was meltwater from a glacier. At the head of this fjord, she assumed, an arm of the inland ice flowed into the bay. The cliffs on either side of them were sheer and vertical. There was no way to walk out of here. Kelly hoped there would be a way as they got further along. Otherwise, she wouldn't be able to get back on track until she could persuade Nivi to turn around and leave the fjord.

This is a nightmare, Kelly thought in exasperation. This entire day is a total nightmare.

She took up her paddle and joined Nivi in pushing the kayak deeper into the fjord. The sooner we get in here and do whatever she wants to do, she decided, the sooner we can get back out. Nivi paddled steadily, humming quietly and contentedly behind her. Her song was rhythmic and surprisingly restful.

They followed a wide curve to the left and suddenly the glacier was visible up ahead. The ice filled a high canyon and flowed down the side of a mountain to the fjord where it formed a calving front about sixty feet tall. The ice river above was striped gray, brown and white, the stripes following the contours of the canyon and revealing the flow pattern in an otherwise solid and motionless looking surface. The front of the glacier was white and cerulean blue, the pure interior that was exposed when the ice broke off. In front of the glacial tongue were several floating icebergs. This glacier wasn't a large one. The little bergs moving through this fjord might not even make it intact to the bay. They were rapidly melting under the summer sun. As they passed close, Kelly could see rivulets of water running off them.

If she had been less anxious and preoccupied, she would have been happy to be here. She would have taken photos of this spectacular scenery. As it was, the only good news she could find in this situation was that they would soon reach the end of the waterway and would have to stop.

A dull echo from their paddles resounded off the cliff walls on either side as they glided easily on the calm surface. Nivi steered them expertly around the icebergs, still humming her melody.

It was the clang of metal that first alerted Kelly to human activity at the edge of the fjord. The sound drew her attention to a smooth, sloping moraine on the north bank. As they came around a subtle curve and the entire face of the glacier came into view, the moraine also became visible in its entirety.

Kelly's mouth fell open as she saw a campsite with several tents erected, tables set up, people milling around and a moored motorboat at the edge of the water. She practically tipped the kayak in her excitement. She spun around to look at Nivi, who nodded up and down, grinning.

Kelly felt tears of relief come to her eyes. She paddled rapidly toward shore where two people and one tail-wagging husky came to greet them. The dog kept close to a stocky, dark-featured young man, a Greenlander, Kelly guessed. But the young woman, the blonde, was somebody Kelly already knew. It was flirty Sonja Holm from the morning tour. What a wonderful stroke of luck. Not only had Nivi taken her to people who could get help, but at least one of them was an American, so there would be no more trouble with language.

"Sonja!" Kelly called, waving frantically. "Sonja!"

Sonja waved back and stepped down to the water's edge to pull the kayak onto shore. "I didn't expect to see you again so soon," she remarked, looking perplexed. Then looking more closely, she said, "You're a mess!"

CHAPTER TEN

Why don't I think to ask these things ahead of time? Jordan wondered, looking up into the greasy guts of the yellow all-terrain vehicle her students had nicknamed Curly after one of The Three Stooges because it could take a lot of abuse. Right now, she wished Curly would live up to his name a little more literally so she could just give him a whack now and then to keep him in line. As part of the recruitment process for this summer gig, she should add some questions to the application about essential skills. *Can you cook? Do you have any mechanical ability? Do you know how to play Canasta?* In some ways, science could be said to be secondary to these other talents when a group of people was stuck on a glacier together for eight weeks.

She lay on her back on a piece of cardboard, tightening the last two bolts that would secure the new belt in place. Of her four students, not one of them had the mechanical ability to change a spark plug, let alone replace a broken belt. You'd think it would have been a safe bet in a group with one guy who loved backpacking and everything outdoors, one athletic lesbian, a female pilot and a native Greenlander that one of them would know how to work on engines. "I can fly a plane," Julie had elaborated. "But I don't work on them." As for Malik, he was the brooding intellectual type. Not a wilderness man like his Inuit ancestors. He had never even driven a car. There wasn't much use for cars in Greenland.

So the job was left to Jordan. She didn't really mind. She enjoyed getting into the muck. It was satisfying to occasionally work with one's hands instead of one's brain.

She snapped the belt to check its tension. Satisfied, she slid out from under the vehicle. Brian took the socket wrench from her and helped her up.

"Is it fixed?" he asked, his asymmetrical face even more than usually askew with concern.

"Yep."

He handed her a rag and she wiped her hands on it, standing back to admire Curly in all his utilitarian glory. Brian loomed over her at six-three, tall and lanky, wearing a knit cap over the careless hair that rarely saw a comb. A heavy brown beard obscured the better part of his face. Earlier in the year, in class, he had been clean-shaven and Jordan preferred him that way. He was shaggy and slapdash enough as it was. But he had decided that a remote Greenland science outpost deserved no less than completely unrestrained hair growth. She couldn't criticize him for that. She herself hadn't shaved underarms or legs for the three weeks she'd been here. With the inadequate military-style shower, about all they could do was keep from being offensive. Malik somehow managed to keep himself groomed to perfection, however, and was always clean-shaven. But Julie, like Brian, had gone primal. Not too often you saw a straight American woman with hairy armpits.

They were a good group, for the most part. All smart and serious about the work. They didn't love each other, but they worked well together. That was actually better than some of the more friendly alternatives, she mused, recalling groups from the past.

It was hard to tell ahead of time how a group like this would function under these conditions, especially with the added element of the unknown member, Malik. He had joined them after they arrived. None of them had known him previously, but he was working out well and Jordan was happy to have a Greenlander on the team. It seemed right. He was responsible for the name Camp Tootega. Before any camp construction began, Jordan always had her team choose a name. This time, Sonja had insisted that it invoke some sort of female spirit because their leader was a woman and she wanted to emphasize female power. Brian had rolled his eyes at that, leaning toward something more natural, like the name of a bird or fish. Of course, he didn't know any Greenlandic names, and a couple that Malik provided were utterly unpronounceable to the Americans. But then Malik had granted Sonja's wish with Tootega, the name of a wise old goddess of Inuit mythology who could walk on water. "Perfect!" she had declared, holding a hand out to present Jordan, as if she were the earthly incarnation of the deity herself. Jordan had burst out laughing. But it wasn't a bad name and they had voted to go with it. So this summer, it was Camp Tootega. From that moment on, Sonja and Malik had been friends. Jordan was glad of that because Malik had not gotten on well with Brian or Julie. But so far, thank Goddess Tootega, no fights.

"Can I start it up?" Brian asked, nodding toward Curly.

"Sure. Go for a spin." She tossed him the keys, then glanced down to the dock to see a bright orange kayak on the beach. "What's this? A visitor? That looks like Nivi's kayak."

"Who's Nivi?" Brian asked.

"She's a local. Lives nearby. I haven't seen her since last summer. Every once in a while she'll come by to sell us fish. Maybe she's brought us a salmon or a halibut. I hope so because I'm tired of eating out of cans."

Jordan walked to the center of camp just as Sonja arrived, her arm around another young woman's shoulder, a shapely brunette wearing a T-shirt, shorts and hiking boots. Her boots and legs were splattered with dried mud and her demeanor suggested weariness.

"There's been an accident," Sonja explained as they approached. "We need to call for help."

The stranger looked up and met Jordan's eyes with her own light brown ones. Eyes the color of amber ale, searching, worried and instantly familiar. Jordan uttered an involuntary gasp. *Kelly Sheffield!*

Kelly's weary anguish was instantly transformed into shock. "Jordan!" she exclaimed, staring unbelievingly.

"You two know each other?" Sonja asked.

"Yes," Jordan replied, rapidly collecting herself. "Kelly used to be a student of mine. What's happened? Are you hurt?"

Kelly looked around in confusion. "Is this your camp?" Her eyes flooded with tears as she pulled away from Sonja and flung her arms around Jordan's neck, leaning on her heavily.

"Jordan," she gasped, "thank God! You've got to help. Pippa's out there somewhere. She's lost or hurt or…I don't know what happened to her."

Jordan held her loosely, stroking her back to calm her, confused and uneasy as Kelly's sobs overtook her.

"Her friend Pipaluk," Sonja elaborated. "She wants us to call a search team. She's been lost for several hours now. She was lucky to run into the old woman over there."

Jordan glanced toward the dock where Malik and Nivi stood in conversation. Still muddled, she gently freed herself from Kelly. "Yes, of course we can call for help. We have a satellite phone. I'll make the call right now. You should come along to answer questions."

Kelly nodded her understanding, her eyes full of emotion and bewilderment. *She's not the only one who's bewildered*, Jordan thought. *What the hell is Kelly Sheffield doing in Greenland?*

Jordan led the way to her tent, Kelly close behind, wiping tears from her face but no longer crying. Jordan couldn't shake her amazement at seeing her here. It had to be a coincidence because Kelly was clearly as surprised as she was.

She held the flap aside, then followed Kelly in. The tent was separated into two distinct rooms by a curtain made of sheets. On the right was Jordan's personal space, her cot, dressing table, a shelf of books, a rack of clothes. On the left was a more public area with several chairs, equipment, stacks of boxes, and a long table containing a computer, radio and telephone, all the tools that kept them connected to one another and the rest of the world.

She led the way to the worktable and offered Kelly a chair, pausing to take a better look at her. She must be thirty years old now. The track of her tears stained her cheeks where they had traveled through a layer of dust. She was beautiful, Jordan noted with awe. Changed but familiar with her clear pale complexion, small ears and nose, delicate features. Jordan observed her full, feminine mouth, as alluring as before, the same mouth she had so foolishly tasted nine years ago.

The last time she had seen Kelly, Jordan recalled, her face had been also been stained with tears.

It had been on her twenty-first birthday. Jordan had invited her out for a drink to celebrate. Her first legal drink and a rare social occasion for the two of them. Jordan didn't usually go out with students, especially not ones who were in love with her. But this was an important day. In addition to the landmark birthday, it was the last time they would see one another and they both knew they were saying goodbye forever.

Ever since Jordan had told Kelly she was leaving to take a position at UCLA, Kelly had been morose. At first, she had said she was coming to LA too, but Jordan talked her out of it. Kelly was in no position to do something like that, in the middle of obtaining her degree and with almost no money. It would have been the height of folly. "The most important thing," Jordan had advised her, "is your education. Don't let your emotions sidetrack you from what's truly important." Don't make the same mistake I made, she could have easily added.

Kelly was fundamentally a practical girl and so she relented. Perhaps she even understood that Jordan's departure meant that she would be free at last from a hopeless infatuation. With Jordan out of the picture, she could move on and find someone more appropriate to love.

With all of this in mind, as they said their final goodbye in the car outside Kelly's apartment house, Jordan had gathered her in her arms for an embrace. Then she pulled back and looked into her distraught, lovely face and the outpouring of love in her eyes, and was moved to kiss her. Very deliberately on the lips, a romantic, tender kiss that lasted only a few seconds, but pulsed with sensuality and focused two years of Kelly's desperate longing into a single moment.

That had been Jordan's parting gift to Kelly, one kiss.

What a hypocrite! she accused herself, grabbing the satellite phone from its charger.

At the time, she had told herself she was giving a gift to Kelly. But she'd been lying to herself. She had just wanted to kiss her, plain and simple. She'd wanted to kiss her for a long time, but she couldn't allow it until she was leaving. When it couldn't lead to anything. Then she had simply walked away. After two years of basking in the warm glow of Kelly's love and giving her nothing but crumbs, she had finally released her. Jordan had given her just enough affection to keep her love alive, but never enough to nourish or satisfy it. She had been utterly selfish.

During her attempts not to exploit young Kelly, that's exactly what she had ended up doing. She had led her on and she was ashamed of it. The only excuse she had for herself was that she too had been young. Younger, at any rate, and still learning how to protect herself from her treacherous emotions.

Back then, she hadn't been accustomed to being worshipped. It had felt wonderful. It was heady and hard to resist. It was easy to understand why so many of her colleagues succumbed to it, taking these girls or boys as their lovers, even though they looked absurd and incurred the ridicule of their colleagues. Inevitably the young devotee was moving on to the next interesting thing, usually within a month or two. But Jordan had kept her worshipper at her feet simply by denying her what she wanted most.

She dialed the local emergency number.

"I hope somebody can get out here fast," Kelly said, clearly distressed. "I'm so worried Pippa is seriously hurt. Or even…" Again her eyes grew moist with tears. She never had been afraid of her emotions.

Is she in love with this Pippa? Jordan wondered as the dispatcher's voice came over the phone: "*Alarm 112, hvad kan vi hjælpe med?*"

CHAPTER ELEVEN

Pippa's situation was now out of Kelly's hands. All she could do was wait and hope the search team found her in good shape.

A few steps away, one of Jordan's students, Brian, the tall, bearded one, stirred a pot of canned stew on the camp stove while Malik, the taciturn Greenlander, stood beside him slicing a loaf of bread into careful, even slices. He was a muscular, clean-shaven man of medium height in a gray wool sweater and dark pants. Kelly found herself staring, fixated, at his head. His fine black hair was cut in a modified mohawk with a ridge of long hair across the crown and much shorter hair on the left side. On the right, it was completely shaved to display a red and white tattoo on his scalp, a depiction of the Greenland flag. The design curved around his ear and extended to his temple. She had never seen anything quite like it. In his left ear, he wore a two-inch long shark tooth earring.

Besides Sonja and these two young men, there was one other student in camp: Julie, a sporty young woman who wore her long brown hair in a ponytail and whose attitude seemed cool and critical. She brought a stack of bowls to the stove and delivered them one by one to the table as Brian filled them. They worked together in silence, a well-orchestrated team used to their routine.

Brian scratched his dense beard with his pinkie, then smiled at Kelly who sat at the table in navy sweatpants loaned to her by Sonja. She felt much better after cleaning up, though removing the mud had revealed dozens of small scratches on her lower legs.

Malik's dog, Atka, lay curled up nearby, dozing. He was a beautiful blue-eyed husky. Unlike all the other dogs she had seen in Greenland, this one was allowed to wander freely. Atka was a pet, apparently, not a working dog.

Sonja arrived and lit a kerosene lamp that hung under the canvas ceiling sheltering the dining space. The sun had dipped below the tall cliff of the fjord, casting the camp into shadow and lowering the temperature significantly. Kelly knew it wouldn't get any darker as the night wore on, but it would get colder. Her mind flew again to Pippa and she had to push back another wave of tears.

"How are you?" Sonja asked, pausing beside her chair.

"I'm fine. Thanks. Feeling much better."

Everyone was present under the dining tarp except Jordan. Kelly waited in tense anticipation for her appearance.

Seeing her again after nine years had sent Kelly into a significant shock. She hadn't been prepared, despite her many mental rehearsals. But they weren't supposed to meet like this. All of her carefully constructed greetings had gone unexpressed. Instead, she had fallen apart all over Jordan—literally—in exactly the way she'd been determined to avoid.

She hadn't expected such a powerful emotional impact at seeing her again. When their eyes first met, a tsunami of emotions had washed over her. She had been so confused and surprised she had been unable to formulate words or thoughts. She couldn't remember what Jordan had said or what her face had revealed, if anything. By the time Kelly had recovered enough to pay attention, Jordan was perfectly composed and treating her like it was just another day at the office. If she had revealed any emotion, good or bad, Kelly had missed it.

It was too late now for the kind of first impression she had planned. All she could do was try to recover some decorum for the remainder of her visit.

Over the years, Kelly had had many fantasies of running into Jordan again, ranging from brief chatty dialogues to life-altering sexual encounters. On occasion, she would imagine a quite different situation in which Jordan would meet her again and be blown away by the woman she had become. She would be sorry they had ever parted and want desperately to be with her. Kelly would coolly rebuff her, saying, "I'm sorry, Jordan. You had your chance and now it's too late."

Despite the occasional revenge fantasy, Kelly had no resentment toward Jordan. Jordan simply hadn't wanted her. Looking back, that made so much more sense than it had at the time when she had asked, "Why not?" The real question should have been, "Why?" She had been an inept and needy girl, a child in Jordan's eyes. As Jordan had pointed out, it would have been unethical. "I would never get involved with a student," Jordan had told her.

As Kelly had told Pippa, she'd had nothing to offer Jordan back then. Even so, Jordan had been kind and indulgent despite what a bother Kelly must have been. She had shown the greatest possible compassion, especially in the end. *That kiss!* So sensual. So moving. It had burned on her lips for weeks and then continued to smolder in her mind for years. It had been the first truly romantic kiss of her life and breathtakingly perfect. She'd given up any hope by then of anything but friendship with Jordan and even that had come to an end. It had been completely unexpected, that kiss. How sad and pathetic she must have seemed to compel Jordan to offer that charitable token at the end.

There was no doubt she'd come a long way since then. She was neither fragile nor pitiable now. She wasn't that girl anymore.

But what about Jordan? Had she changed too? Almost a decade later, she looked fantastic, almost the same. Her face was leaner than it had been, the way a woman's face loses fullness as she ages, and her hairstyle was a shorter, more utilitarian cut than the one she used to have, but still the same dusky brown color. Her eyes, her inscrutable blue-gray eyes, were unchanged, intelligent and penetrating. They were the sort of eyes that seemed to see everything and reveal nothing.

"Where's Jordan?" Brian asked, taking his chair at the table.

"She's in her tent," Sonja answered. "I'll go get her."

As Sonja shoved her chair back, Jordan emerged from her tent and walked toward them.

She wore a green Polartek jacket over a navy turtleneck T-shirt. She walked in a relaxed gait to the table, smiling at the group, her gaze lingering briefly on Kelly before she sat down. There were no rings on her fingers; she wore no earrings or makeup. She was, as always, perfectly natural and effortlessly lovely. Kelly felt tremendously happy to find Jordan so entirely as she remembered her.

"Any word about Pippa?" Kelly asked.

Jordan shook her head. "Not yet. They wouldn't have had time to get there yet. But with the coordinates you gave, the search area can be precisely determined, and I'm sure it won't take them long to find her. They're very practiced at this sort of thing." She glanced around the table at the others as she took her chair. "Nivi didn't stay for dinner?"

Malik put bread and butter on the table and took his chair. "I did invite her, but she wanted to get home. She took a loaf of bread. I hope that is okay." He spoke more haltingly and with a thicker accent than Pippa's, but his English was excellent, smooth and practiced.

Kelly couldn't help staring at the right side of his head and his patriotic tattoo. His eyes were so dark, no pupils were visible.

"Yes," Jordan said. "No problem. She deserved a reward for bringing Kelly to us."

"Absolutely," Kelly agreed, tasting the broth in her bowl.

"I'm sorry we can't offer you something more interesting for dinner. We didn't know we were having company."

"This is perfect," Kelly said appreciatively. "It's funny how good canned stew can taste when you're camping."

Kelly ate while Jordan spoke to her students briefly about the day's work. She was friendly and engaging with them, but also professional. There could be no doubt she was the person in charge in this group.

A few minutes into the meal, the sound of a helicopter reached their ears and directed all their eyes to the sky. The helicopter came into view to the east, then passed rapidly by.

"That'll be the search party," Jordan said. "I hope your friend is safe."

Seeing the helicopter on its way to Pippa gave Kelly some sense of comfort. She made a conscious effort to avert her thoughts from that situation, realizing there was nothing she could do now but wait.

"What was that you were working on this afternoon?" Jordan asked Brian. "With the wood and the hammering and all that?"

"Remember the basketball hoop Malik found for us? We built a stand and backboard for it. We're going to finish it after dinner and get in a little B-ball this evening. Do you want to play?"

Jordan laughed ironically. "No, thank you! Not my thing." She glanced at Kelly with her familiar sly smile. "I have a long-standing policy of avoiding doing anything with balls."

Sonja lurched forward, nearly choking, then burst out laughing. Kelly smiled appreciatively. She noticed that Malik too was smiling, and realized this was the first time she'd seen anything other than seriousness on his face.

"Where do you go to school?" she asked him.

"University of Copenhagen. Dr. Westgate was kind enough to let me join the team, since I am home for the summer."

"Home is Ilulissat?"

He nodded. "This is where I grew up. This is close enough to hang out with my family on weekends. And have my dog with me." He motioned toward Atka who lay nearby, awake and watchful, but making no move to interfere with the meal. "This is perfect for me. It fits so well with my specialty." Anticipating her question, he said, "Paleoclimatology."

Kelly shot a questioning glance toward Jordan, who chuckled.

"It's the study of prehistoric weather patterns. You've forgotten."

"Sorry," Kelly said, "I don't remember much from my science classes. Prehistoric weather patterns? That sounds very technical. How can you look at that? Rocks? One thing I do remember is that Greenland has the oldest rocks on the planet."

"Yes, that's true. I'm glad you remember something." Jordan buttered a slice of bread, her lips turning up slightly in an amused smile. Kelly had always loved that particular understated look of pleasure. "In this case," Jordan explained, "it's ice, which, technically, is a rock. The ice too is very old here. Like the rest of us, Malik is here to delve into the memory of the ice."

"The memory of the ice?" Kelly stopped eating. "I've never heard that phrase."

"It's a poetic way of referring to Greenland's ancient deep freeze. Ice cores have been taken down to a depth of two miles. Each year's snowfall is compressed into a thin layer, so you can read the cores like tree rings. Two miles down equates to over a hundred thousand years, so Greenland's ice sheet is sometimes referred to as the two-mile time machine."

"Wow! But how does ice tell you anything about the past? It's just frozen water."

"Not entirely." Jordan gestured with her spoon as she spoke, her face so familiar and so evocative of past feelings that Kelly found it hard to listen to her words. "With each layer of snow, particles are captured. Like dust, volcanic ash and pollen. Atmospheric gases, too, are trapped in bubbles in the ice. By analyzing each layer, we can reconstruct what the climate was like year by year. How much snow there was, how cold it was, whether there were volcanoes erupting or forest fires burning, what sort of plants were alive. The further down you go, the further back in time." Jordan fixed her gaze on Kelly. "The ice remembers everything."

So photos aren't the only things that capture a moment in time, Kelly thought. "I had no idea you could get that much information out of ice."

"It's amazing," Sonja insisted. "The knowledge and technical skill that goes into this sort of research. There's just so much data, it blows your mind."

"It sounds fascinating," Kelly remarked. "Sonja, I know you're at Boulder. So how did you get associated with this UCLA group?"

Sonja looked perplexed.

Jordan shook her head. "No, no," she intervened. "I'm not at UCLA anymore."

"You're not?"

"No. I was there a few years, but once I got seriously into Greenland research, I transferred back to the Denver area. I'm teaching at Boulder again."

Kelly was floored. "Seriously?"

Jordan nodded matter-of-factly, lifting her plastic water glass to take a drink. "I've been there for the last six years."

"The National Ice Core Laboratory is in Denver," Sonja added.

"Right," said Jordan. "That's where you need to be if you want to study the cores they're pulling out of here."

"Greenland ice cores are in Denver?" asked Kelly, still barely comprehending the fact that Jordan had been back for six years.

"Yes. They're kept there permanently for scientific research. I'm not personally involved in the core drilling operation. Our research here is more about measuring the advance and retreat of glaciers. But the rest of the year, back home, we get to peer into the ice samples and tease out primeval mysteries." Jordan grinned mischievously, as if there was something deliciously wicked about studying old ice. "You clearly didn't stay in science," she said good-naturedly. "What do you do?"

Kelly roused herself from her thoughts to say, "I'm a photographer. I'm here with a journalist. He specializes in Greenland."

"What's his name?"

"Charles Lance."

Jordan nodded. "I know Chuck. He's been here several times before. In fact, I have a message from him asking to come out to talk. So apparently you'll be back here soon on a professional visit."

Kelly couldn't tell if that was good or bad news for Jordan.

"The Arctic must seem like heaven to a photographer," Jordan observed.

"Yes. It's the light, the round the clock light. Normally, twilight is so fleeting. It's that magic time of the evening photographers covet. But here, it's sunset all night long. Perpetual twilight. It's incredible, really. I've been feeling a kind of giddiness ever since I arrived."

"I can imagine," Jordan replied. "Like the feeling I had the first time I came here. Twilight to a photographer must be like ice to a glaciologist. And Greenland has them both in massive quantities."

"Speaking of ice," Brian said, "we lost track of one of our buoys yesterday and I'd like to try to find it tomorrow."

The conversation slipped into work topics again as they finished their meal, leaving Kelly as observer. What she mainly observed was Jordan, who seemed relaxed and sure of herself. To Kelly, she was friendly, but not personal. Not that Kelly expected her to be in front of her students. She hoped to spend some time alone with her later where they could be more open with one another.

She soon discovered Jordan had no such hopes when she pushed her chair back and said, "Sonja, can Kelly bunk with you tonight?"

"Sure. I'll take care of her." Sonja's mouth turned up in a subtle, ironic smile as she struggled to suppress her glee. She gave her head a toss, flinging her straight bangs away from her eyes.

"Great," said Jordan. "I've got some work to do, so I'll say good night. If I hear any news, Kelly, I'll let you know right away."

With that, Jordan left the table and walked rapidly toward her tent, leaving Kelly with the impression that she couldn't wait to be rid of her.

CHAPTER TWELVE

The storm that had come up overnight continued into the day, confining Asa and Gudny to their burrow. They stayed dry and comfortable inside, wrapped together in their furs and skins. But even without the storm they would not have been able to travel today. During the night the child Asa had been carrying, amid much pain and bleeding, had been stillborn. The ordeal left her weak and anguished, and she curled up next to Gudny in her cocoon and slept through most of the next day, comforting herself with the belief that the child, a boy, had been spared a life of hardship.

When she woke, they ate what was left of the food. She hadn't planned on an extra day. Though she was still not fully recovered, she knew they had to push on while the weather allowed or they might be trapped by another storm and starve to death.

It was afternoon when they left the cave, emerging into sunshine and straggling gray clouds. A breeze coming off the icy bay bit at their noses. She knew it wasn't likely they would find any more shelter, so she planned to keep walking as long as possible, through the night, hoping to reach the village by morning.

As evening approached, Asa spotted a herd of reindeer grazing close to the shoreline. She picked up Gudny and placed her on her shoulders so she could see them. There's that smile, Asa thought, leaning her head back to look at Gudny's delighted face. It cheered her to see it, as it always did. Back on her feet, Gudny walked beside her, holding her hand. Their pace was not fast, but it was steady.

Gudny's good mood was short-lived as twilight descended. She was tired and hungry and continued to remind her mother of both conditions. Asa was having her own problems, feeling weak and struggling with the weight of her pack. There was a persistent pain in her abdomen and she knew she couldn't carry both the pack and Gudny. Their rest stops came more frequently, which worried Asa, and when they came to an impassable ravine that stretched far inland, she nearly burst into tears.

"What's the matter, Mama?" Gudny asked, tugging at her clothes.

Asa sighed and slipped the pack off her back, letting it fall to the ground. "I'm tired, hungry and sore. I don't know if I can go on."

Gudny leaned against Asa's legs. "It'll be all right," she said softly, echoing Asa's earlier words to her.

Asa took hold of Gudny's hand and stared into the ravine at her feet. It was deep, jagged and in a strange way welcoming. One step and all of the misery of life would be over. If her hand had been empty, it would have been an easy step to take.

Gudny slipped away and took hold of the strap on the pack, tugging at it. "Do you want me to carry this?" She heaved, gritting her teeth and screwing up her little face, dragging the pack across the ground.

Asa laughed and reached down to take it from her, recommitted to her task. They walked parallel to the ravine until it came to an end at a trickling brook. They stopped at the brook to drink. As Asa squatted beside it, she spotted a patch of bright green further up. She walked up to investigate.

"Kvan!" she shouted with delight.

The large-leaved plants grew in the soft gravel beside the brook. Gudny sat on a rock while Asa cut down several plants with her stone knife.

"You like kvan," she reminded Gudny, handing her a stalk.

Gudny held it in her gloved hand, looking puzzled.

"Eat it," Asa urged. She demonstrated by taking a bite off a stem. Gudny did the same, frowned, then ate some more. She had never eaten raw kvan. Normally, they cooked it in milk, which was much better, but it wasn't so bad this way.

Asa tied a bundle of kvan to the outside of her pack and they set off again, both of them chewing a stalk of the plant. She felt more optimistic now that they had some food. As they worked their way back on the other side of the ravine, she looked south along the shoreline and thought she recognized a certain rocky point. She couldn't be sure, but if it was the landmark she thought it was, they were two and a half hours from home. Two or two and a half hours for a healthy adult. For the two of them, maybe three and a half. Still, that was wonderful to realize…if it were true. She tried not to get too excited. One rocky point looked a lot like another. If it was the one she knew, they would find out as soon as they got high enough to see past it. There was an island on the other side of it, jutting up from the frozen bay. It was a favorite roost of birds and was shaped like Thor's hammer lying on its side. The handle of the hammer faced east. There would be no mistaking that landmark, if it was there.

Asa quickened her step, anxious to get the view that would tell her they were nearly home.

CHAPTER THIRTEEN

Kelly was disappointed that Jordan hadn't offered to share her tent. It was possible she was unhappy with Kelly's sudden appearance here. She'd thought she'd gotten rid of her years ago, that annoying besotted girl whose uncontrolled passions sapped her energy. But *I'm not that girl anymore*, Kelly inwardly objected, at the same time realizing Jordan couldn't know that. That's what Kelly was here to prove.

Exhausted both physically and emotionally, she retired to Sonja's dome-shaped tent. She spread her borrowed sleeping bag on a cot next to Sonja's. Then she took off her boots and lay on top of the sleeping bag, staring up at the bright blue fabric stretched tight across the tent's aluminum skeleton. The sound of music reached her ears indistinctly.

It had been over two hours since she got here. The more time that went by, the more worried she got about Pippa. She had heard nothing yet. *Why was it taking so long?* She yearned for and dreaded the moment when she would hear that Pippa had been found.

A shadow outside the tent distracted her. The flap opened and Sonja ducked inside carrying a cookie. She dropped onto her cot and broke the cookie in half.

"I brought dessert," she said.

Kelly rolled onto her side and took the offering. It was peanut butter, soft and sweet and just the right thing to cap off the night.

"Thanks."

Sonja sat on the edge of her cot facing Kelly. "Are you all set?"

"Yes. All the comforts of home."

"I've been living like this for a few weeks already. It's not bad. I don't mind. The worst thing is the mosquitos."

Kelly nodded and ran her finger over one of the itchy red bumps on her cheek.

"That reminds me," Sonja said, reaching into her front pocket. "I have an antiseptic wipe for that cut on your leg."

Kelly sat up and pulled her pants leg up to reveal several small scratches and one cut deep enough to have bled.

"How did you get so scratched up anyway?" Sonja asked.

"Brambles. I went through a horrible bog. There are some really nasty plants around here."

Sonja rubbed the moist cloth gently across the wound a couple of times, producing a slight sting. "Yeah," she said. "You should stay on the trail."

"I would have if I could have found it."

Sonja caressed Kelly's calf tenderly before rolling the pant leg back into place. Then she looked up and smiled. "You're cute."

"Thanks. I don't feel very cute tonight."

"I admit you looked fresher this morning, but you've had a rough day. Still, pretty darn cute. The way we keep running into each other, maybe the universe is trying to tell us something."

Kelly laughed, then abruptly cut herself off when Sonja leaned toward her, looking like she was going to kiss her. Kelly caught her shoulders and held her off.

"No goodnight kiss?" Sonja asked, rocking back onto her cot.

Kelly shook her head. "No, thanks. I've got a lot on my mind right now. This just doesn't seem like the time and place."

Sonja pressed her lips together in resignation and sighed. "Okay. I understand. It's not that often a rocking hot lesbian shares my tent. I was thinking it was my lucky night."

"Sorry."

"Is Pippa your girlfriend?"

Kelly was surprised by the question. "No. We're just friends." She got inside her sleeping bag and lay on her side facing Sonja. The cots were nearly touching, as the tent was so small it could barely sleep two.

"So you were Jordan's student too," Sonja said, crawling into her own bag. "When was that?"

"Ten years ago. How long have you known her?"

"A year. I've had her for two semesters. She's great, isn't she? I was so lucky to get chosen for this fieldwork. It's a terrific opportunity. Eight weeks in Greenland. Everybody's so envious."

"I can imagine. Eight weeks is quite a while to be gone, though. Nobody brought their spouses, I guess."

"No. Malik's lucky. He's got all his family in town. Brian's wife is back home and he misses her like crazy. And Julie's single."

"What about Jordan?" Kelly tried to make her voice sound as casual as possible. "Did she have to leave someone behind?"

Sonja narrowed her eyes slightly before saying, "Not that I know of. She's married to her work. But she doesn't talk about her personal life, if there is one, which I totally doubt. How about before, when you knew her?"

"She was like that then too."

Sonja's eyes twinkled with mischief. "Her students call her The Ice Queen."

Kelly flinched. "Really?"

Sonja shrugged. "It's not in a mean way. Everybody likes her. Girls especially. When she was your teacher, did you know about her? Did you know she was gay?"

"Yeah, we knew. She didn't discuss it or anything. I mean, she wouldn't talk about something like that, but she didn't try to hide it."

"Were you out then too?"

"I was just figuring things out. Jordan became a role model for me. I was looking for female role models, I guess, lesbians in particular."

Sonja smiled knowingly. "Did you have a crush on her?"

Kelly hesitated before saying, "Yeah, sure. Who wouldn't, right? I mean, don't you?"

Sonja laughed, but didn't seem inclined to answer. Was that a yes? Kelly wondered.

"Do you know anything about her?" Sonja asked. "Her family or background?"

"No, not really." What Kelly did know, she wasn't inclined to share with Sonja. Though the facts were skimpy and of little use to someone trying to force her way into Jordan's private world, Jordan wouldn't like them being shared.

Jordan grew up in a poor, religious farming family in the Midwest, one of two daughters. Her sister had remained there, marrying and having three children. As far as Kelly knew, Jordan had little to do with any of them. Their lives had grown too far apart in every way imaginable. To Kelly, Jordan had seemed isolated with no family, no lover, no close friends. All of her relationships seemed to be purely professional, except her odd friendship with Kelly. It was hard to know how to describe that, hard even to call it a "friendship," but they had been close in a way, and Kelly believed Jordan had been fond of her.

"What about you?" she asked Sonja. "Nobody waiting back home?"

"Nope." Sonja adjusted her pillow and laid her head flat. She held the open edge of her sleeping bag up. "You sure you don't want to zip them together? It's warmer that way."

"Fortunately, it's not a cold night."

Sonja laughed again and zipped up her bag. "Good night." She turned over and grew quiet.

Kelly lay on her back, listening to the soft music drifting through the still night. She gradually recognized it as smooth jazz. She wasn't sure what time it was, but if somebody was still playing music it probably wasn't too late. She soon concluded that she wasn't going to fall asleep so easily after all, despite her exhaustion. She was too worried about Pippa and too aware of Jordan's nearness.

She unzipped her sleeping bag, prompting Sonja to roll over and say, "Where ya going?"

"I can't sleep. Is there any herbal tea?"

"You know where the coffeepot is. It's right there."

"Do you want anything?"

"No, thanks. I'll be asleep in a minute."

Kelly pulled on her jacket and went outside. The music, she discovered, came from Malik's tent, easily identified by Atka lying just outside the entrance. The interior was dimly lit. The other two tents nearby, Julie's and Brian's, were both dark. This cluster of small tents was downslope from the center of the camp where the kitchen and living areas were set up. Jordan's tent, the big one, was about fifty feet further up from there. A lantern was on inside. Jordan was still up.

Thumbing through the teabags, she selected an orange spice, noting a few packets of rooibos. That had been Jordan's particular favorite, she recalled. Maybe it still was.

She turned to the stove to see Malik standing beside her. Startled, she gasped and clutched her chest. His black eyes were cool and expressionless. The Greenland flag on his scalp glowed pink in the night sunlight.

"Sorry," he said in a soft, nonthreatening voice. "I did not mean to scare you. I heard you walk by."

"I didn't think I'd made any noise."

"Only the feet of animals make no noise."

Impulsively, Kelly glanced down at his feet, seeing a pair of Teva sandals and wondering what she had expected to see. Atka sat beside him, tongue hanging out the side of his mouth.

"You are making tea?" he asked.

"Yes. I don't think I can sleep. Too worried about Pippa."

"Let me light the stove," he offered, lifting the lid to reveal two burners. "Pippa is a sweet little girl."

"You know her?"

"We have lived in the same town all our lives. You see how small it is."

"Of course."

He struck a match and lit the stove, adjusting the flame before putting a pan of water on the burner.

"I hope I didn't wake you up with my thunderous tromping through camp," Kelly said.

Malik smiled. "No. I was awake, working. I never sleep well in summer. As a kid, I would stay up sometimes all night in summer. Lots of kids do that."

"I've seen it. At midnight, I've looked out the window to see them racing past in the road on their bikes. It seems so strange."

"Three months of the year we do not see the sun. We hibernate like bears and wait for it. In the spring, when the first ray of sunlight peeks over the hills and touches our cheek with a kiss of warmth, we awake. 'Seqineq nuivoq,' we say with joy in our hearts: The sun has risen. The frozen earth begins to melt. Out flows water, insects, plants and animals, emerging like a flood of life, swelling as the days grow longer and the great summer thaw begins. Then we sing and dance and celebrate life. No time for sleeping."

He spoke like a poet, Kelly observed. "You said you were awake, working on something. What?"

"I am making a collection of Kalaallit stories in English, to save them for the world. It is what I do in my spare time. Some of these have never been written down in English before."

"What a wonderful project!"

"Yes." Malik looked pleased with her response. "I have been searching through old libraries here and in Denmark to find forgotten stories written down by European visitors in the sixteen and seventeen hundreds. I compare those to traditional stories handed down orally, trying to find the roots of our legends. But mainly I talk to old people and ask them what stories their parents and grandparents told them when they were little children. I was very glad to meet Nivi today. She invited me to come to visit her, so she can tell me all her old stories. Just like in your country where every child knows the story of Little Red Riding Hood or the legend of the tooth fairy, I hear many of the same stories over and over and that is how

I know they are part of our culture and have been passed down for many generations."

"I'd love to hear some of those stories," Kelly said. "It's so interesting that you work in both the science of the natural world and the culture of the people at the same time, that you're so interested in both."

"There is no difference to me between the natural world and the people who live in it. It is all Greenland." He smiled, then turned to the boiling water on the stove. "Here is your water ready. I will see you in the morning and I hope to hear good news about Pippa."

He returned to his tent, Atka at his heels, and the camp was silent again. Kelly put a teabag in a mug and poured hot water over it, then her attention was drawn back to the big tent with its circle of white light seeping through the fabric.

She impulsively opened a packet of rooibos and made a second cup of tea.

CHAPTER FOURTEEN

Staring up through the hole above, Pippa could tell it was night by the color of the sky. It was rosy gold. She didn't know what day of the week it was. She didn't know how long she'd been asleep. Her head hurt and her swollen ankle throbbed with pain. She sat up and gritted her teeth through the painful process of removing her boot. Finally it was off and she leaned back with a deep sigh. Her stomach rumbled so loudly it echoed through the small chamber. Too bad she hadn't been carrying her backpack when she'd fallen in here. She could really use that ræklinger now. Not to mention her water bottle. She ran her tongue over her dry lips.

She understood now that she wasn't in America or England or Africa, but in Greenland as she always had been. Her mind had cleared. She had fallen into this cave while picking cottongrass flowers. The ground had given way beneath her feet, plunging her into this dungeon. She also understood that it wasn't really a cave, not in the strict sense of the term. It was a pocket created by a pile of boulders that had fallen in the ravine long ago. The space between them had filled in over time with gravel, sand and dirt, forming an airtight chamber. It wasn't airtight anymore, she mused, looking through the opening above.

It hadn't been airtight earlier either, she thought, not during the Viking days. That is, if everything she had just seen had actually happened.

For several minutes, she had been lying here marveling at the experience she had just had, trying to decide if she had been dreaming or if she had had a vision. It wasn't like any dream she'd ever had. It was vivid and powerful, and the emotions of it still gripped her. She remembered earlier that she'd seen a woman's face in the darkness, and she now knew that face was that of a Viking woman named Asa. She also believed that this was the same cave Asa had happened across in her journey home. Everything about it fit. Somehow that woman was speaking to her across the centuries.

Gradually overcoming the amazement of her vision, Pippa turned her mind to her own situation. Perhaps, she thought tentatively, Asa is trying to help me. She sat up and peered into the gloom. Hundreds of years ago, there had been at least one crevice between the rocks of this structure wide enough for a woman to fit through. If she could find that and open it up again, she might be able to get out. Because there was no way she could get out the way she had come in short of flying.

What must Kelly be going through? she wondered. She hoped she was okay. Being alone in a strange place, not knowing the route or the terrain, would she have attempted going on alone? Or was she still waiting for Pippa to reappear, frightened and huddled behind a rock against the wind?

Driven by this image, Pippa gathered her strength and tried to ignore the pain as she crawled to the edge of the chamber and shined her penlight on the wall, feeling with her fingers for the edges of boulders. The continual low howl of the wind accompanied her orderly progress as she ran her hands over cool stone. After investigating one spot, she moved in a counter-clockwise direction, using the odd rock cairn as her signpost. When she returned to that, she would have made a complete circuit.

Most of the boulders were tight against one another with little space between. About halfway along, she found one place where her hand did not meet solid rock. It was earth, gravel and dirt. She took out her pocketknife and poked into it. It was loose enough to dig into. This was one possible exit. She continued around the chamber until she was back to the rock pile. As she shined her light on the wall, she was startled to see scratches in the rock about a meter from the floor. She peered at them more closely. These were not random scratches. They were a straight line of faint characters etched into the rock. She could barely make them out in the dim light. Only a couple of them looked like letters at all and they made no sense to her. Maybe they were just random scratches after all.

Momentarily distracted by these symbols, she was reminded of her purpose by the renewed pain in her head. She went back to the one spot she had found that seemed like a possible passage through the rocks. She turned off her light to conserve the battery and began to dig with her knife. Little by little, she scraped away pebbles and dirt, creating a pile of debris beside her knee. Periodically she shined the light to gauge her progress. She had exposed plant roots, which encouraged her to continue. Most of the tundra plants were small with shallow roots, extending only inches into the soil. The plants producing these roots couldn't be far away, which meant that the open air had to be close as well.

While she worked, she thought of Kelly, picturing her cute smile and the way her ironic hazel eyes laughed when she was joking. She was really nice. And smart. In the two weeks since they'd met, Pippa had gotten to really like her. She made her laugh. Pippa had never been friends with anyone like Kelly before. Most of the interesting people she met came and went so fast she didn't have time to get to know them.

The best thing about Kelly, Pippa admitted to herself, was that she was a lesbian, a fact that had sent her into flights of ecstasy when she first discovered it. Kelly had mentioned it casually, as if it were a fact about her no different from the town where she lived or her favorite color.

"Is Chuck your boyfriend?" Pippa had asked her that first day when the two of them were on her Rodebay tour.

She had laughed like it was an absurd idea, then said, "Just a colleague."

"Do you have a boyfriend?" Pippa had persisted.

"No. Nor do I have a girlfriend at the moment. I'm a lesbian."

"For reals?" Pippa had nearly pitched herself overboard in her excitement. After that, she'd wanted to know every possible thing about Kelly.

In the two weeks since then, she had made it her business to drop by the boarding house in the evenings to hang out with her, which often meant hanging out with Mr. Lance as well and Mrs. Arensen's boring grandson Jens. The times they were alone, playing a board game or just talking, were the best. Kelly was a super cool woman and Pippa wanted to spend as much time with her as possible. That was why she had suggested this hike. An entire day alone together would be awesome. It had been a good plan and had been going along great…until she'd fallen into this mess.

She pried loose a rock that fell on the floor with a clatter, diverting her from her thoughts. Behind it was a mat of lichen. She put her knife down and grabbed a handful of plant matter, pulling it through the opening she'd made. She pulled in a couple more handfuls until her hand pushed through to the cold night air beyond. She looked out through a clean hole in the earth to the outside. Triumphant, she lay on her back and kicked at the hole with her good foot, knocking more dirt and plants out and widening the opening. Now she could easily see outside to the twilight. There was no way to tell what time it was by the light. It could be ten o'clock or three in the morning. She stuck her head through the opening and felt the cold air on her face. A flash of light caught her eye. She watched as it blinked on and off, appearing to move in a straight line across the sky. Then the faint and distinctive sound of a helicopter reached her. As she watched, she saw a spotlight beam down from it, aimed at the ground.

They're looking for me! she thought, and immediately returned to the task of widening the opening. There was a much better chance of being found if she was above ground and could attract their attention. She pulled out sod and rocks, certain that she could make an opening large enough to crawl through. If Asa could do it, she knew she could, because Asa was much larger than she was.

By the time she had created a passage large enough to squeeze through, the sound of the helicopter was louder. She pulled herself through the tight space with her arms, wriggling her way to freedom. Once her hips made it through, the rest was easy. She rolled onto her back on the bare rock, looking up at the sky, triumphant. She scanned the sky and located the helicopter circling to the north. If she could climb out of the ravine, they should have no trouble spotting her. That could take some effort with only one good foot. In the meantime, she would turn on her penlight and hope it had enough battery power left to attract someone's attention.

She sat up and took it from her pocket, but fumbled when the world began to spin around her. She dropped the light and clutched the ground. Her stomach flipped and nausea assailed her. She curled into a ball on her side, her eyes shut tightly.

While she waited for the vertigo to retreat, images of Asa, one after the other, ran across her mind like scenes from a film: the Viking woman wearing Thule garments marched steadily across a hostile landscape with her child by her side, two desperate and wretched people with a single goal: to get home.

Pippa sank again into blackness. When her vision returned, she was walking, feeling tired, but with no pain in her ankle. A pair of yellow sealskin kamik adorned her feet and the small fingers of a child were encased in her hand.

She walked up a rise and was finally able to see over the promontory she had focused on for the last half hour. She was overjoyed to see that the island she had hoped for lay there, its jagged contours cradling sleeping birds. There was no doubt this was Thor's Hammer. A landmark she knew at last! She whisked Gudny joyfully atop her shoulders and pointed.

"Look! We're almost home!"

Gudny clapped her hands, trusting and believing. The girl had never been this far from home. The island meant nothing to her. But it meant everything to Asa.

The closer they got to home, the more familiar everything was and the lighter Asa's heart became. But now she began to worry about what she'd find when she arrived. It was possible Bjarni had survived his wounds and was still recovering from them, too badly injured to go out looking for her. What of Alrik, her son, she wondered. She hoped he'd had the sense to hide during the Skræling attack. And the rest of the village? Would there be anyone or anything there to welcome them home? She clung to hope in all these matters, and hope would be her companion until she reached her destination when it would be replaced, good or bad, with truth.

She searched the horizon for the church steeple until she remembered that the church had been on fire during her abduction. So she watched instead for the house of Hoskuld, always the first house to come into view because of its high place on a hill. When she saw it, standing there as always, her heart leapt to her throat. It felt like she'd been gone for a lifetime, yet it had only been a matter of days.

Gudny was excited now too because she recognized the scattering of buildings and the enclosures made of rocks that marked their grazing fields, empty of livestock as they had been for some time. Everything was quiet as usual at this time of night. Behind the village was the hill where the cemetery stood. Asa wondered how many new graves had been added since she'd been gone.

As they entered the cluster of homes, she saw that Soldmund's house was a pile of ash. But her own house was still standing. Gudny took off running to it and disappeared inside. Asa was too weary to run. When she entered her house, Gudny was darting from room to room calling for her father. The house was empty. The hearth was cold. The beds had been stripped of their coverings.

"Where's Papa?" Gudny asked, looking up at her mother with innocent confusion.

Asa lowered herself into a chair and pulled Gudny into her lap. "Are you happy to be home?"

Gudny nodded and laid her head against Asa's chest.

"Me too. Very happy."

She sat without moving for several minutes, too tired to rouse herself. Gudny fell asleep in her arms. She noticed it was getting lighter outside. Morning was approaching. She was finally able to urge herself out of her chair. She put Gudny on her bed and covered her with the coat she'd been wearing. Then she went through the narrow passage connecting their house to Bjarni's mother's rooms.

She found Hild asleep, snoring deeply. She shook her gently awake.

"Mother," she said quietly. "Wake up. It's Asa."

Hild opened her eyes and gasped, then sat up and stared. "Asa?"

Asa hugged her briefly.

"Where have you been? What happened?" Hild asked.

"I'll tell you everything later. We are now safe."

"We?"

"Gudny is with me."

"Oh!" Hild clasped her hands together and looked heavenward. "Thanks be to God!"

"Tell me what has happened here," Asa implored. "Bjarni?"

Hild's eyes grew sad and moist. She shook her head and lowered her gaze.

Asa took a deep breath. "Alrik?"

Hild shook her head again, then looked up with tears in her eyes. "Like a grown man, he fought alongside his father. And with him, he went down. Both of them, gone."

Asa slumped forward, her heart pierced through with the news. "Who else?" she finally asked.

"Asa, most of the men are dead. Olaf is alive, but he was injured badly and we had to take off his leg. Old Gest is still with us, but he's useless, as you know. The only strong man left is Asvald. It was a vicious fight. The Skrælings tried to kill us all, but the women and children hid. When we came out from our hiding place, we found a massacre. They took the whale meat. They left us with no hunters and no food." Hild peered more intently at Asa, then recoiled. "These are Skræling clothes you're wearing."

Asa nodded. "They kept us warm on our journey home. What about our goats? Where are they?"

"Gone. After you were taken, Asvald decided to feed the village with your goats. I told him they belonged to me. Bjarni was my son. He said we couldn't have that kind of thinking now. We few left are like one family and have to combine our property to survive."

"How will we survive with no men?"

Hild shook her head. "We can catch birds and fish."

"But we can't catch enough to put away for the winter. We need reindeer and walrus and seal meat."

The prospect of winter always loomed over the village like a shroud of doom. Even when times were good, winter was nearly too much to bear. There were always deaths. The villagers and their livestock huddled together in their homes, waiting for the dark, freezing gloom of winter to pass so they could start living again. If they could have slept through it like hibernating animals, they would have. Finding food in winter was dangerous and difficult. The only way to survive was to lay by enough food in the summer to last. Hild knew that. They all did.

Hild took Asa's hands in hers. "God will provide," she said earnestly, but the desperation in her voice hinted at her doubt.

Asa was too tired and demoralized to reply.

She soon learned that everyone else seemed even more disheartened than she was. Hope, which was always in short supply, seemed to have taken leave completely. Their small group teetered on giving up. Some were preparing themselves mentally for the end, like Hild, who spent all her waking hours in prayer, dreaming of Heaven. Old Gest decided he preferred Valhalla and talked of the old gods as if they were his best friends. He claimed Odin had a fine milk cow he was going to bring by next week along with a dozen sheep, so he needed help repairing his corral. He became angry when no one would help him. Madness was one way to deal with despair, Asa reflected.

With most of the men gone, Olaf with only one leg and Old Gest half crazy, Asvald was now their leader. He sent every woman and child out every day to hunt. Only the elder women stayed in the village to care for the small children.

Asa went out hunting with the others, bringing back enough food to meet their day-to-day needs, halibut, hvan gathered near streams and birds they snared in their rookeries. But they had no luck with large animals. They hadn't even seen a whale or a walrus, and if they were lucky enough to see one, Asa wasn't optimistic they could take it.

One day when she was scouring the coastline in search of driftwood for their winter fires, she spotted a sled in the distance, a Skræling sled with a team of dogs, speeding across the frozen surface of the bay. She watched the sled disappear from view and thought again of the wild idea that came to her more and more frequently. She had so far kept it to herself, hoping their fortune would take a turn for the better. But the weather had already turned colder and their time was rapidly running out.

She took her idea to Asvald.

"You want to live with the Skrælings?" he asked in disbelief.

"I want to live. I want my daughter to live. We will not survive the winter here on our own. And if by some miracle of God's benevolence, some of us do survive, how will we survive the winter after that? We are too few to make it on our own. The Skrælings know things. They are strong. They can hunt. They will not starve."

Asvald shook his head. "Their ways are not our ways. To live with them, we would have to turn our back on God. Then we would have nothing. Forsaking God, we would lose our souls. We will do our best here, Asa, but if God has decided to take us, it is our duty to go in dignity, solidly in His faith. This life is hard, but it is mercifully short."

"But my daughter is only five years old. Doesn't she deserve to live?"

"The time of her body on earth is unimportant. She will have everlasting life in Heaven."

Asa spoke no more about this idea until a few days later when she had made her decision. Then she went to her mother-in-law and told her she was leaving and taking Gudny to live with the Skrælings.

"Have you lost your mind?" Hild asked. "What did those savages do to you?"

"If we stay here," Asa explained, "we'll die."

"You don't have enough faith, Asa. You have to put your trust in God. God will provide."

"I fear God has forgotten us."

"Blasphemy! You would give yourself to the devils who murdered your husband and son?"

"Then you will not come?"

"I would rather die than go begging on the mercy of those heathen savages. At least I will die a Christian."

Asa saw there was no chance of persuading her. "Yes, you will. Goodbye, then, mother."

For Asa, the courage to act came almost entirely from Gudny, that happy child who deserved to live. It was for Gudny she felt compelled to do this.

She gathered a small bundle of belongings from her house. She took only necessities. She stared for several minutes at her family's wooden cross above the hearth. It symbolized a link to her Norse ancestors and to the homeland she had never seen. And never would see. This land, this Greenland, was her homeland. Not Iceland where her grandparents had been born. Iceland was nothing to her. Nor Norway, even further removed in time and space. Why did these people have such a strong bond with a place they had never been? Why did they even call themselves Norsemen? Every one of them was born here in Greenland. They were all Greenlanders, and it was the only place any of them had ever known.

She left the cross where it was. Likewise, she left behind her Bible and her book of Icelandic sagas. In those three choices, she reluctantly turned away from her family, her religion and her history.

She dressed herself and Gudny in their Skræling garments. She felt guilty for leaving and fearful of where she was going. She couldn't be sure the Skrælings, if she found them, would even allow her to live with them. They might kill her or chase her away. Then what would she do? Come back here and endure the scorn of her kinsmen? She tried not to let these fears overwhelm her resolve. Her short stay with the Skrælings had shown her a possibility, one apparently too far-fetched for her kinsmen to consider.

She met the others in the center of the village where they had gathered in a huddle of disapproval.

Olaf, once their best hunter, leaned on a crutch, standing on his one leg next to his fifteen-year-old son Grif. His wife had died last year in childbirth and he and Grif lived alone now. It seemed every household was bereft and in mourning. Old Gest, crazy fool, glared at Asa wordlessly as if she were the Devil himself.

"You cannot do this," Asvald told her sternly.

"Let her go," one of the women said. "She's bewitched."

"She doesn't pray anymore," Hild accused. "Those heathens did something to her."

Gudny clung to Asa's leg, frightened and confused.

After an uncomfortable two minutes of deliberation, Asvald took Asa's hand and said, "I will not stop you. God protect you."

"No!" Hild cried, rushing in to snatch Gudny, pressing her roughly into her garments. "Go if you must," she spat at Asa, "but don't sacrifice the child."

"She's mine and she's coming with me," Asa said firmly, dismayed that Gudny was now in tears.

"Lock her up!" Hild demanded. "She's lost her mind."

Asvald approached Hild and pulled Gudny from her, saying, "Let the child go. Her mother has the right."

Hild released her hold on Gudny and lowered her head between slumped, defeated shoulders. Asvald handed Gudny over to Asa, his expression grim and cold. Unlike last year when the others had departed on their quest to reach Brattahlid, these people had no prayers for Asa. She didn't blame them, nor did she begrudge them their opinions. She wasn't sure herself she was doing the right thing.

Asa nodded wordlessly toward her friends and turned to go.

"Wait," called a deep voice.

She turned back to see Olaf grab his son by the shoulders. He shook the boy, his face a tableau of despair, then clasped him to his chest. Without a word, he turned Grif around to face Asa and pushed him toward her. The boy looked bewildered, turning to his father for an explanation. Olaf jerked his head firmly toward Asa and said, "Go!"

Several gasps of disbelief arose from the group.

"No, Papa!" the boy protested.

Olaf's upper lip quivered through his heavy yellow beard, but his eyes remained stern. "Keep me in your heart. Go now."

Asa felt her eyes sting with approaching tears. She reached an arm toward Grif, whose moist blue eyes, set deep in a hairless face, were wide with fear. He walked into her embrace, then the three of them set off in a northerly direction toward the land of the Skræling, not knowing what fate awaited them.

CHAPTER FIFTEEN

Kelly stood outside Jordan's tent with a mug in each hand. "Jordan," she called quietly.

"Come in," came the immediate reply.

She pushed aside the flap with her foot and entered the tent. Jordan sat at her computer, her back to the entrance, typing rapidly. She wore the same turtleneck T-shirt as earlier over navy blue sweatpants, a pair of thick socks on her feet. Kelly approached and set the cup down on the desk. On the screen was a wavy, grid-like pattern of red lines.

Jordan glanced at the cup, removed her glasses and looked up to meet Kelly's eyes.

"You?" she said, surprised.

"Sorry I startled you."

"Uh, no, you didn't. Actually, you did. I thought it was one of the others." She ran her hand through her hair and picked up the mug, tasting the tea. "Rooibos. You remembered?"

"Sure."

Jordan smiled gently.

"Are you very busy?" Kelly asked, looking again at the odd shapes on the computer screen.

"Routine stuff. Feeding data into this modeling program. It creates a 3-D image of the glacier. Each day we take measurements, plug them in, and once enough data points are collected, it can simulate the movement of the glacier over the course of the summer. Check this out."

Kelly watched over Jordan's shoulder as she clicked a button and the grid lines moved like a flowing river for a few seconds, then abruptly stopped.

"By the end of the summer," Jordan said, "it'll go on a lot longer, of course. Isn't it cool?"

"Yes," Kelly agreed. "Jordan, I was hoping you might have time to talk."

Jordan gulped down a serious swallow of tea before answering. "It's getting late, but a few minutes…"

Kelly pulled a chair closer and sat down. It was nice just to be sitting here, just the two of them, after so long. It took Kelly back many years to those coveted minutes in Jordan's office at the end of the school day, when she would listen raptly to whatever Jordan wanted to talk about. Even her random complaints had found a grateful audience in Kelly. It didn't matter what she talked about. It only mattered that Kelly was allowed into the private company of her loved one, if only on campus. Jordan's secret life beyond the university grounds had remained frustratingly unknown to Kelly. Back then, she had imagined that it was a fascinating world of interesting people and stimulating activity, but she had eventually come to understand that it was more likely spent quietly at home with a couple of cats and a stack of science journals.

"I'm happy to see you again," Kelly said sincerely. "You look great. How've you been?"

"I've been good," Jordan answered vaguely. "How about you?"

"I'm good."

"How's your mother?"

"Her health isn't so great. Heart disease. High blood pressure. I don't see her much. She's still with my sister in Portland."

Jordan nodded and took another leisurely drink from her cup. "So you're a photographer. That's terrific."

"I love it!"

"You always took great photos. I told you at the time you should pursue photography seriously, not just as a hobby. But you stubbornly clung to meteorology, trying to please me."

Kelly nodded. "I did everything I could to please you. I was a silly girl, wasn't I?"

Jordan regarded her with pleasure. "Yes. But charmingly so. You're not a silly girl anymore, are you?"

Kelly laughed shortly. "I hope not. It's embarrassing to think about it…now. I must have seemed like a homeless puppy. You were so kind to me. Anybody else would have told me to get lost."

Jordan's slight smile looked oddly sad. But it was short-lived. She brightened and said, "I told you you'd outgrow it, didn't I? You'd look back and say to yourself, Oh, hell, what was I thinking?" Jordan slapped her palm against her forehead. "But it's very common to have a crush on a teacher. Nothing to be embarrassed about. You survived and went on to have more mature relationships…one assumes."

Although her manner was friendly, Kelly believed Jordan was holding herself at a distance, as she always had. She didn't seem at all relaxed. Kelly had so often yearned to break through Jordan's barriers, to peel her back layer by layer until she could touch her exposed heart.

"I've had a few relationships," Kelly confirmed. "I don't know if they were more mature or not." She laughed self-consciously.

She wanted to talk about her feelings and, more importantly, Jordan's. But it was too soon for that, she knew, after such a long separation. It was a strange situation. She felt both like they had just met and like they had known one another intimately forever.

"I can't believe you've been right there in Boulder for six years!" Kelly shook her head. "Did you ever think of contacting me after you came back?"

Jordan looked momentarily confused. "No, I didn't think about it. I assumed you had moved on, had a full life." She looked apologetic. "There wouldn't have been much point. No place for me in your life anymore."

"Oh, no, I disagree! We could get together now and then. Talk and enjoy one another's company. On a more equal footing. As friends."

Jordan shook her head. "Kelly, I was your mentor. People always leave their mentors behind. And it's okay. It's expected. It's one of the classic rites of passage."

"But I didn't leave you. You left me."

"I know, but you would have left me in time. Besides, I'm speaking figuratively. You left me in the sense that you outgrew your fantasies about me. Once you grow up and find your own way, mentors have nothing left to offer you, not even friendship. Least of all friendship, really, because they were never real people to you. They were an ideal. So when you've matured, they're nothing but a disappointment because you once thought they were perfect."

"I never thought of you as perfect."

Jordan was clearly surprised. "You didn't?"

"No. I don't think I've ever seen anybody like that, to be honest."

"But I remember you saying that I was your role model, that you thought I was the most admirable woman you'd ever known."

"All true. I admired you so much. I still do. But it wasn't a blind admiration. You have shortcomings like everybody else. You hide them well, but if a person is looking closely, she can see your weaknesses."

Jordan cocked her head, curious. "So you loved me in spite of my flaws?"

Kelly shook her head. "I loved you *because* of them. People don't like perfection, Jordan. They may admire it, but they don't identify with it, so it doesn't move them. That's one of the things you learn in photography. Look for the imperfections and bring them to the fore. That's where the interest lies. That's where you can touch someone's heart."

Jordan looked thoughtful. "You seem so mature," she said wistfully. "In any case, you have clearly outgrown your need for a mentor."

"I don't remember you ever saying whether or not you had a mentor."

Jordan hesitated, looking like she was trying to decide how to answer. Kelly had seen this response many times before. Whenever she asked a personal question, no matter how innocuous, Jordan always took her time answering, as if she were considering whether or not it was worth the risk. Kelly assumed this intense need for privacy had been ingrained in her during adolescence. She had grown up in a conservative, intolerant family. Her acceptance among them had required that she keep her emerging lesbianism a secret. One of the most fundamental truths about her had been abhorrent to everyone she knew. Later, as an adult, she had come out of the closet, but she never seemed to have overcome her self-protective evasiveness.

"Yes, I had a mentor," she finally replied. "My professor and advisor at Cornell, Alonzo Marquette. He was a brilliant scientist. As a student, my goal in life was to be just like him, to pattern my career after his and hope to accomplish just a fraction of what he had done for environmental studies." Jordan looked distracted. "He took me under his wing and I'll be forever grateful for the extra attention."

"Cornell? I thought you did your graduate studies at the University of Chicago."

"Yes, that's right. I started at Cornell and finished at Chicago." Jordan crossed her legs and leaned back in her chair, fixing a relaxed gaze on Kelly. "So you're happy working as a photographer. Tell me what you love about it?"

* * *

Kelly was setting her mug down to consider her response. Jordan was relieved to move off the subject of herself. This whole situation was nerve-wracking with Kelly showing up here so unexpectedly. Even worse, here she was dredging up the sore old topic of Professor Marquette and, by extension, his beautiful and passionate wife. That was not something Jordan wanted to talk about. Or even think about. That disastrous chapter of her life was long over. She wished it could be forgotten. Actually, she wished it had never happened. There was no way it could be forgotten. After nearly twenty years, the memories had barely dulled at all.

She could still bring to mind the pale, translucent skin of Teresa's shoulder, a blue vein trailing down across the curve of her breast. Lying beside her, Jordan had often traced that vein with her forefinger while Teresa lay on her back, her body's heat waning after lovemaking. Teresa Marquette had been forty-three, nearly twice her age, a buxom brunette. Her husband called her Terry. Though Jordan didn't know it at the time, their marriage was full of resentment, discord, perhaps even hatred, at least on the part of Teresa, a woman possessed and driven by a bitterness Jordan couldn't guess at until years after.

From their first meeting, Jordan had found Mrs. Marquette sexy in an intoxicating, carnal way, but it had never crossed her mind that the attraction could be mutual or that anything would ever happen between them. She never suspected that Mrs. Marquette had begun to take an interest in her husband's favorite graduate student, the brainy young lesbian he was molding in his image. Until one day when she came by their house to deliver a set of student papers she'd graded and Professor Marquette was not at home.

Teresa asked her in for a drink, then told her how smart and special she was, and told her something she hadn't heard before, that she was a desirable woman. After a second drink that left Jordan light-headed, Teresa made her move. She pulled Jordan against her and kissed her, deep and luxuriously, easily coaxing her body into a desperate longing. Lonely and unsophisticated, Jordan offered little resistance to the older woman's advances.

Teresa easily won her and they became lovers. There was guilt, but not enough to drive Jordan away. She rapidly became obsessed with Teresa, spending almost every afternoon in her bed, ignoring her thesis, skipping classes, employing every excuse to keep her in the blissful embrace of her illicit lover. Within days, she was hopelessly in love. Teresa used her body every way imaginable, invaded her mind and possessed her heart. She thought of nothing else day and night but the craving need that overwhelmed her. So much so that she worried that the rest of her life was turning to shambles. But when she tried to resist, Teresa would call her and say, "Oh, sweetheart, please come to me today. I'm so lonely and I love and need you so." Jordan had no power to say no.

It went on for weeks and it was magnificent!

Until Lonnie, as his wife called him, found out.

He was deeply hurt and betrayed...by both of them. He quit as Jordan's advisor, of course. His wife told him that it had been a lark, that she had no feelings for the girl. Jordan didn't believe it and decided Teresa was merely saying that to avoid hurting her husband. But Teresa wouldn't see her again and was thoroughly cold when Jordan tried to talk to her.

Somehow, news of the affair was leaked to the rest of the faculty, percolating down through the student body as well. Years later, Jordan finally began to understand that the only person who could have spread the rumor was Teresa herself. Alonzo Marquette had been thoroughly humiliated.

He had always told Jordan that she would someday be a valuable asset to science. But after the affair was revealed, he told her, with uncharacteristic disgust, that she had thrown away everything she could have been for "a piece of tail." It was possible he was more disappointed in her than he was in his wife.

Jordan was devastated. She had lost the woman she loved and the man who believed in her all in one blow. She had lost her place of privilege and her path to glory. She had lost everything, in fact, that mattered to her.

The soaring star of her career fell from the sky. The story thankfully never reached a court or a newspaper. It was a scandal contained within the halls of academe, but the halls of academe were Jordan's world, so it was sufficient to destroy her. She left Cornell. It was too uncomfortable there with everyone knowing what had happened. Besides, she couldn't bear to approach another member of the staff to work with her.

Once she had had time to reflect and recover, she began to believe that all Teresa had ever wanted, from the beginning, was to inflict pain on her husband. She had wanted to take away something that represented hope, the offspring of his intellect. Eventually, she understood that she'd been used. She'd been a fool.

After a period of painful recovery, she decided there was nothing more important to her than finishing her degree and doing the work she had set out to do. She decided she could do it without the endorsement of her mentor, of any mentor. At least she hoped she could, so she applied to Chicago and worked hard with a single-minded focus and a determination greater than any she had felt before.

Above all, she pledged to herself that she would never again be derailed by her emotions. Her career was the most important thing in her life. To jeopardize it for "a piece of tail" was the most idiotic thing imaginable. It would never happen again. She would be beyond reproach in every way. She would never win back Professor Marquette's respect, she knew, but there would be nobody else who would ever find her foolish or frivolous.

By the time Kelly came along, Jordan had gotten her toe in the door and was on her way. Kelly had always seemed mildly threatening to her, even as an innocent young woman without an ounce of guile in her. She'd been infatuated with Jordan, but she hadn't been a seductress by any means. She'd been shy and earnest, easy to predict and easy to control. She had lacked self-confidence, so she never pushed for what she wanted.

Kelly had also seemed a little sad in those days. Her parents were divorced and her mother, with whom she lived, suffered from depression and alcoholism. She was a sloppy, self-pitying kind of drunk who could make a child feel guilty for merely existing. Kelly never said anything like that about her mother, but it was evident from what she did say that her home life was oppressive and her spirit yearned for an escape. Her two older sisters had already left home, so it was just Kelly and her defeated mother.

Jordan had been moved by her, and had wanted to be the one to rescue her and give her every possible means of reaching her goals. She had felt a tenderness toward her that hadn't happened with anyone else. Not a student, not even a lover. Jordan had advised her, encouraged her and tried to make her feel capable, but had kept her at a distance all the while. Despite her innocence and transparency, Kelly had been a beguiling temptress.

The temptation of Kelly had been a test Jordan had passed. Except for that one goodbye kiss. That had been a mistake. A foolish risk. Fortunately, it hadn't turned into anything. But it had shown Jordan that she wasn't completely immune to her self-destructive impulses. Since then, she had steeled herself even more against her treacherous heart, determined that it would never undermine her again.

When she said goodbye to Kelly for the last time, she felt she had barely escaped a disaster that could have ruined her. An affair with a student, especially one so virginal and impressionable, would have been the height of folly. She never let a student get that close to her again. Anyone else who had gotten close had touched only her body.

Incredibly, here she was again, nine years later, evoking an old ambivalence in Jordan. She was happy to see her, but keenly on guard against the feelings of fondness seeping in from the past.

"One thing I try to do," Kelly was saying, gesturing with an open palm, "is capture the truth of a subject. To catch it in just the right light, at the right angle, at the right moment so it reveals itself, or at least an aspect of itself that is so true it looks like something you've never seen before. To capture it at its most pure and honest, when it's nothing but itself."

Jordan made an effort to concentrate on the present. "Are you talking about inanimate objects?"

"It doesn't matter. It applies to everything, including people. I think photography is unique among the arts because it's the only one that doesn't invent its own reality. With music and writing and painting, the artist creates something that doesn't exist in the real world. Even a painting of an object isn't a replica of it. But a photograph is an exact likeness of something that's already there. The real value of a photograph is that it freezes a moment in time forever. Just like the ice does." Kelly paused, looking suddenly self-conscious.

Jordan gazed patiently at her, listening, looking at the light in her eyes, thinking about the changes in her looks and manner. She had been attractive back then, no doubt about it, but now she was much more beautiful than she ever was as an undeveloped, untested, unscarred girl of nineteen. Jordan had never much liked the looks of young women of that age. They were so unfinished, as if a painter had done a preliminary sketch and hadn't yet filled in all the fine details. It's the details that make a person's face resonate interest. And details come from living.

"Some people don't see the art in a photo," Kelly said. "Because it's a replica made by a machine. Like what I was just saying. It's not something invented. But a good photographer can add something so there's no way you would have had the same experience of the subject if you'd just happened past it on the street. Do you know what I mean?"

Jordan nodded. "I think so. A photographer sees something other people don't see and then tries to convey that vision in the photograph."

"Exactly! Ordinary scenes or objects that you'd never think of as photo-worthy, even. Like a worn-out saddle on a fence post. In the photo, it's presented with as much of its raw beauty or ugliness or whatever is true about it that people look at it with new eyes and feel something they couldn't have felt without the photo." Kelly's shoulders relaxed and she smiled.

She had changed. She seemed full of confidence and poise. And passion for her work. Jordan felt enormously proud of her. Not that she could take any credit for it. Whatever sort of woman Kelly had become, she had achieved it on her own. The best Jordan could claim was that she hadn't damaged her in any way. Kelly had come to her with her delusions about love intact and had left in the same condition. If she had grown cynical since then, she had someone else to blame for it.

"That was extremely eloquent," Jordan said. "I'd say you've chosen the right career."

Kelly sighed. "I guess I wasn't that good at science."

"Oh, you were a good student. But I don't think your heart was ever at home there. I'm really happy to see you've found your calling. I know Chuck wouldn't have asked you along if you weren't good."

* * *

While they had been talking, especially once Kelly started talking about her work, Jordan had seemed to relax and warm up. She had managed to deflect the conversation away from the subject Kelly had come to talk about, their relationship. Truthfully, she wasn't sure what she'd come to say. She had just wanted to have a private chat and see where it led, get to know Jordan again. In her mind's rehearsals, she had often poured out her heart to Jordan and declared, "I still love you!" Invariably, in these failed fantasies, Jordan would shield her face with her hands and say, "Oh, no! Not again!"

Kelly would spare her that tonight. She had matured enough to know that saying "I love you" to someone who couldn't reciprocate was a demanding and selfish act. Not that she didn't feel it. The way she felt tonight she might have been that silly girl all over again. It would almost be worth making a fool of herself if she could inspire Jordan to kiss her once more like she had all those years ago. The first kiss had lasted her nine years. Maybe the second…

"Thank you for the tea," Jordan said decisively, putting the empty cup on the edge of the table.

"Thanks for the chat," Kelly replied. Understanding it was time to go, she stood and collected the mugs. "I just wanted to tell you," she ventured, "that I appreciate everything you did for me back then and how kindly and wisely you handled it."

Jordan nodded. "I'm glad to see how well you've done, Kelly. See you in the morning."

CHAPTER SIXTEEN

Jordan woke to a beeping sound. She rolled over and opened her eyes, noting the stiff muscle in her neck. It had been a restless night. As she sat up, she remembered Kelly's visit from the previous evening. She was sure there had been some purpose to that other than chatting over a cup of tea. Or maybe not. She had no reason to be suspicious. Maybe Kelly just wanted to catch up.

There was that beep again. She glared at the sheet hanging between her and the computer, then slipped on her thongs and walked over to discover a message from Ilulissat Search and Rescue. She read it, then quickly dressed and went outside into the cool morning air. Malik was in the kitchen mixing something in a bowl.

"Good morning," he said cheerfully.

"Morning. Is there coffee?"

"Yes. It has just finished perking."

She poured a mug and took a temperature-testing sip. "What are you making?"

"Pandekager," he replied with a grin.

Of course, she thought. When it was his turn to make breakfast, it was always pancakes. Last week he had proposed making them for dinner as well, but Brian had a fit, so they had hot dogs instead.

"Greenlandic pandekager," Malik elaborated.

"Really? How so?"

"I picked some fresh bilberries yesterday." He tipped the bowl so she could see the berry-studded batter.

"Sounds good." Jordan sat down at the table as Julie arrived and grabbed a mug from the counter. "Julie, could you wake up Kelly? I have some news for her."

Julie nodded and walked over to Sonja's tent. A few minutes later Kelly emerged wearing a sweatshirt and Sonja's too-long sweatpants, her hair askew, her eyes bleary. She looked adorably disheveled. Jordan felt lighthearted at the prospect of delivering good news to her.

"I hope it's not too early for you," Jordan said. "But I thought you'd want to hear the news as soon as possible. Your friend Pippa was found and flown back to town last night. She's okay."

"Oh!" Kelly's hands flew to her face, then she heaved a deep sigh.

"I suppose you want to get back as soon as possible to visit her in the hospital."

"Hospital? But you said she was okay."

"She has a concussion and a twisted ankle, so they're keeping her for observation. They said she was conscious and alert when they found her. Just a little dehydrated. Apparently she'd fallen into a ravine or something. Thanks to you, she's safe now."

Kelly sank into a chair. "Jordan, thank you so much for everything."

"You're welcome. I'm glad we could help. Malik's going to town in a while to get some supplies. He can take you back. So I'll see you when you come out with Chuck." She turned to Malik. "Malik, when the pancakes are ready, could you bring me a couple? I've got some work to do this morning before we head out to the field."

She walked rapidly to her tent, glad to be away from Kelly's stare. As long as Jordan had been able to see her as a child, she didn't have to be taken seriously. But now she was a woman. Beautiful and complex with depth and nuanced hues. There was no denying the physical attraction Jordan felt toward her, but it wasn't a comfortable feeling. When Kelly looked at her, she seemed to be looking right inside her. It made it hard to look her in the eye and it made her want to run and hide.

She went to her bed and lay back down with her cheek on the cool pillowcase. She closed her eyes, remembering the one kiss they had shared. She had kissed Kelly too long and had wanted so much more than one kiss. But the circumstances were wrong in every way.

There were plenty of her colleagues who had no qualms about relationships with their students, often with a greater age disparity than between her and Kelly. It was a common enough phenomenon to be a cliché: the middle-aged professor and his young protégé. He strutting about looking ridiculous with that self-satisfied coquette on his arm. How could he be so pompous as to think she wouldn't open her eyes someday soon and see him in all his wretched ludicrousness?

Not to look ridiculous was one of Jordan's chief goals in life. She had earned the respect of her colleagues, but one stupid mistake could change everything. Besides, men didn't suffer loss of reputation as easily as women did, even in the modern world. She knew how much harder a woman had to work to hold onto credibility. She couldn't allow herself to show weaknesses associated with her gender, like sentimentality, passivity and self-doubt. Her rule was that it was okay to feel those things, but it was not okay to let others see them. Which made it hard sometimes to ask for help...or understanding. Or anything, really, because needing something, anything, automatically put her in a position of vulnerability.

She had been lying on the bed for several minutes when she heard Sonja's voice.

"Jordan, I've got your breakfast. Are you sick?"

Jordan rolled over and sat up. "No. Just tired. I didn't sleep much last night and I woke up with a stiff neck."

Sonja smiled sympathetically, her bangs hanging halfway over her eyes. She set a plate of syrup-covered pancakes on the side table, then sat on the edge of the bed. "Sorry," she said, putting her hands on Jordan's shoulders and massaging gently. "Why don't you lie back down and I'll give you a massage. I'm pretty good at it. So people tell me."

Jordan brushed her away and swung her feet to the floor, facing her pancakes.

"Good news about Pippa, isn't it?" Sonja asked.

Jordan nodded. "Quite a relief for Kelly, I'm sure."

"I bet you were totally blown away when she turned up here out of the blue like that."

"Uh-huh. The last place I would have expected to see Kelly Sheffield. Actually anyone from home."

"She said you haven't seen one another for nine years. Why is that?"

"She was my student," Jordan said flatly. "I don't keep in touch with many students."

"I get the impression she was a special student." Sonja looked up to catch Jordan's eye. "*Very* special."

"Not *that* special," Jordan said sternly, cutting a triangle out of her pancake stack.

"Oh, it doesn't matter. Whatever you were to her once, that's in the distant past. She's got Pippa now, hasn't she?" Sonja looked pleased with herself. "And it's apparently serious. They're totally devoted to one another."

Jordan stiffened, dropping her fork in the plate. "Did Kelly say that?"

"More or less. It was her explanation for blowing me off when I made a pass at her last night."

Jordan laughed, noticing it came out sounding more bitter than amused. "You made a pass at Kelly?"

"Uh-huh. Why shouldn't I? She's super hot. Anyway, she turned me down flat."

"Maybe she just isn't interested in…" Jordan reconsidered her insult. "Blondes."

"Maybe. Or maybe I'm just too old for her." Sonja tossed her bangs and strode out.

Jordan brushed off the implied insult about her age and took a bite of her breakfast. She shook her head at Sonja's seduction technique. Apparently she thought she could goad Jordan into bed. She plied her as often with abuses as compliments. This morning her argument seemed to be, "Nobody else would want you, you old hag, so you may as well take me." It didn't much matter. It was a lost cause whichever way she played it.

Sonja was one of several students who had made a play for her over the years. Jordan had plenty of experience in this department. The thing to do was pretend not to notice that they were sitting in your class fantasizing about slithering into your lonely spinster life and blowing your mind. They imagined that you weren't getting any and they were going to rock your world. They were so naïve and so arrogant, most of them. Because of their youth, they didn't know how obvious they were. Or how boring.

That Kelly had turned Sonja down pleased Jordan, but didn't surprise her. Kelly couldn't have changed so much that she would be so cavalier about sex. It was totally out of character to think she would go for a cuddle in the sack with Sonja. Especially if she was seriously involved with someone else. But an eighteen-year-old? That seemed out of character too.

There was always the chance Kelly was in love with Pippa and couldn't stop herself from what looked to an outsider like folly. Maybe Pippa was really something special. Age wasn't always an accurate gauge for a person's maturity.

I'd like to meet this Pippa, Jordan thought, stuffing a forkful of pancake in her mouth.

CHAPTER SEVENTEEN

For the last hour, Kelly had been listening to a remarkable story that Pippa had kept quiet about until today. They sat side by side on the couch in the boarding house living room, drinking hot chocolate while rain banged on the windowpane behind their heads. Work plans for everyone had been canceled due to bad weather.

Pippa had been home from the hospital two days and said she felt fine. No more pain in her head. No more dizziness. Her twisted ankle was rapidly improving. Though she limped, she was walking unaided.

As soon as they'd been reunited at the hospital, they had both eagerly told the other about their adventures. Kelly had been touched to hear how anxious Pippa had been about her in the midst of her own ordeal, and how she had fired a half dozen questions at the rescue team the moment they had found her, like, "Where is Kelly? Is she safe?"

Kelly had already heard the story of Pippa's accident and her rescue. But today she learned that the most important part of the experience for Pippa wasn't any of that. It was what had been going on in her mind during her many hours in the cave, an elaborate and surprisingly coherent dream about a fourteenth-century Norse woman named Asa.

There was nothing truly strange about the story. It seemed historically reasonable. There were a lot of similar stories about how the Viking settlers lived and how they ultimately died out. What was weird was that Pippa was convinced it wasn't a dream. She seemed to think it had all really happened just as she dreamed it, that centuries ago the Viking woman had hidden from the Thule in the very cave she herself had fallen into. Had not only hidden there but had miscarried her baby there.

"This has been on my mind every minute since I got back," Pippa said. "But what I didn't realize before is that the baby has to be buried in that cave. Where else would it be? She didn't take it with her."

"It might not have been buried at all," Kelly pointed out, going along for the sake of conversation. "She had a lot on her mind. She might have just left it there and some animal took it away."

Pippa shook her head. "She wouldn't have done that. These people were devout and superstitious Christians. It would be important to her to bury it. I know it's there. It's under the rocks, the pile of rocks I told you about. It's not just a random pile. It's a burial mound. She carved a message there. I saw it. That has to be an epitaph."

Kelly shivered. "You're freaking me out here, Pippa."

"I knew I shouldn't have told you." She frowned and took a drink from her mug.

"No, no," Kelly objected. "It's good that you told me. I really enjoyed the story. But, you know, it's just a story. A vivid dream."

"What if it wasn't a dream?"

"What else?"

"A vision," Pippa replied solemnly. "Like a message from the past."

"You don't believe that."

Pippa shrugged. "Nivi believes it. She believes I can see into the future and the past."

"That's just folklore. You know that. What happened to you is just the combination of the concussion and the suggestion that Nivi planted in your mind. You said yourself you were drifting in and out of consciousness and you even hallucinated that you saw someone in the cave. Obviously, there was no one there. You can't really trust your experiences from that day."

Pippa shrugged. "Maybe. But I can't stop thinking about her. I want to know what happened to her. Did she survive? I've tried to conjure it up in my mind again, to continue the story. But it's no use. I get nothing." She set her mug on the table, looking morose.

She was obviously feeling very close to this story of hers. It was real to her. These people were real to her.

"I just have a feeling about Asa," she said. "She's trying to tell me something and I don't believe it's just that she died of starvation with the rest of them. I think there's something special about her."

Because she's the heroine of your story, Kelly thought, and you don't want to think of her perishing so ingloriously. Kelly pulled Pippa's head under her chin, giving her a bracing hug as Mrs. Arensen appeared in the doorway in a shapeless floral dress.

"I am taking a count," she announced. "For supper. Jens and Mr. Waddell are going to the Disko Hotel." She shook her head disapprovingly. "How can a student afford a forty-krone hamburger? Mr. Lance, he is also going."

"What are you cooking?" Kelly asked, making a mental note that extravagant meals were on Mrs. Arensen's list of moral weaknesses.

"Laks," she replied.

Kelly turned to Pippa. "Salmon?"

Pippa nodded.

"That would be great," Kelly said. "I love salmon."

"Good." Mrs. Arensen smiled, stretching her thin lips even thinner. "Nice fresh fish caught this morning. I have been having it all day in a pot with sugar, salt and onions. Nice pickled fish. What about you, Pippa? Will you be having supper with us?"

"*Nej tak*. I'll be going home."

Mrs. Arensen withdrew from the doorway.

"What's wrong?" Pippa asked. "You look like you've been stabbed in the stomach."

"Pickled salmon?"

"You don't like it?"

"I have no idea. I've never had it, but to do that to a beautiful, fresh piece of fish, it's just criminal. I mean, holy cow, we're going to eat it tonight, not for Christmas! I know you can't get fresh fruit and vegetables, but you definitely have fresh fish. So why go and do that to it?"

"The Danish like things pickled. You might like it too."

Kelly shook her head dejectedly and looked at the window where the rain still blasted against it. "When do you think you'll be back to work?"

"A few more days. In the meantime, as soon as the weather lets up I'm going back to the cave."

"What?" Kelly was alarmed.

"I have to go back to finish Asa's story. I don't think I can connect with her anywhere else."

"I hope you're not serious."

"I *am* serious. If I go by boat, I can get close enough for a short walk. It's less than a kilometer inland, don't you think?"

"Your father will let you take a boat out alone?"

"He gave up a long time ago trying to force me into a traditional mold. I'm a modern woman."

"But your ankle," Kelly objected.

"It's a lot better. It's a short hike. I can take a walking stick. I'm fine, really. Don't worry." Pippa peered earnestly into Kelly's eyes. "I've just got to go back. I have to find out what happened to Asa and her daughter."

Kelly could tell she had her mind made up. "Then I'll come with you. Even if your ankle's okay and you're a modern woman, nobody should take a boat out alone."

Pippa nodded her assent as they heard the front door slam shut. Kelly glanced at the antique-looking cuckoo clock on the wall to see that it was five thirty.

"Must be Annalise coming home from work," she said.

Annalise, who taught a business course in town, was the only person in this house who could go to work on a day like this. A moment later she wandered past the open doorway.

"Hi, Annalise!" Pippa called.

The young woman stopped to look in, blinking through her water-spotted glasses. She wore a navy blue skirt, pale stockings and black flats. She was short and plump and extremely conservative looking, especially for a woman in her early twenties. She wore no makeup, no jewelry, and looked a lot like a Catholic schoolgirl. Kelly knew almost nothing about her, except that she lived in Nuuk and would be returning there at the end of the summer.

"Hi, Pippa," she responded, smiling. The rest of their conversation was in Greenlandic, a hasty dialogue of small talk before Annalise retired to her room.

"She's nice," Pippa remarked.

"Yes, and very quiet. No trouble at all. I think Mrs. Arensen is in love with her."

Pippa giggled as Chuck came in and grabbed his heavy coat off the rack.

"Hey," Kelly called, "why's everybody going out tonight?"

"Aren't you coming?" He put on his worn Panama hat. Like his Van Halen T-shirt, it was a treasured part of his wardrobe.

"I think I must have missed this memo. What's going on?"

"Oh, sorry. I was supposed to tell you. Slipped my mind." He pulled on his coat, wrapping the muffler around his neck. "It's a birthday party for Waddell. He's thirty-five today. We're all invited. Come on. We've got the hotel van coming to pick us up. You too Pippa. I'll go tell Elsa we're all going, then I'll meet you out front."

Kelly sprang off the couch. "The good news is that the pickled salmon will still be edible tomorrow."

"And the bad news?" Pippa asked.

"The pickled salmon will still be edible tomorrow." Kelly laughed and extended a hand to help Pippa off the couch.

CHAPTER EIGHTEEN

Out of utter frustration, Julie half screamed, half growled and let go of the corner of the plastic tarp she was trying to tie down. It flapped wildly in the wind. The rain pelted relentlessly down on them as they worked to cover the supplies and equipment. Jordan hugged the hood of her parka closer around her face, feeling chilled through.

"I'll do it," she offered, stepping in and grabbing the rope. "Go inside."

While the rain bombarded her, she managed to tie the corner down over their food supplies. Everything that could be damaged by water was now either inside or covered. But the camp was a sloggy mess and all of them were wet and cold. The sky was still dark gray and the rain showed no sign of letting up. It was going to be a miserable night.

"Fuck!" muttered Brian, standing in front of her with his arms laden with blankets.

"What's the matter now?" Jordan asked.

"Our spare blankets are wet. All we've got is what's already in the tents."

Jordan observed his grim expression, then looked at her bedraggled group. Water dripped from the tip of Malik's nose and Sonja bounced up and down on the balls of her feet trying to generate warmth.

"We're going to town!" Jordan declared. "Three weeks of cold, dirt and mosquitoes and we deserve a vacation."

"What?" Sonja asked, stepping under the tarp. "We're going to a hotel?"

"Yes. There's a gorgeous, modern hotel with a great bar and restaurant."

"How expensive?" Julie asked.

"Don't worry. My treat. Let me call and see if they have rooms."

"We can't leave all the equipment," Malik interjected.

Jordan glanced around the camp, realizing he was right. It was extremely unlikely that anyone would happen along and take anything, but they couldn't risk it. For a brief moment, she had felt buoyant, contemplating a long soak in a deep, hot bubble bath.

"No, of course we can't," she agreed. "I'll stay. The rest of you can go."

She moved toward her tent to call the hotel.

"I can stay," Malik called after her, his voice buffeted by the wind. "It will not bother me. This is just a balmy summer rain."

Jordan turned to observe his reassuring smile. He nodded his encouragement. One woman's freezing monsoon…, she mused.

"Yes!" he assured her. "You go enjoy yourself. I used to camp out here all the time. This is nothing to me. It is just rain. Atka will keep me company and we will have a good time."

She hugged him gratefully. "I owe you one, big time."

She called the hotel and reserved three rooms, one for the girls, one for Brian and one for herself. It was an expensive indulgence, but she knew it would be worth it.

After hastily packing overnight bags, they piled into the boat. Malik untied it from the dock and tossed the rope on deck. He waved as they pulled away, his face in shadow under the hood of his parka, his dog sitting calmly beside him as shimmering sheets of water covered them both.

"Don't you get the feeling," Julie said, "that as soon as we're out of sight, he'll turn into a wolf and the two of them will go running over the mountains howling at the moon?"

Jordan chuckled. "I don't know about that, but I do think he'll enjoy the solitude."

An hour and a half later, Jordan was alone in her hotel room. She drew a hot bath and sank into it, the chill in her bones gradually dissipating. She washed her hair, working up a rich lather and enjoying the long, sensuous experience of both abundant hot running water and privacy. She washed herself all over with a soapy washcloth, slowly and thoroughly, then she shaved her legs and underarms until they were silky smooth. She finally and reluctantly left the bathtub, drying herself with a thick towel, rubbing lotion into her arms and legs, then drying her hair with the hotel blow-dryer.

This luxurious ritual took nearly two hours from start to finish. Afterward, she finally felt civilized. She enjoyed field camp, but among the things she missed most was clean hair. What the others missed most, she imagined, was their families, friends and lovers. It seems a little pathetic, she thought, that the main thing I miss is clean hair. But there was no one waiting for her at home.

During these summer sojourns, that was usually the case. Even when she was dating someone, it wasn't the sort of situation that left anyone yearning for nightly online video chats like Brian and his wife. Her relationships were often casual and short-lived. If the length of a relationship was a measure of its success, then hers were all failures. Luckily, she had her career as a measure of her success.

Through the course of these several short, unsatisfactory relationships, one important lesson she'd learned was never to date someone you couldn't afford to lose from your life. Like a close friend or a great doctor or your favorite barista—all people she had lost after a brief love affair. These people were hard to replace. The barista more than most, she lamented, recalling that she could no longer stop at The Jumping Bean on her way to class because of Absinthe. Going there had been one of life's simple pleasures. Absinthe had seemed a little odd to Jordan at first, somewhat edgy with her numerous tattoos, intimate piercings and her in-your-face insolence, but she made a damned good cup of coffee and never failed to swirl a cheerful image on top of her latte. Originally it had been the letter "J," but after she started her romantic pursuit of Jordan, it had been the shape of a heart, touchingly perfect in creamy beige foam.

Maybe it was Absinthe's appearance of hardness that had appealed to Jordan in the first place. After her humiliating love affair with Teresa Marquette, she had avoided dating completely until she had obtained her doctorate and secured a position at Boulder. Even then, when she ventured out again, she did so with extreme caution. She eventually learned something that Teresa had demonstrated well, that one could enjoy the company of a lover and the intimacy of lovemaking without the debilitating component of love. In Jordan's experience, being in love was too much like being insane, and she had no intention of inviting that disaster on herself again.

For all her outward show of bitterness, Absinthe had turned into a too saccharine refreshment. After a few weeks, she began to voice the usual recriminations. "Don't you have any feelings for me at all?"

"Of course I do," Jordan had answered. "I think you're fun and sexy and good in bed."

"That's not what I mean," Absinthe replied, shoving Jordan into that uncomfortable corner that she dreaded, where anything honest she could say would be a disappointment.

These sorts of questions or their counterpart statements, like, "I love you," always signaled the end of a relationship to Jordan. Those three words were a blaring alarm, an attack, like a torpedo sent to blast her out of the water, calling for evasive maneuvers.

Since Teresa, she had never said those words to anyone. She didn't think she ever would. When she had said them to Teresa, her response had seemed one of triumph. So Jordan had interpreted it later, the satisfied smile, the sigh of contentment, and the anticipated echo of, "Oh, my darling, I love you too!" At least Jordan had never said it falsely, nor would she consider it, even as a patch over the insecurities of someone like Absinthe.

"Because of you," Jordan had said, trying to lighten the mood with Absinthe, "I now know the unique joy of metal as a component of lovemaking." She had drawn Absinthe close and sucked on the ring through her bottom lip. "Before you, it was all feathers and silk and leather. Now, the cool sleek sensation of steel quickens my pulse."

Absinthe had pulled away, saying, "I'm serious, Jordan."

Seeing that the question had to be answered, Jordan relented and told the truth. "I like you," she said. "We have fun together and I enjoy your company. I hope that's enough."

But it wasn't enough, as Jordan knew it wouldn't be as soon as Absinthe had asked the question. If it had been enough, she wouldn't have asked.

Absinthe and The Jumping Bean were part and parcel, so there was no going back there now. Jordan sighed. She missed Absinthe. Not Absinthe the lover, but Absinthe the barista.

These days dating just didn't seem worth it anymore. The pleasure of having a woman in her bed was erased by the emotional demands that inevitably emerged as predictably as thunder after lightning, usually by the third week. She was beginning to think that she preferred being alone. Life was so much easier that way.

She finished dressing in a lightweight sweater and casual pants, luxuriating in the feeling of real cleanliness, and went upstairs. At the entrance to the bar she noticed Julie carrying two brandy glasses toward the restaurant. Normally in a ponytail, her hair was loose tonight, flowing over her shoulders, giving her a decidedly softer than usual look.

"That looks good," Jordan remarked, tapping one of the brandy glasses.

"Oh, hi. We were beginning to wonder if you were coming out at all tonight."

"The truth is, I could easily just crawl into bed until morning and be happy."

"We're in the restaurant having dessert. Come on in."

"I will. Let me get one of those first."

After ordering a brandy, she entered the restaurant, searching for her group. Just as she spotted them, a noisy table distracted her and she glanced over. The first person she recognized was Kelly. Jordan caught her breath. She'd already forgotten what Kelly looked like in this older incarnation. The image in her mind the last few days had reverted back to the twenty-one-year old. The thirty-year-old, unaware of her admirer, sat so her reflection in the window provided a three-dimensional view of her face. She wore a long-sleeved topaz-colored blouse over brown pants. Her legs were crossed at the knee and she appeared relaxed and engaged with her friends.

Sitting next to her was a petite young woman, a Greenlander with incredibly beautiful blue eyes and long brown hair. The girl bumped playfully against Kelly, smiling happily at her. She looked all of sixteen, the picture of joyful innocence. Pippa, Jordan presumed. Not what she had expected. She had thought she'd be more sophisticated, that she would transcend her physical age in bearing and appearance. But it was just the opposite.

Chuck Lance was also present, accounting for the boisterousness of the group, and a couple of young men Jordan didn't know. She proceeded to her team's table and put her glass down at an empty spot, noting their half-eaten desserts.

"Hi, Jordan," Brian said. "Do you want something to eat?"

"I'll have one of those brownies." She pointed to Julie's plate. "Can you order that for me when the waiter comes by? I'll be right back. There's someone over here I want to say hi to."

She walked back to the other table and laid a hand on Chuck's broad shoulder. He turned and looked up, his cheeks blazing red from the alcohol, heat and excitement of their celebration. As he recognized her, his eyes opened wide with delight and he sprang up, hugging her enthusiastically.

"Jordan!" he cried. "So good to see you again. What are you doing in town?"

"It wasn't planned," she said. "We decided to get out of the rain for the night."

"Sure. Nasty day. Good for you, then. Did you get my message?"

"Yes. You can come out any day it suits you. We're always there."

"Except for tonight," he pointed out.

"Yes, right. Hopefully, we won't see any more weather like this. Just send me a message before you come and I'll be prepared to give you a tour."

Chuck moved aside to open her view to the rest of the table. "I know you've already met my photographer, Sheffield, during that crazy hike gone wild."

Kelly smiled politely.

"Yes," Jordan said. "Hi again." His phrasing suggested he hadn't been told they'd known one another before. It didn't really matter. It was none of his business and Kelly wasn't the sort of person to go blabbing about her private affairs. Jordan suspected she maintained a mostly professional relationship with Chuck.

"And this is Pippa," he continued. "Pippa, this is Jordan Westgate, the woman responsible for your rescue."

Jordan reached across the table to shake the girl's small hand. "I'm not responsible. All I did was make a phone call. I'm glad it turned out so happily."

"We're so lucky you were there," Pippa said gratefully, then smiled warmly at Kelly.

Chuck proceeded around the table, introducing Jens Arensen, a pale young man with a thin face and two days' worth of a sparse blond beard sprouting on his chin.

"Arensen?" Jordan asked, shaking his hand. "Any relation to Elsa Arensen?"

"She's my grandmother," he answered. "I'm staying with her this summer."

"That's where we're holed up," Chuck interjected.

"I've spent a few nights at the boarding house over the years," Jordan said. "How is Elsa?"

"Same as ever," Jens said, a tipsy smile on his pallid face. "You should stop in for a visit."

Next, Chuck turned to the man to his right, a tidy fellow in a satiny blue shirt and striped tie, who stood as he was introduced. "This is Trevor Waddell. He's with JPI Petroleum."

Jordan reached over to shake his hand. "Looking for oil, Mr. Waddell?"

"We're in the early exploration stage. JPI is negotiating for a contract with NUNAOIL. I'm here to determine drilling sites for us to bid on."

"Drilling sites? I didn't think oil drilling had begun in Greenland."

"Oh, it hasn't begun, not yet, but negotiations for licenses are ongoing. Everyone is jockeying for position."

"I see. You're all lining up offshore with your drills at the ready, waiting for the starter pistol to go off."

Waddell smiled. He was probably used to that sort of mockery.

"Are you a geologist?" Jordan asked.

He nodded.

"Oh!" Chuck blurted. "I'd completely overlooked that. Dr. Westgate is a geologist too. You two are in the same field!"

"The same field?" Jordan caught Kelly's eye, noticing a smile of amusement curling up at the edge of her lips. "Hmm. Perhaps not."

"You know what I meant," Chuck said. "Same discipline. But nearly antithetical applications. Jordan's a glaciologist."

"Clearly," Jordan said, "we're working on very different problems."

"I suspect Dr. Westgate doesn't approve of my application of geology." Waddell took his seat. "But until you all quit being oil consumers, you'll expect somebody to pump it out of the ground for you. You get awfully damned outraged whenever the supply drops and prices go up."

"You're right," Jordan said. "We all have to share the blame. But I sometimes wonder, necessity being the mother of invention, what would happen if we simply quit pumping it out of the ground. How long would it take civilization to rebound with some fascinating new solutions to fossil fuels? That's out of the question, I suppose, but wouldn't it be interesting?"

Her gaze landed on Chuck, who seemed highly entertained, looking like somebody had lit a fire under him and he was preparing to rocket into space. She remembered how he loved a good argument.

"Join us!" he suggested, reaching for a chair from a nearby table.

"No, thank you. My students are here." She nodded vaguely toward the other table, regretting that she wasn't able to join this company.

Chuck was visibly disappointed. "That's too bad. I'd love to hear the ice woman and the oil man talk about the future of Greenland."

Jordan laughed. "Wouldn't you, though? I'll see you soon." She glanced toward Kelly. "Both of you."

She returned to her table and seated herself between Sonja and Brian. From that position she could easily see Chuck's group. She found herself drawn often to observe Kelly and the childlike Pippa whose gestures and expressions were familiar and affectionate. It was easy to see she adored Kelly. For her part, Kelly was attentive and seemed fond of the girl. Pippa pulled out a digital camera and took a photo of herself and Kelly at arm's length, then she looked at it on the camera and giggled with delight.

This pairing was perplexing. But in the nine years since Jordan had known Kelly, she didn't know anything about what she had been through, emotionally or romantically. Maybe this girl was just what she needed now.

Whatever the reason, all of this was good news, Jordan told herself. It meant that Kelly had moved on and wouldn't be mooning over Jordan anymore. That was a relief!

"Are you all having a good time?" she asked, focusing her attention back to her own table.

"Awesome!" Brian replied. "Thanks for footing the bill. You're gonna freak when you see what our meal cost. But it's not like we had caviar and champagne. I had a hamburger and a local beer, Erik the Red. Let me tell you, this beer rocks! Actually, this is my second bottle."

Jordan waved dismissively. "Don't worry. I've been here before. Food is always expensive in Greenland. This place, even more so. And I agree about the beer. It's one of the not-to-be-missed treats of Greenland."

"It's really generous of you to do this," Julie said.

The waiter came by with Jordan's dessert, a small plate containing a gooey brownie sitting in a pool of silky crème Anglaise topped with shards of pecan brittle.

"To Jordan!" Sonja interjected, raising her glass. "For saving our asses from the wrath of the Arctic night."

In concert with the others, Jordan took a sip of her drink. It slid warmly down her throat. She glanced around the room to take in the space. The restaurant was roomy and modern with high ceilings and a wall of glass facing the bay. Tonight there wasn't much to see. With the storm, it was dark out and the windows were streaked with running water, reminding her crew how happy they were to be here.

She tasted the brownie. "Um, this is so good!"

"It's too bad Malik couldn't be here," Sonja lamented.

"I feel bad about leaving him out there by himself," Jordan agreed, causing herself a momentary shudder with the thought of Malik and the oil man sitting under the same roof. Oil drilling in the Arctic was one of his serious hot buttons.

"I think he's happier by himself anyway," Julie suggested.

Brian huffed. "And we're certainly more jolly without him here."

"What's that supposed to mean?" Sonja asked resentfully.

"Just that he's so intense and serious all the time. If he were here, I'd have to have a debate about the political ramifications of my hamburger, for Christ's sake."

"So he cares about things," Sonja said. "There's nothing wrong with that."

"Nothing wrong with it, no, but tonight I'd just as soon relax and forget about all that. Yeah, Greenland has problems, but so does every country and you just have to let it go once in a while and have a good time or you'll go nuts. I wonder if that dude ever has a good time."

"He doesn't smile much," Julie commented.

Sonja wrapped both hands around her glass. "He's concerned about the state of the world, particularly Greenland. He's just patriotic."

"So am I," Brian said, "but I'm not going to tattoo the American flag on the side of my head like some dweeb. I have nothing against the dude. He's just kind of a drag, so if you're having a party, it's better he's not there. If you're having a political rally, he's your guy."

Jordan took another bite of her dessert, glancing Kelly's way. As if Kelly could sense it, she turned to catch Jordan's eye. For a second, they seemed locked together before Kelly was distracted by Pippa.

"Since we're here to learn about Greenland," Sonja said, "I think we should listen to what Malik has to say. He's our authority on everything about this place."

"I agree," Jordan said. "His contribution is valuable. The science we're doing here is globally important, but we don't want to lose sight of where we are. His perspective will remind us of the long history and rich culture of the people who live here."

Sonja smiled and sat back in her chair, satisfied. She gave Jordan a look that suggested they were somehow in synch on a higher plane of understanding than the other two.

"Let's bring him back something nice," she suggested. "To thank him for this little vacation."

"Good idea," Jordan agreed.

"Maybe we should bring him a case of Erik the Red," Brian suggested with a smirk. He drained his bottle, then scratched his beard under his chin and stood. "After three weeks with no TV," he announced, "I'm looking forward to checking out the sports channel tonight. Thank you for a lovely evening, ladies."

"Good night," Jordan said. "Meet up in the lobby at eight tomorrow."

As she sipped her brandy, she listened distractedly to Julie and Sonja discussing the prohibitive cost of higher education, specifically *their* higher education, and why things that benefit society as a whole, like education and health care, shouldn't be free to everybody. Soon, Jordan wasn't hearing them at all. Instead, she withdrew into her own thoughts.

Kelly was like her younger self in many ways. One who listened carefully and didn't speak often. When she did speak, it was well considered and intelligent. She hardly spoke at all tonight, overshadowed by the garrulous Chuck and eager Pippa demanding her attention.

Not that Jordan would ever take the chance of letting Kelly get close to her again, but if Pippa were not in this picture, she reflected, what a perfect night this would be for an erotic adventure. Kelly might still find her attractive, she reasoned. If such things were possible, they might have been able to come together on a night like this for one night of pleasure. Nothing more. Yes, that would be enchanting, she thought, taking another sip of brandy and focusing on Kelly's sumptuous mouth. The liquor ran like a warm, thick ribbon of velvet down her throat, spreading smoothly in every direction, the warmth moving further down where a delightfully fluid tingle appeared.

Delicious, she thought, watching Kelly closely. What was once an immature fruit was now a succulent delicacy.

Encouraged by the brandy, she fell into a vivid fantasy of taking Kelly to her room, crushing her tightly against her body and kissing those incredible lips. Not like she had that one time years ago, but with complete abandon. The buttons on that silky blouse would come apart easily, allowing her access to the heaving, anxious bosom beneath. When she touched her lips to that velvety soft skin, both of them would go weak with hunger and melt like an ice cube in an oven.

"Jordan, what do you think?"

She started, nearly tipping over her glass. A drop of brandy fell over the rim onto her hand. She carefully put the glass on the table and faced Sonja, who was clearly waiting for her response.

"Sorry, what?"

* * *

"The polar bear," Chuck said, continuing his story, "was just trying to get the hell out of there. But Sam was convinced he was about to be eaten and both of them tore through the camp doing their own versions of screaming bloody murder. The bear got tangled in one of the tarps, the rope wrapped around his hind leg, so he's running in circles, this wild blue tarp flapping behind him, catching on everything and knocking our shit all over the place, making the bear crazy berserk." Chuck leaned back in his chair, raising his hands to emphasize how crazy the bear was. "Sam's yelling at me, 'Shoot him! Shoot him, you motherfucker!' Then Sam trips over one of the tent spikes and takes off like a toboggan. Whoosh! across the ice, face first. The bear, madder than hell, turns on the tarp and starts ripping it to shreds. There was nothing I could do but stay clear of him." Chuck shook his head and snickered. "It was the funniest damn thing I've ever seen. The bear finally got free of the tarp, but in the process he destroyed our camp. Meanwhile, Sam had belly sledded all the way to the bottom of the hill and was walking back up. The bear finally got free and went tearing off as fast as he could, by chance running straight toward Sam." Chuck howled with laughter, remembering, and had to stop his story until he recovered.

Kelly took the opportunity to glance toward Jordan's table and catch her eye. Jordan held her gaze momentarily, her expression passive, before taking a sip from her brandy glass. Kelly couldn't stop thinking about the fact that Jordan was staying right here in the hotel for the night and how easy it would be to show up at her door and ask to come in. Was there any chance Jordan would welcome her? Her mind continued to work on how that might be achieved. Drink up, Jordan, she silently urged.

Chuck wiped his watering eyes with his napkin and continued. "So of course Sam sees the bear heading straight at him and shrieks. He drops and covers his head and waits for the end. The bear leaps clean over him and takes off across the ice. I just wish I had it on film. It would be priceless."

Kelly ate the last of her pasta, noticing Jordan's group preparing to leave. A minute later, they passed by on their way out.

"See you soon," Jordan called to Chuck, her cheeks flushed from the brandy.

Then she smiled at Kelly, such a sincere, purposeful and affectionate smile that Kelly felt a wave of warmth flow through her, and along with it renewed hope that Jordan's heart wasn't completely closed against her.

Following Jordan, Sonja winked at Kelly and tossed her bangs out of her eyes.

"That's really a weird coincidence," Pippa remarked after they'd gone. "That she was your teacher in college."

"Uh-huh," Kelly muttered.

"What?" Chuck asked, coming to attention. "You already knew Jordan?"

"Yeah." Kelly was suddenly uncomfortable. "I had her for a couple classes."

"Why didn't you say so?" Chuck asked.

Kelly shrugged. "That was a long time ago. It didn't seem important." She picked up her water glass to take a big swallow, hoping the conversation would change course.

"Did you know she would be here?" Pippa asked.

Kelly reluctantly put her glass down. "Not until Chuck showed me the schedule. When I knew Jordan, she wasn't doing this kind of research."

"I remember the first year Jordan Westgate showed up here," Chuck reminisced. "That was about five, six years ago. She was with a team on the interior ice run by old Three-Finger Carter."

"Did he lose the other two to frostbite?" Jens asked.

"Naw. He had all his fingers. That was just how he drank scotch. Three fingers at a time." Chuck tipped his chair back on its two rear legs. "Holy shit, that man could put it away! And then get up the next morning and put in a full day's work like nobody's business. Liquor just didn't affect him. I saw him drunk, like seriously slurring his words drunk, maybe only twice in all the time I knew him."

Chuck proceeded to tell the story of one of those times. When the waiter returned, he ordered another round of drinks.

"No more for me," Kelly said, still mulling over the affectionate parting smile Jordan had given her. "I've had enough."

She shoved her chair back from the table and Pippa followed suit.

"See you tomorrow," Chuck called, then launched back into his story.

As Kelly stood at the cashier station waiting for her change, her eyes lingered on another bill on the counter, Jordan's. She had signed it to her room, number 147. Kelly committed the number to memory and met Pippa in the lobby.

"There's a shuttle about to leave," Pippa said. "We should take it. It might be the last one."

"You go ahead. The rain's stopped so I'm going to hang around here for a while and walk back."

"Why?"

"To take some photos. There's a lot more elevation here than in town. I might be able to get some good shots of the bay with the clouds and all. Interesting light going on tonight."

"Do you want me to stay? I don't mind."

"No, that's okay. You'd better catch the shuttle so you don't have to walk back with that ankle." Kelly laughed nervously. "I don't want to have to carry you. I'll see you tomorrow."

After hugging Kelly goodbye, Pippa limped out the front doors to the waiting bus. Through the rain-splattered front windows, she watched until Pippa got on the bus, assuring herself that she was actually leaving.

Now to Jordan, she thought, leaving the lobby.

CHAPTER NINETEEN

Her heart pounding wildly, Kelly walked down the stairs to the first floor. Her plan was unformed, but seeing Jordan's room number had seemed like a message from Destiny herself. She and Jordan belonged together and here was her chance to press her case. There was nothing to lose except a little pride. And that was nothing compared to what she could potentially gain. If she offered her heart to Jordan and was turned down, so what? She already knew that wouldn't destroy her.

And if she wasn't turned down? If Jordan welcomed her? Her mind reeled at the thought. She didn't want to imagine it could really happen for fear of disappointment. She didn't expect wishes to come true, but hope still welled up in her. Besides, this wasn't something impossible. Jordan had been fond of her once. Why shouldn't it grow into love now that all the circumstances were right between them?

Sometimes she had imagined that parting kiss not as a goodbye but as a promise to hold on to for the future. A promise that Jordan would wait for her, wait until she was ready.

At the bottom of the stairs, she turned left down a long hallway, then right at the next corner. At the end of the hallway was a glass door leading to the outside. Through the glass, she got a glimpse of the rugged shoreline and a sliver of the bay itself, pinkish in the cloud-filtered light from the low-lying sun. As she had told Pippa, the light was exquisite tonight. But even that wasn't enough to deter her from her purpose.

As she read numbers on doors and made her way down the hall, one of the doors further along opened. Feeling like a burglar, she ducked into the alcove of the nearest room, out of view, realizing that if someone came past and saw her hiding like this, it would look a lot more suspicious than if she were simply walking down the hallway. She peeked out to see a woman walking the other direction, toward the far end of the hall. She was long-legged, wearing an oversized sweater that reached to her thighs. As she tossed her blonde head, Kelly realized it was Sonja. She stopped at one of the doors closest to the end of the hall and glanced in Kelly's direction. Instinctively, Kelly pulled back into the alcove. When she looked out again, she saw Sonja knocking on the door. A couple of seconds elapsed before the door opened and Jordan appeared in a floor-length bathrobe. A few words were spoken quietly between them before Sonja went inside and the door shut behind her.

Kelly leaned heavily against the wall, stunned and disbelieving. To prove to herself that her eyes had not deceived her, she continued down the hall to the door in question to verify the room number. There it was on a brass plate, 147, unmistakably. She could hear the muffled voices of the two women inside.

Sonja? her mind screamed at her. *It wasn't possible!* Sonja, the woman who had flirted unapologetically with Kelly? How could it be that Jordan would take Sonja, one of her students, as her lover? Students were thoroughly off limits, she had maintained. No exceptions. That had been her firm rule, one of the main reasons she gave for keeping her relationship with Kelly purely platonic.

Oh, Jordan, how could you?

Kelly closed her eyes and breathed deeply, feeling weak. Then she moved closer to the door, holding her breath and listening. She heard nothing. Were they kissing?

I could bang on the door, she decided. *I could interrupt*. And then what? Obviously, if they were meeting like this tonight, it wasn't the first time. Interrupting would do nothing but embarrass everyone.

She pivoted to the side and let the wall support her, feeling betrayed and hurt.

Why her and not me?

Kelly had always suspected, but hoped otherwise, that she had been nothing but a thorn in Jordan's side, that the excuse about no fraternizing with students was a smokescreen. She'd wondered if the real reason she'd been rejected was simply that Jordan wasn't attracted to her. And here was proof of that. For some reason she couldn't understand, Sonja had succeeded where Kelly had failed. She closed her eyes and swallowed down the pain rising in her throat.

All those years ago, Jordan's wrongdoing, if any, had been being too soft and too compassionate. Not rejecting her completely and outright had fueled Kelly's hope that one day Jordan would be hers. She had lived on the keen edge of that hope for two years. In vain.

As she leaned against the wall, she felt despair wafting over her as hope died. She simply wasn't what Jordan wanted, not then…and not now.

The sound of Jordan's laugh, so familiar, jostled her from her thoughts. Dejected, she fled out the back door into the damp and frigid night, not bothering to button her coat or pull on the hood. She walked to a gravel trail that led to the road. She passed a few sleeping huskies chained to the rocks. One of them opened his eyes as she passed, then closed them again, lying half in and half out of his doghouse.

It was as close to dark as she had seen since arriving in Greenland. Steely gray clouds obscured the sun, creating an outline of soft luminescence at their boundaries. She continued on the path past the hotel's unoccupied outdoor deck. Through the restaurant windows, she saw Chuck, Trevor and Jens at their table, still drinking and telling stories. She stood above on the road for a few minutes, watching from her place of invisibility, feeling alone and full of regret as the rain fell on her bare head. She had arrived in the Arctic with a renewed dream only to have it shattered. She would have been better off never having come here, left with her wistful memories and purely imaginary fantasies. Even if she had never been able to see Jordan again, at least her false pathetic belief that Jordan had cared for her would still be intact.

This was the lesson her mother had so frequently tried to teach her, that these infantile hopes of the perfect true love would destroy you if you kept believing in them. She had thought she understood that lesson. She had thought of herself as a realist. But apparently she was as foolish as she had ever been.

While raindrops ran down her face, she numbly watched the silent scene through the restaurant glass. Jens reeled back in his chair and slapped the table with his palm. Those guys would be there until the place closed, but she had no interest in returning to their cheerful company.

She pulled her hood over her head and snapped it in place, then walked briskly to the long, sloping road into town. Ilulissat lay below, an unusual sight with the buildings lit up, lights on the boats in the harbor, the few cars with headlights on. One of those wound its way up the hill toward the hotel.

This was a rare opportunity for photos. The light was so different tonight. But she kept walking, unable to interest herself in photography, trying to concentrate on the crunching of gravel from her boots in the hopes of driving Jordan, and even more so, Sonja, out of her mind.

* * *

"What is it you just had to tell me?" Jordan asked impatiently, clutching the lapels of her bathrobe to be certain she revealed nothing to Sonja.

"Malik called," Sonja reported, sitting on the arm of the sofa. "He says the box with the cereal and pancake mix got soaked through and he wants us to get some more. You know how he loves his pandekager."

Jordan laughed. "Yes, he definitely does. Is everything else okay?"

"The rain's stopped and he says nothing else was damaged. Just a lot of slush and mud."

"Good. We can pick up some supplies before we leave in the morning. Now I'm way past ready to go to bed, so if you don't mind…"

Sonja stood and approached Jordan, a sultry look in her eyes. Jordan was fully aware that this report on the state of the camp was a flimsy excuse to wheedle her way into the room.

"I could stay," she suggested, standing close, her lips curled into a simpering smile.

Jordan frowned, indicating her disapproval.

"Why not?" Sonja whined. "What harm would it do?"

Jordan took a step back. "I'm not interested."

"Why aren't you interested? We're both single. Am I that horrible?"

"You're very attractive and you know it. But that's completely beside the point. Our relationship is a purely professional one and it's going to remain that way."

Sonja was attractive in the abstract, but even if she weren't a student, she would hold no allure for Jordan. It had nothing to do with her physical appearance. Jordan resented her arrogance. She had no humility. Without it, her attitude lacked respect. Respect, maybe more than love, was what Jordan craved. She didn't need veneration, just honest, simple respect.

Sonja sidled closer and put a hand on her cheek, caressing her gently. "You're so hot," she breathed. "You know I'm crazy about you. Let me stay. You won't be sorry."

She moved to land a kiss and Jordan caught her by the wrist and held her firmly at arm's length. "Is that what you said to Kelly?" she demanded.

Sonja blinked, looking startled. "What?"

Jordan released her. "When you made a pass at her. Don't you remember that?"

Sonja sputtered dismissively. "That was just harmless fun. I knew she wouldn't take me up on it. I was just flirting. But with you, I'm deadly serious. I really want to be with you."

"Yeah," Jordan said flatly. "I get the impression you'd have said the same thing to Kelly if she'd shown any interest."

"That's not true! I love you, Jordan." She adopted her most sincere look, but it came off so utterly phony that Jordan sputtered a derisive laugh.

"God, Sonja, I'm surprised you would even try that one!"

Sonja's shoulders slumped in resignation. "Okay, okay. But I still think you're hot. I've been out here three weeks. Three weeks! A girl gets desperate. What am I supposed to do?"

"Not my problem," Jordan said, irritated with Sonja's flippancy.

"Jordan," Sonja whined, "I really like you. Give me a chance."

"Not in this universe," Jordan replied firmly. "You've been pushing the limits all along and now you've crossed the line. You don't have any special status with me, Sonja. Not any more than Julie, Brian or Malik. Out here, you're working on my team and that's it. We're doing a job. I know I've been lax around camp because I want it to seem like we're a group of friends so we can have fun. But there are still rules."

Sonja pouted with mock remorse.

"I'm serious," Jordan emphasized. "I hope you believe that because there won't be another warning. If you try anything like this again, you're on a plane back to Denver. Now you need to go."

Sonja nodded, her eyes lowered. Then she looked up and said, "You know, Jordan, you really should let yourself have some fun once in a while."

"I don't need your advice."

After Sonja had gone, Jordan got into bed, berating herself for mentioning Kelly. That was stupid. She'd done it on impulse, reminded by Sonja's clumsy seduction routine that she'd made a pass at Kelly. It had angered her as soon as she'd heard about it. But why? Sonja would've made a pass at any woman sleeping in her tent. Somehow it was worse that it was Kelly. It felt like a betrayal. But, really, how could Sonja possibly know about the feelings she was treading on?

Jordan lay in bed tormenting herself with the fantasy of what might have happened if it had been Kelly knocking on her door tonight instead of Sonja. Stupidly, that was the conclusion she had jumped to when she heard the knock. She'd thrown a bathrobe over her nightgown and flown to the door, hoping it was true. Remembering her reaction, she was embarrassed by her giddy demeanor and how disappointed she'd felt when she had opened the door to see Sonja standing there instead.

Poor Sonja, the unwitting recipient of all of that disappointment.

Of course Kelly had not come to her room. There was Pippa. Now that she had seen Pippa for herself, she could imagine that she had a kind of adorable charm that might appeal to... Jordan flung herself over onto her other side and punched the pillow. What difference did it make? It was irrelevant. It was just sex, her attraction to Kelly. Just lust. Kelly had blossomed into a gorgeous woman. Any lesbian would have to be dead not to notice that. Nothing would ever happen between them anyway, Pippa or no Pippa. Kelly wasn't the kind of woman who would ever settle for just sex. Unless she had changed a great deal, she would want it all. And that was the last thing Jordan wanted.

She was determined not to let Kelly keep her from another night's sleep. *Just sex*, she told herself again, trying to calm her mind. It had been a while since she'd been with anyone. She just wanted a woman. The hot bath, the luxurious bed, the brandy, all of that had put her in the mood for lovemaking. She took a deep breath, trying to relax. That's all it was, she thought, reassured, and closed her eyes. She just didn't want to waste the room.

CHAPTER TWENTY

The first time she had come to Camp Tootega in Nivi's kayak, Kelly had been exhausted, dirty and mosquito bitten. After nine years, that was far from her chosen reintroduction to Jordan. So today she was determined to look good. She wore her most flattering jeans and a sweater that accentuated her bust. She had taken special care with her hair and wore no hat to make sure it stayed just so. Why was she trying to look sexy for a woman who wasn't interested in her? She'd been asking herself that question all morning and had settled on the answer that she simply wanted Jordan to regret having rejected her all those years ago. She wanted Jordan to look at her and think, "Damn! I could have had that!" So it was a kind of revenge, she admitted to herself, aware that it was a petty move. But it would still be satisfying if it had the desired effect. Especially because of Sonja and the new wound Kelly bore from that discovery.

For the last two days she had been plagued with thoughts of Jordan with Sonja. Their coupling seemed like a cruel joke the universe had played on her. It had occurred to her that

Sonja may simply be a sexual diversion, that there was no real connection between them. Even that didn't sit well with her, but it was easier to understand than the alternative, that Jordan had sincere feelings for Sonja. If it were just sex, she reasoned, then maybe there was a place for her in Jordan's heart after all. Against her will, that tiny remnant of hope began to flutter back into existence.

Whether to exact revenge or incite desire, her strategy for today was to get Jordan's attention. She knew she looked good. This morning when she'd come out to the shuttle stop, Chuck had looked her over with interest and raised one eyebrow as the left side of his mouth had twitched indecisively. Her usual work clothes consisted of a T-shirt under an oversized, long-sleeved shirt and cargo pants with pockets full of gadgets. Today there was no room in her pockets for even a memory card.

Ever since she had told him she was gay, Chuck had respectfully avoided any remark that might appear to acknowledge that she was a woman, even opting to address her only by her last name. They were just buddies doing a job together. She knew that was hard for him. He wasn't the sort to overlook gender, not in word or deed, so she appreciated his discretion.

"Go ahead," she told him, observing his twitching lip. "You can say it."

Encouraged, he sucked in a deep breath and said, "You look hot! Who knew you had an ass like that! You know I'm no Bible-thumper, but this morning I'm ready to fall on my knees and pray the gay away." He swallowed, openly leering. "Curves! Sheffield has curves!"

"Okay, that's enough," she ordered.

He complied, saying no more, but she had caught him looking at her more than once with a covert sideways glance. Good, she thought, hoping Jordan would have the same response.

They hired a boat and pilot to take them up the coast to their destination. The sky was clear and the morning light so bright that Kelly could barely open her eyes without sunglasses on.

At the mouth of the fjord the floating ice became denser and the pilot slowed the engine, carefully steering to avoid collisions as Kelly took pictures. She knelt low on the deck to catch shots of water dripping off the sculpted edge of an iceberg, several strings of sparkling drops backlit by the sun and looking like a multistranded diamond necklace.

Her experience of this scenery was completely different today from what it had been last week when she and Nivi had paddled through this gorge. Today she could enjoy it and it was truly awesome.

As they approached the glacier, they veered left toward the moraine. Kelly mentally prepared herself for seeing Jordan. Her plan was to be cool and professional, cheerful and carefree, to reveal nothing of the hurt she carried in her heart or the feelings she had once worn on her sleeve.

Brian met them at the dock and helped Kelly unload her tripod, cameras and lens case.

"Jordan's expecting you," he said, walking with them toward camp. "You picked a great day for taking photos. Plenty of sunshine."

"Hi, Kelly!"

She turned to see Sonja under the kitchen lean-to and felt an automatic wave of jealousy. She inwardly scolded herself and forced a smile.

Jordan emerged from her tent to greet them, dressed in Dockers and a long-sleeved polo shirt.

"Good morning!" she called cheerfully. "Welcome to Camp Tootega!" She gave Chuck a friendly hug. She turned her attention to Kelly and hugged her too.

If Jordan noticed how good Kelly looked, she didn't show it. But she wouldn't. Jordan never let her cards show. And that was exactly how Kelly would play her hand as well.

"How do you want to do this?" she asked.

"Maybe we could just chat for a few minutes," Chuck suggested. "Get some of the basic questions out of the way. Then you can show us around."

"Perfect. We can talk inside." She indicated her tent.

"While you two are talking," Kelly said, "I'll take some shots around camp."

Chuck followed Jordan into her tent while Kelly took her equipment and walked back downslope toward the dock, looking for a good view of the camp. Sonja was suddenly at her side.

"How's your little friend?" she asked.

"Pippa's doing well. She's nearly recovered."

"That's great."

Kelly put her equipment down and took some overview shots of the camp. With her camera in hand, she could ignore Sonja without appearing completely rude.

"There's a nice view from up there," Sonja advised, pointing to a ridge to the west. "You can see the camp with the glacier behind. Pretty cool."

"Thanks," Kelly said. "What's the best way up there?"

"I'll show you."

Sonja, it seemed, wasn't inclined to leave her on her own. She carried the tripod and led Kelly to a steep but manageable path up to the ridgetop. She was right. The ridge gave a photogenic view of Camp Tootega set against the Langenford Glacier with its blocky white and blue face. Kelly took some shots while Sonja sat cross-legged on a smooth slab of rock nearby. When she paused to change her lens, Sonja said, "You look great today."

"Thanks." Kelly dug in her bag for the lens and grabbed a wad of cotton cloth. She pulled out a rolled up pair of sweatpants. "I almost forgot I brought these back. Thanks for the loan."

"You're welcome." Sonja winked, taking them from her. "You can get in my pants any time."

Kelly eyed her critically. "Why are you coming on to me?" she demanded coolly.

"Why wouldn't I?" Sonja hopped to her feet. "You're freaking gorgeous. Not to mention the only eligible lesbian in the country." Sonja laughed.

"What about Jordan?"

Sonja looked startled. "Well, technically, Jordan *is* an eligible lesbian, I guess. But I think she's more likely to mate with a polar bear than me. Or you. Or anybody else."

"I don't understand. I thought you—"

"I like her. I do. But it won't do me much good. It's okay to admire from afar. Well, you understand that. You once had a crush on her too, right?"

"Yes, but nothing happened."

"Sure. Of course!" Sonja looked like the idea of something happening was outrageous. "Same for me. Nothing's ever going to happen there. She's impenetrable. There's a reason she's so comfortable here in the frigid Arctic. The Ice Queen, remember?"

Kelly held Sonja's gaze, studying her to see if she was telling the truth. Or if she was just a player trying to ally herself with Kelly by pretending a shared defeat.

"So you've gotten nowhere with her?" Kelly asked hopefully, recalling the one treasured kiss she had received from Jordan. "Not even a kiss?"

Sonja laughed shortly. "No! All I've gotten is a lecture about staying in my place and the threat of being sent home. And, believe me, she means it."

Kelly did her best not to reveal how welcome this news was. If true, it seemed that Jordan was less concerned about the feelings of her admirers than she once was. She had been so gentle with Kelly, her rejection so diffused by kindness that it had barely discouraged her. Maybe Jordan had grown harder with time. Maybe she had earned her nickname, a thought that made Sonja's news both welcome and troubling. Even if Sonja had struck out with Jordan, it didn't mean she was available to Kelly. Maybe The Ice Queen really was impenetrable.

After Jordan's interview with Chuck, the clan of Camp Tootega lined up for group shots for the article. Kelly took several, then took a few with just Chuck and Jordan, enjoying looking at Jordan through her lens. After the shoot, the group went on a hike along the path of the glacier. Julie and Brian drove ahead in the ATV while the rest of them walked.

"We've placed three buoys on the glacier," Jordan explained to Chuck. "We've got cameras mounted alongside at regular intervals as well. Stitching all that film together gives us a movie of the ice flowing."

Chuck had his voice recorder clipped to the front of his jacket, as usual, recording the conversation. He didn't take notes. He said that got in the way of listening.

"Here's the first one," Jordan said, halting at the edge of the glacier where an orange flag was clearly visible halfway across the ice. It protruded from the top of a teardrop-shaped device about the size of a beach ball.

"Kelly!" Chuck called, waving her closer. "Get a shot of that buoy."

"It's a Westgate buoy," Sonja offered. "It's named after Jordan because she designed it."

Chuck turned an inquiring glance toward Jordan.

"Yes," she acknowledged. "A lot of teams have gone to these now. They replaced the more fragile ones we used to use."

"The Marquette buoys," Sonja elaborated. "They were a piece of crap."

"Oh, Sonja!" Jordan said, frowning her disapproval. "They were *not* a piece of crap. These buoys float up better under pressure, so they last longer. Grinding ice is pretty darn powerful and destroys a lot of expensive equipment."

"She's always telling us the cameras are worth more than all of us combined," Sonja quipped.

"Chuck," Jordan pleaded, "please don't say the Marquette buoys are crap."

Chuck laughed. "Don't worry." He screwed up his face and closed one eye. "Marquette? I think I know that guy."

"I'm not surprised. He was a pioneer in this field. He worked in Alaska primarily, not in Greenland. He's retired now."

Kelly took several shots of the orange and white buoy embedded in the surface of the glacier.

"Now I remember!" Chuck blurted. "I met Marquette last year at a conference in Dallas. They were giving him an award, some lifetime achievement thing."

"I heard about that," Jordan said.

"I had a chat with him after dinner that night. I told him what I did, you know, spending the summers out here. I mentioned you, among others, as one of the scientists I've been following. He remembers you."

Kelly was puzzled to see the sudden look of alarm on Jordan's face, short-lived but unmistakable.

"Of course he remembers her," Kelly intervened. "He was her mentor."

"What did he say?" Jordan asked, her tone casual, but the look in her eyes suggesting anything but.

"He said you were one of the finest researchers in the field. He was glad to see how well you'd done."

"Oh," Jordan said, looking relieved, "that was nice of him."

* * *

Jordan's knees had gone weak when Chuck mentioned talking about her to Marquette. But Marquette had been the flawless professional, giving no hint of the scandal Jordan had caused him.

"What's the purpose of the buoy?" Kelly asked.

Jordan shook off her anxiety. "The buoys are great. They have a transmitter that sends us their position at regular intervals throughout the day. We can track not only how fast and how far they travel, but since they flow with the ice, we can model the flow patterns as well. So far this summer we've calculated the speed of this glacier at ten meters per day. That's five meters a day faster than last year."

Chuck whistled. "Are you kidding? That's nuts!"

"Yes, it is. Just galloping along." Jordan appreciated Chuck's experience, that he had taken the time and trouble to educate himself about his subject matter. She hated talking to journalists who knew nothing about the interview topic. It invariably led to mistaken conclusions she worried would be attributed to her. But Chuck had been on this beat for years and he understood the science better than most of her students.

"Why the huge jump in one year?" he asked.

Jordan continued walking. "Ice is extremely sensitive to temperature changes. One or two degrees can cause enough of a difference to start a cavalcade of events. You go slow and steady up to a point, you know, and then suddenly you're past equilibrium and all hell breaks loose."

Chuck sputtered. "Doesn't exactly look like all hell breaking loose here, Jordan."

"Maybe not to you. But ten meters a day, to me, is all hell breaking loose. The Jakobshavn Glacier, the big one in Ilulissat, is now moving at an unheard of thirty meters a day. It's happening all over the country."

He nodded. "Global warming."

"Uh-huh. In addition to measuring the rate of travel, we're also measuring the amount of meltwater coming off this glacier. We've discovered the same sort of increase there. A huge jump in water output. Some of the water that melts ends up creating a layer of liquid between the bedrock and the ice. It acts as a lubricant, making the ice move much more easily and therefore faster. So the more the ice melts, the faster it moves. It's a cumulative effect."

"Sort of changes the whole definition of the word 'glacial,' doesn't it?" Chuck observed with an ironic smile.

"These glaciers aren't acting much like glaciers these days. If this glacier maintained its speed and rate of melt, it could last for thousands of years more. But it won't. It will recede at a greater and greater pace each year. It's on an unstoppable course toward its demise."

Kelly was in full view in front of them, lining up her shots. Jordan couldn't help admiring with an almost painful longing her perfect ass encased in those teasingly tight jeans. That can't be the best outfit for climbing over rocks and crawling into tight spaces, she decided. But it did provide some terrific sightseeing for Jordan.

"What about the interior ice?" Chuck asked.

"It's more stable, but it's melting faster too. The smaller it gets, the faster it melts because the ice sheet reflects less of the sun's radiation, so the temperature in the vicinity rises and accelerates the process. Who knows how long it will last at this rate."

Chuck narrowed his eyes at her. "I don't like to hear a scientist say 'who knows.'"

Jordan shrugged. "Too much of this is new territory for us. It may already be too late to stop it. Even if we were able to completely halt the rising temperature at this point, which doesn't seem likely, it wouldn't reverse the process. When the ice is gone, we're looking at a seven meter rise in sea level and a climate none of us can predict. Many scientists believe we're past the point of no return."

"Do you agree with that conclusion?"

Jordan hesitated. "Let's just say I prefer to live in a place with a little elevation."

"I'd like to walk out on the glacier," Kelly called, jogging toward them.

"You'll have a chance to do that further up," Jordan said. "Believe me, it's worth the wait. We've got something very special to show you."

Kelly nodded and went back to her work. As she squatted beside the glacier to take a shot across the surface of the ice, the denim across her rear end stretched so tight a flea could have used it as a trampoline. Jordan tore her gaze away to glance at Chuck, who smiled roguishly.

After another half hour of walking, Jordan heard the noise she was anticipating, running water, lots of it. Back home, this sound would signal the approach of a waterfall, as it did here. But this was a waterfall unlike any Jordan had ever encountered and she was excited to be able to show it off.

Their ATV Curly was parked up ahead where the others awaited their arrival.

"Oh, my God!" Jordan heard from the front of their group as Kelly made it there ahead of them. Hearing her, Chuck took off at a trot to catch up, moving surprisingly nimbly for his size.

Jordan approached the spot where they stood, knowing they were both blown away by the sight as she had been when she first saw it. In front of them was a fifty-foot wide bottomless blue pit carved deep down into the ice, so deep they couldn't see the bottom. Across the pit, about thirty feet below the surface of the glacier, was a massive stream of meltwater emerging from a hole in the ice and freefalling into the pit.

Both Chuck and Kelly looked down with their mouths open, stunned into silence. Jordan caught Malik's eye and the two of them smiled knowingly at one another. It was a magnificent sight to behold the first time. And the second and third and fourth.

"It's a waterfall!" Chuck finally said.

"In a glacier," Kelly added.

"How far does it go?" asked Chuck, turning to Jordan excitedly.

"To the bottom," Jordan answered. "Right here, the ice is three hundred feet thick. We put a line down and that's what we concluded, that this waterfall has carved a hole all the way through the ice to the bedrock."

Chuck turned his gaze back to the waterfall and whistled appreciatively. "Where does it go after it gets to the bottom?"

"We think it turns into a stream down there just like any waterfall anywhere. So it flows under the ice to the sea, through natural contours at the base of this canyon. It forms a kind of slip-and-slide for the ice above. And that's what I believe is the reason for the rapid movement of this glacier, all that liquid water carrying it along."

"This is mind-blowing!" Chuck remarked. Obviously, even with all his experience, he had never seen a sinkhole quite like this before. "Sheffield, you wanna…" He turned to locate her. She was at the edge of the ice, camera clicking. "Ah. She's got it."

"This feature hasn't been here very long," Jordan said. "It probably won't hang around much longer with the movement of the ice. Your timing was lucky."

"It's incredible!" breathed Kelly, pausing in her picture taking to simply stare. Then she turned to them, energized, and said, "I have to go down there!" Her face blazed with excitement.

"It isn't safe," Jordan informed her. "You can walk out on the glacier and get some different angles, but you'll want to stay well clear of the edge."

"No," Kelly contradicted decisively. "I have to go down. I need to get below the top of the waterfall so I can shoot it looking up. You've got equipment, right? Ropes, rappelling gear? I've done it before, in caves."

"Caves are a lot more stable than ice," Jordan stated.

"Sorry, but this isn't something I can pass up." She strode to the ATV, motioning for Malik to accompany her. "Where's the gear?"

"Chuck," Jordan implored, "aren't you going to stop her?"

He shook his head. "Nope. That's her job and that's why I brought her along. Shit, this girl's got the goods." He winked at Jordan. "Besides, she's not going to listen to me."

They watched as Malik helped Kelly suit up.

"She's a good photographer, then?" Jordan asked.

"Hell, yeah! She's still young. She'll get better. I don't think she knows what direction to go yet, how to specialize. She's really great at seeing something profound in ordinary objects and teasing a surprise out of it. She's going to be an artist, a real artist someday. But personally, I wouldn't mind if she catches the itch to do this kind of thing permanently. I could use a regular photographer to go down in sinkholes and shit like that."

Wearing a harness, fingerless gloves, helmet and crampons, Kelly traipsed over and handed her camcorder to Chuck. "You shoot me while I'm shooting this," she instructed. "Film the whole thing and don't forget to zoom in a few times. Oh, man, this is going to be awesome!" She walked to the edge of the pit, seeming not the least bit frightened.

"Chuck," Jordan began, speaking quietly, "did she know ahead of time I'd be here?"

He nodded. "I gave her a list of our contacts."

"Did she tell you she knew me?"

"No." His gaze lingered on her face, as if he were trying to read her. "Should she have? Is there some issue?"

"No!" Jordan rapidly asserted. "None at all. I was just curious."

"Here goes," Kelly announced, giving them a thumbs-up as she leaned back at the edge of the ice pit, her camera over her shoulder, both hands on the rope. She carefully lowered herself over the smooth edge and down the vertical wall, planting the claws of her crampons firmly into the ice with each step.

The rest of them watched her go down. Chuck stood with his feet firmly planted, filming with a steady hand. Jordan gulped nervously as Kelly's head disappeared from view. Nobody spoke. Jordan and Chuck moved closer so they could keep her in view.

At regular intervals, she stopped, leaned back with her weight on the ropes, and shot photos. Then she descended a few more feet. The lip and walls of the pit were smooth, sculpted by flowing water like the rocks of any river, but this had happened over a matter of days instead of centuries. Kelly's main line had already carved a groove four inches deep at the lip.

The ice in the pit darkened the deeper it went, starting at the top as stark white and gradually changing to sky blue, then a haunting cerulean and eventually midnight blue far below.

Kelly had gotten to the cerulean layer where she could look upward into the spray of the waterfall, capturing the photos she had lusted after.

She's really something, Jordan thought. Not everyone would be able to hang on the edge of a vertical wall above a bottomless pit. No matter how much you trusted the security of a nylon rope, it was scary. Jordan didn't think she could do it. She had a fear of heights and knew from past experience how immobilizing that panic could be. But Kelly showed no hesitation at all as she proceeded through her methodical work.

She looked up and caught Jordan's gaze. She grinned, her eyes sparkling with happiness. Jordan smiled back at her, full of respect and admiration.

"We're at twenty-five meters," Malik reported. "Eighty-two feet."

"That's far enough," Jordan said to Chuck.

He gave a short nod, then shouted into the pit. "That's as far as you're going, Sheffield! Get your butt back up here!"

Kelly nodded her understanding, took a few more shots, then began her steady ascent back to the surface. When her head finally appeared over the rim of the pit, Julie took the camera from her, then Brian pulled her out.

As she unbuckled the harness, she exclaimed, "That was so cool!" She looked at Jordan as she exuded triumph. "That was so cool!" she repeated, bouncing on the balls of her feet.

Chuck gave her a one-armed hug as he handed the

camcorder to her. "Damned fine job!" he beamed. "Now that's not something you're going to see every day! Not even in Greenland."

Jordan was happy too, happy to be able to share the experience and happy to see Kelly so exultant.

CHAPTER TWENTY-ONE

Kelly walked up to the sink where Jordan was piling dishes into sudsy water.

"It's my turn to clean up," she explained.

"I'll help," offered Kelly, picking up a dish towel. She took a plate from Jordan and wiped it dry with the towel.

Lunch had been a satisfying but odd combination plate of macaroni and cheese and canned tamales. Predictably, the conversation had hinged on global warming, the disappearing Greenland ice sheet and Greenland's changing culture. Chuck and Malik, standing by the big tent, were still engaged in that discussion, their expressions suggesting that Chuck was enjoying the debate and Malik was frustrated. Kelly wasn't surprised. It was Chuck's typical position to play devil's advocate, to draw people out and get them to talk candidly in an impassioned defense of their position. It was a journalist's technique he had employed so long that it had become his ordinary mode of conversing.

"You were impressive today," Jordan remarked. "You didn't seem scared at all."

"I was too excited to be scared. It was the most thrilling thing I've ever done. I can't wait to see the photos."

"I'd like to see them too." Jordan gazed at her with an expression of admiration, holding out another plate.

Her eyes fixed on Jordan's, Kelly reached for the plate and grasped Jordan's hand instead. The aluminum plate fell to the ground, clattering briefly on the gravel.

"Oh, sorry," Kelly said, reaching down to pick it up.

She felt light-headed, struck again by how inviting Jordan's demeanor seemed. She wondered if she was imagining it. But the woman beside her was no Ice Queen. Her eyes were full of warmth. Kelly was moved to speak from the heart and confess her feelings.

"Jordan," she ventured, putting the plate back in the suds. "There's something I want to tell you."

Just then, the sound of raised voices distracted them both. Malik loomed threateningly near Chuck, blurting in his hesitant English, "You do not know what you are talking about! An ancient culture is being lost here because of global climate change."

Atka stood beside Malik, looking alert, aware of his master's increasing anxiety.

"What the..." Jordan uttered, drying her hands on the towel.

"Adapt or fucking perish," Chuck replied calmly.

Jordan walked toward them and Kelly followed.

"How do you expect the Greenlander to adapt?" Malik asked contentiously. "This is the Arctic. Without hunting and fishing, what do we have?"

"Oil," Chuck answered matter-of-factly. "As soon as this country starts drilling for oil in earnest, everything will change. Hell! Cut yourself loose from Denmark and you'll be swimming in money. Imagine all that wealth being divided among a mere sixty thousand citizens. You'll all be fucking rich. You won't have to eat whale meat anymore."

Malik's glare had not diminished. "We like whale meat."

Chuck gave a slight nod to the women as they approached, the twinkle in his eye suggesting he was having a grand old time. "I don't know what you're complaining about," he said to Malik. "Look at you. Your father was a hunter. Barely scraped by, I'm guessing, with nothing but essentials. You're going to be a scientist. Geologist? Oceanographer? Something like that, right? Some big shot egghead type with a comfortable apartment and a fancy car. Thanks to global warming."

Malik bristled. "Global warming is a huge, devastating and avoidable crime against the planet."

"Uh-huh," Chuck agreed. "And traditional Greenland hunting, in the opinion of the world, is a huge, devastating crime against marine mammals."

"No endangered species are hunted. This practice is sustainable."

"Don't tell *me* that, pal. I know all about it. I'm just telling you how things are in the real world. Once Greenpeace started publishing photos of cuddly baby harp seals back in the seventies, you guys were sunk. People don't want you killing anything cute. Maybe you can't make a living hunting anymore, but you can make a living farming shrimp or drilling for oil or as a scientist studying the disappearing ice sheet." He exhibited a self-satisfied smile. "Adapt...or fucking perish. Like every species ever has done since life on earth began."

Malik gritted his teeth and sputtered, "You are full of shit!" He threw up his hands and walked rapidly to his tent, his dog at his heels.

Chuck shrugged and faced Jordan, smiling. "That guy's got a big chip on his shoulder."

"You're diddling with what he's most passionate about," Jordan commented.

"Diddling?" He pressed his lips together. "You're right. That's exactly what I was doing." He turned to Kelly. "Let's go, Sheffield. Get your gear."

"But..." Kelly began, turning a questioning glance toward Jordan.

"I have to be back by four," Chuck explained. "No time for any more diddling around here."

Jordan laughed. "Thanks for coming out, Chuck. I hope you got a good story. And, Kelly, send me a few of those photos, okay? I'm sure they'll be amazing."

Jordan's expression was thoroughly public again, showing no sign of the earlier openness she had extended to Kelly. There would be no further opportunity for a private conversation today and Kelly didn't know if or when another would present itself.

Frustrated and disappointed, Kelly took her cameras to the boat and prepared for the trip back to town.

CHAPTER TWENTY-TWO

Despite her agreement with Kelly that they would go together to the cave, Pippa couldn't wait. It was her last day off work and Kelly was with Mr. Lance at Camp Tootega for the day. Besides, Kelly didn't believe in Asa, and Pippa worried that her negative energy would interfere with her ability to reconnect. So she took her family's boat out alone and piloted up the coast, pulling in as close as she could to the location of the cave, and limping with her walking stick over the coastal terrain to the ravine. From the edge she could easily see the patch of cottongrass below that had drawn her there in the first place, white heads bobbing in the breeze. Near them was the opening in the cave roof she had fallen through.

She made her way down to the side entrance she had created and squeezed into the cave, shining a flashlight around the interior. It was as she had left it. On the floor were scattered a few wilted cottongrass flowers, left where they had fallen on that day. The pile of small rocks stood near one wall as before, imbued with a new significance now that she understood its purpose. The sight of it filled her with tense expectation, sending a chill down her spine. Under those rocks was the proof. A tiny skeleton, maybe an animal skin wrapped around it, lay protected there where Asa had left it hundreds of years ago.

Pippa wanted so badly to pull the rocks away. But she knew enough about archaeology to know she had to leave the grave marker intact, to preserve the integrity of the site. Her presence here may have already compromised some of the evidence, such as footprints, hairs and fibers left by Asa and Gudny. But the most important evidence, the grave and the baby, had to remain untainted until someone qualified and impartial could gather the evidence that would prove Asa's story. Then everyone would believe it, even Kelly.

She knelt beside the pile of rocks and shined her light on the wall to illuminate the carved symbols. "These *are* letters," she announced triumphantly, her voice echoing in the chamber. She traced the markings with her finger, trembling with the force of knowing that Asa herself had made this message with her own broad, freckled hand, and that the only person ever to see it was Pippa, as if it had been meant for her, like the entire story, sent to her from the past to find a voice, finally, after such a long silence.

She roused herself to take photos of the runes and the rock pile before sitting cross-legged on the floor and turning off the flashlight. She closed her eyes and tried to empty her mind of every thought except an image of Asa, that willowy blonde woman with eyes the color of her own, her ancestor, her grandmother whose DNA lived in her cells, carrying the memories of her life.

She reran the episode of Asa arriving home in triumph only to find her family and village decimated. As she remembered these facts, she began to feel sad and hopeless. She focused her mind on those emotions, willing herself to be Asa, a woman fighting against nature, her countrymen and history itself to survive, to allow her child to survive, to allow her story to survive down through the generations and generations until one of her progeny would finally remember it.

After several silent minutes had elapsed, Pippa felt a mild wave of nausea overtake her. When it had passed, she found herself sitting inside a dome-shaped room, the air warm and heavy, smelling of soot. She looked up to see a grid of whale bones forming the ceiling, packed over with animal skins and turf. A fire burned on one side of the room and smoke curled out through an opening in the ceiling. Sitting beside her was a brown-skinned woman in her late forties with sable-colored eyes and long black hair punctuated with strands of white. Her upper lip was creased with a fine network of wrinkles. Her hands, working with needles made of bone and thread of caribou sinew, moved rapidly to make fine stitches, binding together two pieces of seal skin.

Saamik, that was the woman's name. She smiled at the children at their feet, stretching her mouth wide and causing the wrinkles above her lip to disappear. The children were playing on the fur-covered floor. As far as Asa could tell, they were acting out a story about a bear and a fox. At least it was supposed to be if Gudny had her way. Gudny was the bear. She commanded her little brother Jaaku to be a fox, but he had his own ideas. Crawling around his sister where she stood on all fours, he growled deeply and shook his head so that his black, shoulder-length hair flew side to side. Gudny's pale eyebrows were knit together in consternation as she complained at him to no avail. She then looked to her mother, hoping for an intervention.

Asa shook her head and continued her sewing. She was making a pair of pants for Jaaku. He was growing so fast, he kept her busy making clothes.

Asa's husband Ortuq was outside repairing the sled, but he wouldn't stay out there for long in this bone-chilling weather. Inside, they were cozy and warm. Shadows flickered on the walls, cast by the flame of whale oil lamps with their cottongrass flower wicks. Asa thought wistfully about those fluffy white flowers and how the Norsemen trampled them underfoot, giving them no thought, while their sheep dwindled to nothing and even a cotton wick became scarce and precious.

She reflected that if she were still in her old village during a dark winter day like this, she would be huddled under a deep pile of skins, shivering in her wooden house. She thought of the village less and less often. It had been four years since she left. There had been no word from or about the village since. In the beginning, Asa had dreamed of returning to her kinsmen, but as time went on, she no longer had that desire. Especially once Jaaku was born. Besides, she knew the Norsemen would never adopt any Skræling ways. Even if life could be better. Sometimes she thought the Norse way was to suffer proudly. Skrælings, she had learned, did not invite suffering. Their disposition was much more lighthearted.

Grif, Olaf's young son who had come with her, was now a young married man with a baby. His second child was on the way. He said he was going back to the village next summer when they moved south to the hunting grounds. He wanted to see his father and persuade him to come live with them…if Olaf were still alive. He also wanted to introduce his father to his son and his wife. Would Olaf be happy about this? Asa wondered. Most likely he would. This was what he wanted for his son. The others would be horrified that Grif had taken a Skræling wife and that neither she nor their son had been baptized as Christians. They would feel the same about Asa, Ortuq and Jaaku. Hild would not welcome Jaaku into her house, despite his beautiful, innocent smile. As for Ortuq, Asa knew Hild would see him merely as one of the savages who had murdered her son. But the Norsemen had killed Skrælings too and Asa no longer saw any difference.

She was grateful that Ortuq and Saamik and the others had not held views similar to Hild's about her little party of refugees and turned them away.

No, she thought, there was no going back, even if there was a village to return to. She was afraid for Grif, that he would go there and find no one left. The last few winters had been hard. She could only hope that some of the others had become desperate enough to do as she had done and were safe with other Skræling families. She was certain that was the only way she would ever see any of them again. When she heard of Grif's plan to visit the village, she urged him not to go, saying, "It will be a miracle if anyone still lives."

"Then I will go and bury the dead," he replied fatalistically.

Grif was an admirable young man. He was respected and well liked. His father would be proud.

Saamik chewed on an aku root, sucking out the sweetness. "Naja," she called to Gudny, for that was her name for her. "Since he's growling like a dog, let him be a dog, then he has it right."

Gudny answered to both her Norse and her Skræling name, but she had lately exhibited a preference for Naja, introducing herself to strangers that way. Because of her fair skin, blonde hair and blue eyes, she was often fussed over, and she savored the attention.

Gudny shook her head at Saamik. "He has to be a fox," she insisted.

"I think Jaaku wants to be the bear. Why don't you be the fox."

"I have to be the bear because I'm bigger," Gudny explained with patience beyond her nine years.

Expecting Ortuq to return at any moment, Asa put down her sewing and poured boiling water over some crushed aku root to make him some tea. Like his mother, he had a weakness for sweets. Once in a while Asa wished she could make him some sweet milk because she knew he would have liked it so much. Gudny had missed milk more than anything. But there were no cows or goats left in Greenland, as far as Asa knew. Without milk, she could not make one of her favorite dishes, creamed kvan. Ortuq had never eaten kvan at all before Asa came. But he ate it now because she stewed it for him, without milk, and he liked it. That wasn't the only thing of value she had brought with her, she liked to think. But the truth was that the Skrælings knew how to make good use of everything available to them on the land and in the sea. If her kinsmen had known how to do all these things…

Gudny had gradually forgotten about milk. She had forgotten many things. She had almost forgotten Bjarni. Thankfully, she had forgotten how he died. Now her father was Ortuq and she loved him dearly. He had taught her about fishing and hunting and carving bone. He said she had special sight in her light-colored eyes, that she could see things nobody else could see. Before a hunt, playfully, he often asked her to guide the hunters. "Naja, where will we find the musk ox?" he would say, then point one direction or the other and ask, "Over there? Over there?" Gudny would look self-important and point in some random direction and confidently pronounce, "Over there!" Then Ortuq and the entire hunting party would set off in whatever direction Gudny had pointed. If they turned and went another way after leaving the camp, she never knew.

"Mama," begged Gudny with irritation, "can you make him bark like a fox?"

Asa turned from the hearth. "Jaaku," she called. He sat up and turned his lovely moon face to her, giving his full attention. She made a yipping sound like a fox to demonstrate. *Yip-yip-yip!* Gudny rolled over on the floor laughing hysterically. Saamik giggled. Why is it so much funnier when your mother does it? Asa wondered. Then she yipped some more, sending both children into ecstasies of laughter.

When Jaaku recovered himself, he sat up and imitated his mother, laughing between his yipping barks. Gudny, happy and triumphant, clambered around him growling like a bear, her plan finally realized.

A scuffling at the crawlspace announced the arrival of Ortuq. The children stopped their game and came to attention, waiting to pounce on their father as soon as his head poked into the room. Asa sat down next to Saamik to watch them.

"Do I hear a bear inside my house?" Ortuq called, crawling in and looking like a bear himself in his thick coat and hood, a fine dusting of snow clinging to the fur.

"It's me!" Gudny cried, beside herself with excitement.

Ortuq moved toward them on all fours, glancing briefly at Asa and Saamik with a twinkle in his dark eyes. "Here is a bear trying to eat my family." He grabbed Gudny, rolled over on his back and held her above him as she giggled and kicked the air. The hood fell from his head, revealing his silky black hair.

"I'm a fox!" Jaaku boasted and climbed on his father, yipping at him.

Ortuq wrestled with them, all three of them laughing, until he was out of breath and overheated in his heavy clothing. Saamik squeezed Asa's hand fondly, sharing a look of maternal satisfaction.

CHAPTER TWENTY-THREE

Having spent most of her time so far in Greenland shooting scenery, Kelly decided a look at Ilulissat itself was in order. She'd go for a walk around town today and shoot the people, the buildings, the ordinary life in this extraordinary place. She liked shooting people more than scenery anyway because there was more to discover. The camera became a more active participant with a human being as its subject, not just a passive recording device.

As she sat on the edge of the bed to tie her shoes, she was startled by Pippa's friendly face at her window. She was peering in through the glass with her intense blue eyes. Seeing that she'd been noticed, Pippa waved.

Kelly stepped over and raised the window. "Hi. You're out awfully early."

"I was hoping you'd have time to talk about the cave before I go to work."

Kelly sat on the bed again. "Okay. Chuck's working on his story today so we're sticking around town. I'll meet you in the living room."

She reached down to tie her other shoe. When she turned back to the window, she saw that Pippa had hoisted herself onto the windowsill and was squirming through the opening. When she'd gotten halfway through, she let herself fall in. She landed with a thud on the floor.

"What are you doing?" Kelly asked impatiently.

"Coming in," Pippa answered matter-of-factly, then got to her feet.

Kelly sighed. "What did you want to talk about?"

Pippa sat on the end of the bed, bending one leg up under herself and producing a small digital camera. "I went to the cave yesterday. I took some pictures this time."

"You went out there by yourself?"

Pippa nodded emphatically. "I got the rest of the story! It's so amazing. I went right home last night and wrote it all down because I didn't want to forget a thing."

"That was a good idea, but you should have waited for me."

"I just couldn't wait. Now I need to get an archaeologist out there. Dr. Westgate probably knows an archaeologist, don't you think? She could help."

"Oh, I don't know." Kelly was reluctant to get Jordan involved in Pippa's fantasy.

"I know you don't think it really happened," Pippa said. "You think I'm just inventing it."

Kelly shrugged. "I guess it's more important that *you* believe it really happened."

"I don't blame you," Pippa admitted. "But it isn't like a ghost story. It doesn't have to be like that. You know how some people believe in reincarnation because they have these memories of previous lives, memories of things that happened but they know didn't happen to them, not in their present life?"

"Sorry, Pippa, but I can't go along with the idea of past lives. If that's your explanation of Asa…"

"No, not exactly." Pippa grew more serious. "What if there are these, like, threads of memory that get passed along in our genes from our ancestors just like instincts do? There's an awful lot of mysterious stuff in our subconscious minds. If even simple animals can inherit awesome bits of information like how to fly south for the winter, why can't we inherit specific memories too? Maybe they're in there wherever your baby memories are and you can't get to them except under hypnosis or something. Or when you have a concussion."

"What are you saying exactly?"

"I don't think Asa is me in an earlier time. I think she's my ancestor. Maybe we can inherit memories the same way we inherit everything else, through our genes. Maybe memories of past lives aren't our own lives, but the lives of our ancestors."

Kelly considered the idea. "I guess it's not impossible, put like that. Like you said, our minds are full of mysteries."

"It would certainly explain a lot of these crazy memories people have."

"It's an interesting idea," Kelly relented sincerely. "Whatever it is, this story seems to have had a profound effect on you."

"It has. She was a very brave woman to have left everything she knew, especially to go trust her life to people she thought of as heathen savages. Do you want to see the pictures I took?"

"Sure."

Pippa extracted the memory card from the camera and handed it to Kelly, who sat at her computer and opened a folder containing a half dozen photos. On the screen was a series of angular scratches on stone.

Pippa stood behind her chair and pointed. "These are letters."

"They don't look like letters to me," Kelly said, peering at the scratches.

"Because they aren't your kind of letters. They're runes."

"Runes?" Kelly looked again. "Really?"

"Yeah. Viking runes."

"What does it say?"

"I don't know. I recognize some of the characters, but I don't remember enough to read them. It's been a few years since I studied this in school. It's very exciting, though, isn't it? I bet nobody has ever seen this before. Not since it was created, I mean, almost seven hundred years ago."

Kelly was skeptical, imagining some prankster with a penknife. But she kept her thoughts to herself and looked at the other photos. There were a few more of the runes and a couple of a pile of rocks.

"That's where the baby's buried," Pippa announced. "It gives me goose bumps just thinking about it. That's what I want the archaeologist for, mainly. To dig it up. Then you'll see!"

Mrs. Arensen appeared in the open doorway with an armful of bedding. "Here are your clean sheets." She saw Pippa and looked startled. "Where did you come from? I did not hear the doorbell."

"I came in the back way," Pippa said, trying unsuccessfully to suppress a giggle.

"The back—"

"Thank you," Kelly interjected, taking two sheets from the top of her pile.

Mrs. Arensen wordlessly removed herself and moved off. Kelly dropped the sheets on the bed just as a piercing scream emanated from the end of the hall. She darted to the hallway to see Mrs. Arensen standing in the open doorway of Annalise's room, a heap of sheets at her feet. Pippa stuck her head out under Kelly's arm to get a look.

Mrs. Arensen launched into a Danish tirade, luring Chuck out of his room next door. Bare-legged and wearing a T-shirt and boxer shorts, he peered into the hallway. Mrs. Arensen continued her incomprehensible harangue, waving her arms vigorously, until a skinny, smooth-chested young man emerged from Annalise's room. He wore thick glasses, no shirt, unfastened trousers, no shoes and socks, and carried a bundle of wadded up clothes in his arms as he dashed past them down the hallway, sprinting out the front door.

Mrs. Arensen trod stiffly after him, still railing. The only words Kelly understood were "hanky and panky." Just like that, as a phrase: "Hanky and panky!" She didn't need to understand more than that to know what was being said. The rest of them hung halfway into the hall to watch their landlady slam the front door and bolt it. Then she shook her fist at the ceiling and strode into the kitchen.

Annalise appeared in her bedroom doorway wearing a bathrobe. She looked defiantly at her audience, knit her thick eyebrows into one long tobacco-colored unibrow, then bent to pick up her sheets, taking them into her room and soundlessly shutting the door.

"Woo-whee!" Chuck whistled. "Who would have guessed?" He ducked back into his room.

Kelly and Pippa did the same. Pippa appeared to be wildly stimulated by the excitement. She ran and bounced on the bed, tumbling over and springing off to land on her feet on the floor like a gymnast.

"That Annalise is in big trouble!" she announced gleefully. "Do you think she'll get kicked out?"

"I guess it's possible."

"Do you think Mrs. Arensen was suspicious to find me in your room?"

"Why would she be?"

"She might think I'd been here all night like Annalise's boyfriend." Pippa looked thrilled with the idea. "She might think we had a secret rendezvous." She pronounced the last word lingeringly, as though savoring it.

Kelly frowned. "I'm sure she wouldn't think that."

"Why not?"

Kelly opened her mouth to speak, but realized any explanation she could come up with was a little insulting to Pippa. She shrugged and changed the subject. "I didn't tell you about the amazing day I had yesterday out at Camp Tootega. There was this sinkhole in the ice with a waterfall in it and I went down inside it."

"You did?"

"Let me show you." Kelly returned to the computer and brought up a photo of herself inside the eerie blue depths of the sinkhole, dangling at the end of a rope, her camera held in front of her. "Isn't that cool?"

"Wow! That's awesome! Majorly awesome!"

Looking at the monitor over Kelly's shoulder, Pippa leaned in closer and planted an unexpected kiss on her cheek before jumping back. Kelly spun around in her chair to see Pippa looking wide-eyed and expectant, a crooked grin on her face.

"You're so lucky," she said breathlessly, "to go all over the world and see so many amazing things. I wish I could go somewhere."

"You can," Kelly said. "Eventually. I wasn't traveling around the world at your age either."

"If I had a friend in some awesome place, it would be easy to travel. Like Colorado, for instance."

Kelly laughed at Pippa's poorly-disguised request for an invitation. "You're welcome to come visit me any time, Pippa."

Pippa's mouth fell open. "For reals?"

Kelly nodded.

Pippa bolted toward her and put her arms around Kelly's neck, hugging her tightly. Then she knelt in front of her chair with her arms crossed over Kelly's knees.

"Well, then," she said with finality. "That will be my goal for next year, to come to America and visit you. It'll be my graduation present to myself."

"Terrific. I'll look forward to it."

After a moment, during which Pippa didn't seem inclined to move, Kelly squirmed away from her grasp and stood. Pippa stayed on the floor.

"Do you think I'm pretty?" she asked suddenly.

"Of course. You're beautiful. Don't you think so?"

"I guess."

"Then why did you ask?"

"I just wanted to know what you thought. If you find me attractive."

Kelly balked, trying to read Pippa's meaning. "You're a pretty girl," she repeated, unsure where this was going.

Pippa jumped up and ran to the door, shut it, then leaned against it facing Kelly with a broad smile and a sense of purpose.

"What are you doing?" Kelly asked, starting to worry.

"Just giving us a little privacy."

"Uh, well, I don't—"

"I think *you're* beautiful," Pippa said. "And amazing. You're the most interesting person I've ever met."

Kelly laughed nervously. "That's nice of you, Pippa, but once you get out in the world, you'll meet lots of people more interesting than me. Believe me, you will."

"I can't imagine that. Now that I've met you, it doesn't matter anyway."

Pippa lunged across the room and pulled Kelly into a tight embrace, wrapping her arms around her and leaning her head against her shoulder. Kelly stood with her arms limp at her sides, afraid to move.

"I don't know what I'll do when you leave in a couple weeks," Pippa said mournfully. "But if I know I'll be able to visit you next year, I can bear it."

"Pippa," Kelly said gently, "remember that theoretical other lesbian in town you've had your eye out for?"

"Uh-huh."

"Are you still looking for her?"

Pippa didn't reply for an uncomfortably long time, then finally said, "No."

Kelly swallowed hard. "Why not?"

Pippa lifted her head so she was looking directly into Kelly's eyes. "Because of you, of course."

Oh, God! Kelly thought, suddenly understanding the full impact of the situation. She put her hands on Pippa's shoulders and pushed her gently away. "I think you should keep looking for her."

"She probably doesn't even exist. It's okay. I can take the loneliness now because I'll know you're out there somewhere and I'll get to see you again."

"I think you might have gotten the wrong idea about what's happening here. Between us."

Pippa looked up at her inquiringly.

"I think of you as a friend," Kelly said cautiously. "It sounds like you think I might be interested in you some other way. Like romantically."

"I hoped you might," Pippa admitted. "You still might, right? We're friends. You like me. I adore you. That seems like a good beginning."

Kelly winced, trying to conjure up the right words. "I do like you, Pippa. But not like a girlfriend. More like a kid sister."

Pippa's shoulders slumped and her smile faded. "But that can change, right? I'm not a kid. I'm a grown woman. Look." Pippa stepped back and held out her arms to display herself.

"You *are* a grown woman," Kelly agreed. "Physically. But you're still a lot younger than I am. And inexperienced."

"We can fix that!" She rushed in to embrace Kelly again, but this time, she pressed herself closer so that Kelly could feel the pressure of her thighs against her own and the full round pliable softness of her breasts against her ribs. There was no doubt Pippa was sexually excited at this close contact. She closed her eyes, raising her face toward Kelly's, her lips parted, indulging her fantasy. Her eager, hormonally-charged body quivered with its unambiguous need, begging to be plucked from its chaste solitude.

Kelly bit her bottom lip, staring down at that glistening, anxious mouth with a combination of compassion and alarm.

"That's not what I mean," she finally said, pulling away. "I didn't mean *sexually* inexperienced, although that's part of it."

"Then what do you mean?"

"I mean inexperienced with people and with life. You're so innocent and trusting and full of happy dreams. You need to find someone else like that. You need to go to college and meet a girl your age and spend your days holding hands and learning about life together."

Pippa looked downcast. "That isn't going to happen."

"It *will* happen. You just have to be patient. I know it's hard, but it will be worth waiting for."

"But I love you." Her eyes, her beautiful blue eyes, teared up and her lip began to quiver.

Kelly was at a total loss. She sputtered, trying to think how to respond. "I'm sorry, Pippa," she finally said, "but I can't return those feelings."

After a moment during which Pippa got her sobs under control, she said, "Could you just teach me, then, without being in love? I don't mind. One person in love is better than nobody.

It will still be wonderful. I know it will. Just once? Then I'll have that for the rest of my life to remember."

Kelly shook her head. "No."

"Why not?" She seemed suddenly very childlike.

"Because it wouldn't be right. You're not really in love, you know. You've got a crush on me because you're lonely and isolated and I'm the first lesbian you've known." At the sound of her own words, Kelly was transported several years back to the moment she had confessed her love to Jordan. She'd heard the same thing. These words, she realized, would offer no comfort. "Believe me, this isn't a good idea."

"Isn't that for me to decide? I can make my own decisions. And I want you, however it turns out."

"It's not going to happen," Kelly said more firmly. "I'm happy to be your friend, but we aren't going to be lovers."

Pippa choked back another sob, then screwed up her face and said, "Because I'm pathetic and you feel sorry for me? You think I'm a stupid child!"

She grabbed her camera off the bed, then streaked across the room. She was through the window and running away before Kelly had a chance to say a word.

She remembered all too well what it felt like to be rejected by a woman she adored. I didn't handle that very well, she thought. She suddenly had a tremendous appreciation and sympathy for Jordan's position all those years ago.

She closed the window and went to the kitchen where Mrs. Arensen was at the stove, stirring a large pot.

"Where is Pippa?" she asked.

"She left."

"I did not see her come by."

"She went out the back way."

Mrs. Arensen stared for a moment, her mouth held in a thin, hard line. She was clearly still fuming over Annalise's indiscretion.

"What are you making?" Kelly asked.

"Reindeer stew."

Kelly sighed.

"Oh, you will like it!" Mrs. Arensen said defensively. "Ja, it is like *coq au vin*."

Kelly smiled to herself. It wasn't the reindeer stew she had sighed over, though it easily could have been. It was poor Pippa. She hoped she wasn't hurt too badly. Kelly berated herself for not having seen this coming. She'd been too preoccupied with her own romantic longings to notice Pippa's increasing attachment to her.

Chuck appeared in the doorway, wearing a pair of shorts and flip-flops, his hair damp.

"Elsa, what is that?" he asked, sweeping past Kelly on his way to the stove. "Don't tell me you're cooking up your famous reindeer stew!" He hovered over the steaming pot as Mrs. Arensen broke into a beaming smile.

"Ja, sure," she confirmed. "Special for you."

He put his wide palm on her back. "Aren't you a sweetheart? I can hardly wait!" He turned to face Kelly. "You're gonna love this. It tastes just like—"

"*Coq au vin*, yeah, I know."

He shook his head. "No, nothing like that. Not everything tastes like chicken, Sheffield."

Mrs. Arensen held the spoon up for him to taste the broth. "Ummm," he said. "Perfect. Can't wait."

Kelly left the kitchen and returned to her room and her computer where she noticed Pippa's photo card was still in her machine. Good, she thought. That would give her an excuse to visit Pippa. Maybe tomorrow after she had a chance to think things over.

Despite what Pippa had said about being willing to settle for a loveless sexual encounter, what she really wanted was a true-blue love affair with all the bells and whistles, and there was no way she could get that from Kelly. Ultimately, she must know that herself. A summer fling or, even worse, an initiation ritual, would end in devastation for her. Not that Kelly was in the business of doling out initiation rituals. Once Pippa reflected on it, surely she would see that Kelly was merely trying to protect her.

As Jordan had once done for her.

The photos from yesterday were still on the screen. She clicked on one of the thumbnails to enlarge it. Of the several candid shots of Jordan she had snapped, this was her favorite. Jordan's body was relaxed, yet held an edge of wariness. Like a wild animal, she was ready to flee from danger. Her expression, too, reflected a slight restlessness. Her eyes were just shy of fully open, the slight squint creating a ridge in the center of her forehead. Kelly didn't know what she was looking at or looking for, but she seemed to be watching for something.

What she liked about the photo was how well it captured the essence of Jordan, a woman standing at the top of the metaphorical ladder, surveying her domain with serene self-satisfaction, but expecting at any moment for someone to dash in and knock the ladder out from under her. Nobody would guess that last part unless they looked past the bearing of her body, past her calm face and unrevealing expression to the subtle hint of fear in the depths of her eyes.

This was the sort of photo she was always after, the one that captured something you would never see with the naked eye. Some pictures were like that, revealing something that happened too fast or was too small or too indistinct to notice otherwise. That was where the real value of a photo lay. With her mother, despite her smile, the camera captured her air of defeat. With Jordan, it probed below her exterior confidence. A single frame of time and space, frozen, allows you to see the subtleties in a way you couldn't do during the unfolding of real time. In real time, too much happened too fast. This expression of Jordan's happened in an instant and nobody saw it, not even Kelly. But her camera had.

In a sense, this photo revealed what Kelly had always known about Jordan, that at the core of her was a mild but ever-present fear. Though Kelly had sensed the fear, she didn't know what caused it.

She stared into the dove-colored eyes on her screen, trying to tease out the mystery of Jordan's unease, but even the truest photo couldn't reveal that.

CHAPTER TWENTY-FOUR

Jordan pulled on her shirt and buttoned the first two buttons as she walked toward the opening of her tent. She pushed through the flap and nearly collided with Pippa. Jordan yelped and clutched her open shirt to her chest.

"Oh," she said, relaxing. "Pippa! You scared me."

"Sorry," Pippa said. "Where is everyone?"

"Up on the glacier, setting out geopebbles."

"Geopebbles?"

"It's a GPS tracking device." She buttoned her shirt the rest of the way. "I was taking advantage of being alone to have a shower. The feeling of clean won't last long, but it sure feels good while it does." She glanced around. "Did Kelly come with you?"

"No. I'm here alone."

"I was just going to make a cup of herbal tea. Do you want one?"

"Sure."

After Jordan turned on the stove to heat water, she sat at the table where an in-progress domino game was laid out. Pippa sat in the chair next to her and folded her hands together primly in front of her on the table.

"I guess I should have called first," she said apologetically.

"Who are you here to see?"

"You."

"Oh! Well, then, you're in luck."

"Do you mind if I ask you a personal question?"

Jordan shrugged. "Depends."

"It's about Kelly."

Jordan nodded, feeling uncomfortable. She wondered yet again what Kelly was doing with this girl. It boggled her mind. Not that Pippa wasn't cute and likable, but there was no escaping her youth and lack of sophistication.

"Do you like her?" Pippa asked pointedly.

Jordan adopted her most casual tone. "Sure, I like her."

Pippa shook her head impatiently. "I mean, you know...*like* her."

"Why would you ask me that?"

"She told me about you, about how she felt about you before, that she used to be in love with you."

Jordan stared, wondering why Pippa was interrogating her. What was she worried about? Had Kelly said anything to make her think there was still something between them? Finally, she smiled and said, "She was my student and I was her teacher. She had a schoolgirl crush on me, and that was a long time ago. I'd have to say I barely know her now. But, you, clearly, are in love with her."

Pippa stiffened, her mouth falling open. "How did you know that?"

Jordan laughed. "It's obvious." She got up to take the boiling water off the stove.

"I *am* in love with her," Pippa admitted, sounding reluctant to say it out loud. "What do you think about that?"

"Pippa, it's none of my business. If Kelly has said something that makes you think there's anything between us now—"

"She hasn't said anything at all. I just wondered because of how she used to feel, if maybe she still had feelings for you. Or maybe you do."

The last thing Jordan wanted was to be involved in a love triangle, even if only in the mind of one young woman. "You have nothing to worry about," she assured Pippa. "Not from me. It's possible I will never even see Kelly again. Our paths crossed here by accident in a purely professional capacity. She outgrew her infatuation with me years ago. And whatever affection I had for her back then was entirely platonic. She's all yours, Pippa."

The girl smiled with relief. Jordan turned back to the counter and put tea bags in two mugs and poured hot water over them. She brought the tea to the table.

"Is that what you came to talk to me about?" she asked.

"Oh, no!" Pippa bounced in her chair, suddenly full of excitement. "It's about the cave I fell into. I was hoping you could help. I think it might have some archaeological value."

"Really? I understood it was just a rock fall type of thing. Never inhabited. Do you want sugar?"

"No, thank you. It wasn't permanently inhabited, but I think somebody used it as a temporary shelter."

"What's there? A firepit? Tools or something?" Jordan took her chair.

Pippa shook her head. "Better than that." She leaned forward and whispered, "There's a body."

Jordan stared into Pippa's earnest face. "Is it possible you want the police instead of an archaeologist?"

Pippa snorted a laugh. "It's a very ancient body. The thing is, it's so amazing to get DNA samples from that time period. I mean, there might even be hair, and you know how valuable that would be."

"What time period?"

"Fourteenth century. A Viking body from the fourteenth century."

Jordan took a sip from her mug before asking, "What did you see in that cave, Pippa? Did you actually see a body?"

Pippa leaned back into her chair. "Not exactly. I don't really want to draw conclusions. A professional should do the excavation."

"Excavation? So these remains are buried?"

"Right. There's a rock cairn. I think they're under it. Like a burial mound. And an epitaph scratched into the wall above it. You know that wouldn't be an Inuit grave."

"Because of the epitaph, you mean."

"Yes. The Inuit don't write epitaphs because of the name souls. They don't want to fix the name to a person who's dead. They use the name again so it keeps living."

"I've heard of that. The cemetery over by the airport, for instance, has blank crosses marking the graves. But that hardly qualifies as evidence that there's a Viking body buried there. Why do you conclude that?"

Pippa looked evasive. "I can't say. When the excavation is finished…"

"But, Pippa, to get an archaeological team out here is a big deal. You have to give us a reason. Who's going to send a team all the way out here on the strength of your hunch?"

"But if I'm right, if a body of one of the Norse settlers could be found, it could open up all sorts of research possibilities. I mean, how often does that happen?"

"It's extremely rare," Jordan agreed. "Most of them seemed to have just vanished. Obviously, if there is a Viking body in that cave, scientists would be seriously interested." Jordan observed her silently, debating the merits of her request.

"Please," Pippa begged. "I know it sounds crazy, but it would mean so much to me."

Jordan set her mug on the table. "I know an archaeologist working on Disko Island. Dr. Salvatore Lund from UCLA. We used to work together. Maybe he would take a look. If he thought it was a valuable site, he would be able to inform the right people and get something going. Would that work for you?"

Pippa smiled and nodded enthusiastically.

"I'll give him a call," Jordan said, "and see if he can find some time to come over."

"*Mange tak!*" Pippa blurted, jumping to her feet. She hugged Jordan impetuously.

Just then, the sound of laughter drifted down to them from the east.

"That'll be my team," Jordan said. "Let me call Dr. Lund before it slips my mind."

"I really appreciate your help."

Brian, Julie, Sonja and Malik came hiking into view, followed by Atka. Brian waved and Jordan returned the gesture, then went to her tent to call Dr. Lund. It's probably nothing, she would tell him. A young girl's romantic imagination gone wild. But she felt the need to show Pippa she had no ill will toward her, that what she had said about Kelly was true, that there was nothing between them, no residual feelings. It wasn't entirely true, but Jordan was accustomed to this sort of subterfuge. Burying the truth about her emotions when they might lead to pain or ridicule was her usual strategy. There was no harm in it, she reasoned, because she would never act on those emotions. Pippa had no reason to know that Jordan was attracted to Kelly. Pippa would never know that, nor would anyone else.

As long as they still call me the Ice Queen, she thought with a smile, I know I'm pulling it off. That nickname, whispered behind her back, was supposed to be an insult. She didn't mind, because along with the intended slur about her lack of tenderness was an implied respect.

So there was not much chance, in this universe, that she would have poured out her heart to Pippa. And if she had, she wondered, what would her heart have said? Her heart had been silent for so long. It may have forgotten how to speak. And that's the way she wanted it, she reminded herself.

* * *

Pippa recognized Malik as soon as he arrived in the kitchen, despite his new haircut and the amazing tattoo on his head. He greeted her in Greenlandic, asking how she was, and she told him his hair was awesome. They were in the midst of their conversation when Sonja walked up and slung her arm around Malik's shoulders. "English, people!" she commanded.

Malik laughed. "Pippa and I are practically neighbors, but I haven't seen her in a few years."

"Hi, Pippa," Sonja greeted her. "Small town, sure, everybody knows everybody."

Malik nodded and went to get a soda.

Sonja grabbed an energy bar off the counter. She wore a flannel shirt open over a tight-fitting T-shirt. She removed her sunglasses and propped them on top of her head. "How are you feeling?"

"I'm fine now."

"Well, you look good." Sonja winked at her before unwrapping her snack.

Pippa got instantly hot in the face, suddenly remembering that Sonja was a lesbian. Malik came by again, popped the top of his soda can and said, "Watch out for this one." He jerked his head toward Sonja. "She is a dangerous woman." He smiled and walked away.

Sonja frowned disapprovingly. "Bullshit!" She took a bite of her snack. "Where's Kelly?"

"Why does everyone keep asking me that?" Pippa complained.

"Hey, don't get sore. It's just that every time I've seen you, she's been there too."

"Not today," Pippa stated flatly. "She's just a friend of mine, you know, not my conjoined twin."

"Yeah, I know." Sonja took a bite off her energy bar, then stared at Pippa, chewing methodically, one hip thrust out, letting her gaze meander unapologetically down the length of Pippa's body. "What're you doing here?"

"I came to see Jordan." Pippa was nervous but also excited at the idea that a lesbian was checking her out.

Sonja was actually nice looking, she thought, with her spiky blonde hair and hazel eyes. Her face was round and girlish with a pouty-sexy mouth.

"What'd you want with Jordan?" she asked with her mouth full.

"Just a science question."

"You like science?"

"I love science!"

"What's your thing?" Sonja took another bite.

"Genetics. Biophysics. Paleomorphology. Anything to do with evolutionary history, really."

Sonja nodded appreciatively. "So you're a little brainiac. What about fossils? You like those?"

Pippa nodded. "Love 'em."

"I found one last week. Wanna see it?"

"Sure."

"Come on. It's in my tent." Sonja led the way to the blue and orange dome, unzipped the flap and ducked through.

Pippa followed. Inside was a cot and sleeping bag, a couple of boxes and some canvas bags. There was a battery-powered lantern on an upturned box for reading. Sonja popped the last of her energy bar into her mouth, wadded up the wrapper and tossed it toward a paper bag serving as a trash can. She missed. Pippa scooped it up and dropped it in.

"Have a seat," Sonja said, indicating the cot.

Pippa sat while Sonja dug through a duffel bag for a wad of newspaper. Then she came over and sat on the cot so close to Pippa that their thighs pressed against one another. Sonja unwrapped the newspaper to reveal a gray oval rock. She handed it to Pippa, who took it in both hands, recognizing immediately the clear black impression of a trilobite.

"It's amazing!" she pronounced, running her index finger over its well-defined ridges. "A nice one!"

"It *is* a nice one. Who would have thought there'd be trilobites in Greenland?"

"Is it Cambrian? Greenland was near the equator then and had tropical forests."

"Brian thinks it's Ordovician. He's more of a fossil geek than I am."

"Where did you find it?"

"About five miles up. According to Jordan's records, that spot was covered with ice just a few years ago. As the ice melts, I guess there will be a lot of things uncovered that haven't been seen for millions of years."

"Yeah, like the ice mummies."

"The what?" Sonja wrinkled up her nose.

"The ice mummies they found a few years ago. Inuits frozen under the ice for centuries. The ice melted and there they were. All dried up, but still with patches of clothing and hair and everything. They're in the national museum. You should go see them."

"No, thank you! I have no interest in looking at freeze-dried humans. Rocks, inorganic stuff, that's my thing. Not mummies or zombies or shrunken heads."

Pippa snorted and handed the rock back. "That's really cool."

Sonja wrapped the newspaper around it and placed it on the box next to the lantern. Then she turned back to Pippa and smiled at her. "You're cute. A cute little imp."

"Thanks," Pippa replied, embarrassed. "You're a lesbian, aren't you?"

Sonja laughed. "Yes. What about you? Are you into girls?"

"I would be, if there were any girls to get into."

Sonja's eyes widened suddenly as her lips curled into a smirk and Pippa realized what she'd just said.

"That came out wrong," she quickly blurted.

"I don't know. I think it came out unexpectedly right." Sonja tilted her head, looking curious. "So there's a shortage of lesbians around these parts?"

"A regular drought. Not a one in sight. Other than Kelly, but she's just visiting. Not that it would matter. She wouldn't be interested anyway."

"Really? Why not?"

"She thinks I'm too young."

"How old are you?"

"Eighteen."

"Then you're not too young. Eighteen's legal."

"Not here."

"No?"

"Legal is fourteen here."

Sonja's eyes widened. "No shit?"

"No shit."

"Hmm." Sonja tilted her head, gazing thoughtfully at Pippa. "I don't know how it's possible that Kelly isn't interested in you. You're the cutest thing I've seen since I got here. I think you're the bomb, little mama."

Pippa giggled, glancing sideways at Sonja. "For reals?"

Sonja nodded, leaning closer. "In fact, I think you're irresistible."

"Wow! Nobody's ever said anything like that to me before."

"Then it's about time they did. I don't know what Kelly's problem is and I don't care. You're a little hottie. I mean, just look at that beautiful complexion." Sonja touched her fingers to Pippa's cheek. "And those incredible eyes. And those lips, so soft and sexy and…" Sonja's fingers moved to her lips and ran lightly over them before her hand slipped to the back of her neck and she leaned in for a kiss. It was soft and gentle and thrilling.

"Ummm," Sonja murmured, pulling back. "Did you like that?"

Pippa gulped, staring into Sonja's eyes. She was so overwhelmed with wonder, she couldn't speak, so she simply nodded.

"Me too."

Pippa closed her eyes as Sonja kissed her again. Sonja's arm tightened around her and her mouth became more ardent. Pippa returned her kiss awkwardly, overjoyed that a woman was interested in her at last. She let her body mold itself against the soft curves of Sonja's. They continued kissing, Sonja coaxing Pippa's mouth to follow her lead until it felt more natural. They sat side by side on the cot kissing for several minutes until Pippa began to understand the rhythm of their mouths and felt the fluttery feelings deep inside that she felt when watching love scenes in movies.

Sonja leaned into her, pushing her back gently on the cot, then lay on top of her. She kissed her neck, then sucked her earlobe and licked the outer curves of her ear, her breath hot and moist on sensitive nerves that seemed to connect to all parts of Pippa's body.

"I'm going to make you feel so good," Sonja whispered.

Pippa lay stiffly, flat on her back. "I don't know what to do," she squeaked.

"You don't have to do anything. Just relax. Let your body do what it wants to. Your body knows what to do."

Sonja ran her hand slowly across Pippa's clothed body, over her thighs and chest. She kissed her again, probing with her tongue. Pippa was at a loss. What was she supposed to do? She recalled passages from books and thought she was supposed to breathe hard, maybe moan and thrash about. But if she was to do what Sonja said, to let her body do what it wanted to do, it would remain scared stiff, immobile and silent. She began to panic and her limbs started to tremble. She had no idea what Sonja would do to her, she realized. Not that she hadn't read things. But there were some things she'd read about that she'd rather not do. A lot of things, in fact, and she was beginning to think Sonja intended to do them all.

Pippa attempted to sit up, saying, "I think I should go."

Sonja leaned more heavily on her, pushing her back down. "No, no, no," she said softly. "Don't be scared. I'm not going to hurt you. I'll be very gentle with you. This is what you've wanted for a long time, isn't it? A woman to make love to you."

"Uh-huh," Pippa agreed uncertainly.

"Of course you have." Sonja took hold of her hand and pressed it against the thin T-shirt over her chest. "Well, I'm a woman and I want to make love to you."

Sonja kissed her mouth deeply, rousing her body into a state of excitement. Where her hand still lay against Sonja's breast, she felt the firm lump of a nipple through the cotton T-shirt. She squeezed tentatively, then allowed her fingers to move over the soft curves, mesmerized by the sensation and the sound of Sonja's murmur of pleasure.

Sonja's body moving over hers felt so good it was scary. She wanted to stop, but she couldn't…until she felt Sonja's hand on the bare skin of her stomach, sliding upward toward her bra. She jumped, startled, and lurched away with an involuntary cry of alarm.

"What's wrong?" asked Sonja.

Pippa shook her head, embarrassed. "I don't think I'm ready for this," she said, her knees bent up between them and clamped tightly together. "I…I'm sorry."

Sonja eyed her over her knees, looking seriously displeased. After a moment of silent contemplation, she sighed and moved aside. "Get out of here, you little squirt," she said in exasperation.

* * *

Jordan was on her way to the clothesline to hang up her towel when she saw Pippa half crawl, half hop out of Sonja's tent and take off running toward the fjord like a jackrabbit.

"Pippa!" she hollered, bringing the girl to a sudden and total stop.

She approached her, observing her state of breathlessness and the wild-eyed look of a hunted animal.

"I didn't know you were still here."

"Just leaving."

"Are you okay?"

Pippa nodded vigorously.

"What were you doing in Sonja's tent?"

Pippa's eyes widened even more. "She wanted to show me a trilobite fossil."

"Uh-huh." Jordan inspected her wordlessly, waiting to see if she would volunteer anything more, but she stood mute and resolute like a soldier at attention. Jordan decided not to press her any further, for it was obvious there was more to it than a fossil, and she was clearly embarrassed.

Pippa still stood stiffly, looking like she was expecting a dressing down.

"Dr. Lund has agreed to come look at your cave," Jordan informed her.

The girl visibly relaxed. "Awesome!"

"I'll let you know exactly when."

Once she understood they were finished, Pippa took off at a sprint to the dock. In a few minutes, her boat was speeding away.

Jordan strode purposefully to Sonja's tent. She entered without announcing herself, startling Sonja where she lay on her cot reading a magazine.

"Jordan!" She put down the magazine and sat up.

"What did you do to that girl?"

"Pippa? Why? What did she say I did?"

"No games!"

Sonja swung her legs over the edge of the cot, recovering her defiance. "Whatever I did, it's a private matter between me and Pippa."

"My God!" Jordan fumed. "Are you really that depraved?"

Sonja frowned. "Are you really that big of a prude? Make whatever rules you want for yourself, Jordan, but this is none of your business!"

Jordan made a conscious effort to stifle her rage, but she could sense it was futile.

Sonja got to her feet and appeared to relax. "Look," she said, dropping the antagonism, "nothing happened. I admit I tried to seduce her, but she chickened out. All I did was kiss her. So it's official. I have now struck out with every lesbian within five hundred miles. But even if we'd finished the job, I don't know what you're so upset about. She's an adult."

"You don't know what I'm upset about?" Jordan was flabbergasted. "This is all just a joke to you, isn't it? Do you really think it's okay to seduce a girl who's in a relationship with another woman? You don't have any qualms about that?"

Sonja looked confused. "Huh? Pippa? She's not in any relationship. She's never even been kissed if I can judge by what happened here a few minutes ago."

Jordan balked, shaking her head. "But you told me she and Kelly—"

Looking suddenly enlightened, Sonja sucked in a breath. "Oh, right!"

The contrite look on Sonja's face gave Jordan her first clue that she had been misled about Kelly and Pippa. Oh, my God! she thought. Pippa has a crush, but Kelly... It all made so much more sense now. Suddenly her head was whirling.

"They're not in a relationship, are they?" she asked evenly.

Sonja shook her head. "Just friends."

"Then why the hell did you say they were?"

Sonja winced at the volume and tone of Jordan's voice. "I...I just..." She shuffled her feet. "Aren't you glad I wasn't trying to steal Kelly's girl? Pippa just wanted her cherry popped and I was happy to oblige. Just doing a good deed. Or trying to. So no harm done."

"No harm done?" Jordan sputtered, her body shaking with rage. "Pack your stuff! I'm sending you home!"

"What? Why? I didn't do anything! So I told a tiny lie. What difference did it make?"

Jordan turned to leave.

"Jordan!" Sonja begged, grabbing at her arm. "I don't understand."

Jordan wrenched herself free and ducked through the flap to emerge in front of the others who stood gathered around, all three of them looking stricken with disbelief. They had heard every word.

She brushed past them and took refuge in her tent where she fell onto her cot and lay on her back staring at the green fabric above her, distraught and embarrassed at her behavior. She had behaved like a lunatic. She'd let her emotions overwhelm her, something rare and terrifying that took her back all those years to those disastrous days at Cornell.

She didn't like the way she'd been feeling since the night Kelly first showed up in camp. She was distracted and on edge and she wasn't sure why. So what if there was a good-looking, sexy woman around? It wasn't like that hadn't happened before. But it had never affected her like this.

Now she had to ask herself the same question Sonja had asked her. What difference did it make if Kelly was seeing Pippa or not? She had to get hold of herself. Thankfully, Kelly's business here was done. She wouldn't be showing up anymore with her big soulful eyes and her disarming smile.

Then everything could get back to normal.

CHAPTER TWENTY-FIVE

Kelly peered at the black-and-white photo in her hands, blown up to an 8 x 10 but still inscrutable. At least to her. This was the clearest of the photos Pippa had shot of the strange markings in the cave. Thin, angular lines formed characters arranged in two rows. Maybe they were words, if she could believe Pippa's conclusion that these were runic letters. In the enhanced photo, the marks looked less like random scratches than they had before. They were still faint and imprecise, but it was harder to dismiss them now.

"What've you got there?"

Kelly jerked her head toward the doorway to see Chuck walking toward her in shorts and a short-sleeved T-shirt.

She handed him the photo. "What does that look like?"

He stared at it, squinting to correct a mild astigmatism. "Runes," he said at last.

She sat at attention. "No doubt?"

"I'm no expert, but it looks like others I've seen."

"Can you tell me what it says?"

"No. It's like Arabic or Chinese. I can recognize it without being able to read it." He handed the photo back. "Where'd this come from?"

"The cave Pippa fell into."

"No shit?" Chuck looked suddenly interested.

"She's trying to get an archaeologist to come take a look. I wish I knew what this said...if anything."

"Why don't you have Elsa look at it?"

"Huh?"

He responded to her confusion with a look of mild disapproval. "To you she may just be a sour old landlady who doesn't know how to boil a potato. But before she retired she had a long and not completely obscure career as a museum historian. In Nuuk. She's an expert in Viking culture. I'm sure she'd leap at the chance to solve your puzzle here."

Kelly was stunned. How superficial of her, she chided herself, to know nothing of her landlady's life.

"I'll ask her!" she said decisively.

A few minutes later she was in Mrs. Arensen's small sitting room. She sat in a threadbare easy chair listening to classical music with her cat Paluaq sprawled on the arm beside her, sleeping. When Kelly handed her the photo, she put on her reading glasses and scrutinized it closely for a long, silent minute. When she looked up, she said, "This is interesting. They are not deep or uniform. Seems like a...how do you say...quickie?"

"I think you mean a rush job."

"Ja, seems like a rush job."

"Can you read it?" Kelly asked anxiously.

Mrs. Arensen nodded, pressing her lips tightly together. "Some of these letters you could take two ways. But, ja, I think so."

"Do you think this is authentic? Do you think it's old, I mean?"

"Old like Viking age? I do not know. Not from a photo. You have to see the original, see what mold or dirt is in the grooves. And see if you can tell what kind of tool was used. You look in a microscope. It is a complex matter to determine if it is authentic."

"But you can decipher the message at least."

"Ja. It looks like Younger Futhark period." Mrs. Arensen's eyes lit up as she said, "Bring me some paper."

Kelly brought a tablet of lined paper and sat on the floor next to Mrs. Arensen's chair while she unhurriedly drew the symbols on the pad. Paluaq, now awake and curious about what was going on, butted her head into the back of the photo. Kelly distracted her by petting her.

"Mrs. Arensen," Kelly said, "I'd be interested in your opinion about what happened to the Viking colonists."

"Ja," said Mrs. Arensen, not looking up from her work.

"I heard they were assimilated into the native population."

"Ja, sure, that is one hypothesis."

"Do you think it happened?"

Mrs. Arensen looked up. "There is not much evidence. But there is not much evidence to support *any* hypothesis, so it is okay. It is a possibility. I would not discount it." She waved her pen. "The Norse who were left would have been a tiny number compared to the native people. If they joined them, it is possible they left no mark."

"Left no mark? Not even in the DNA of their descendants?"

"Ah, well, sure, what do I know about DNA?" She rolled her eyes dismissively. "I am talking about culture. Language and customs. Inuit culture shows nothing of the Vikings. But what would they want of Viking life anyway? They would have no use in the Arctic for wool clothing and wooden houses. If they had taken those things, they would have died out too." She laughed abruptly. "There are a few old Inuit stories told of white people, but they are legends. Some are for sure fiction, so these stories cannot be used as evidence." She shrugged and returned her attention to the runes.

Kelly hoped she could present a translation to Pippa that would please her. Pippa had not returned her calls and was presumably still angry at her for turning down her shocking offer of love. Kelly felt sorry for hurting her and wanted to make it up to her somehow.

As Mrs. Arensen worked, Kelly tried to imagine what the runes depicted, but she had no idea what a Viking might write on the wall of a cave. Maybe something equivalent to "Kilroy was here." Or "This is Erik's cave. Keep out!" Or something more poetic like, "There was a young girl from Elnesvågen…"

"This is an epitaph," Mrs. Arensen announced, startling Kelly.

She rose to her knees to look at the paper with its many notes and scribbles. "An epitaph? Are you sure?"

"Ja, well, it is the most common thing we see. Stones erected at gravesites. They are all over the northern countries, in Iceland, Norway, the UK, everywhere the Vikings lived. Even after they took the Latin alphabet, they still used runes for gravesites because of the spiritual meaning. They usually say something like, So-and-so erected this stone or cut these runes for so-and-so, daughter or son of so-and-so. Some are long and complicated and some are simple, like this one."

"What does it say?"

Mrs. Arensen read the message clearly. "For Torben, son of Asa."

Kelly fell back to a sitting position, a chill running down her spine. "No, no," she muttered. "It can't say that."

Mrs. Arensen took off her glasses and frowned with indignation. "It is a simple message. Not hard to translate. I have seen hundreds of these."

Kelly struggled to recover from the shock of this discovery, her mind immediately grappling for logical explanations for the unbelievable coincidence of the name "Asa" from Pippa's dream.

She leaned over the photo and said, "Where does it say Asa?"

Mrs. Arensen pointed to a series of three characters. "Right here. There is the character for 'a'."

"It looks like an 'f'."

"They do."

But it wasn't possible Pippa's vision was real!

Maybe she was better at reading runes than she knew. Maybe, in her fevered state, drawing on subconscious knowledge, she had read this correctly and it had been the seed for her entire dream. Or maybe she had carved this message herself, in her delirium, and didn't remember. If so, the official analysis would show that these markings were recently made.

Having latched onto two acceptable explanations, Kelly relaxed. But now she questioned the wisdom of presenting these findings to Pippa. She didn't want to encourage her fantasy because of the inevitable disappointment she would face when the experts discovered the truth. If Pippa had made this carving herself, she was in for a seriously embarrassing outcome. Kelly was left with the unhappy conclusion that she couldn't tell Pippa what the runes said after all.

CHAPTER TWENTY-SIX

Jordan sat by herself under the kitchen canopy drinking a beer. Fifty yards away, Brian, Malik and Julie played basketball on their makeshift court. The night was mild, still and comfortable. The sky was clear and the sun hung above the horizon, shining a golden orange light across the ice at the head of the fjord. It would have made a lovely picture, Jordan thought, and her mind conjured up an image of Kelly standing on the shore with a camera in hand.

Sonja wandered in and positioned herself a few feet away, leaning casually against the counter. Jordan ignored her and took another swallow of beer.

"I've just had a very interesting online chat with an old friend," Sonja announced. When Jordan didn't respond, she asked, "Do you want to know what it was about?"

"What possible reason could I have for wanting to know what you were chatting about to an old friend?"

Jordan was surprised and irritated that Sonja had sought her out this evening. She was still smarting from losing her temper earlier in the day. She was angrier at herself than she was at Sonja, and was embarrassed that all of her students had witnessed her breakdown and were moving gingerly around her as if they were afraid of setting her off again. She had taken dinner in her tent, eager to escape the awkwardness of a group meal. She had expected that Sonja would stay away from her tonight. By tomorrow it would all have blown over and they could go on as before, everybody pretending the whole thing had never happened and Sonja grateful for being given another chance. That was the plan in Jordan's mind anyway, but Sonja was foolishly pushing her luck.

"I think you might be interested," Sonja said smugly. "You see, my friend went to Cornell University. Years ago."

Jordan's interest was piqued, but she kept her eyes on the basketball game. "Good for her."

"It was about eighteen years ago, actually."

Jordan stiffened and lowered the beer bottle to the table.

Sonja swung into view in front of her, looking crafty and self-congratulatory. "I was just telling her about our work here and about you. Turns out she recognized your name. You didn't know one another back then, but she had heard of you. You were at Cornell at the same time. She was just a freshman then and you were a graduate student."

"What's your point, Sonja?" Jordan was beginning to feel queasy, but doing her best to appear unruffled.

"She told me the whole story. Quite a little scandal, wasn't it? You and your professor's wife."

"What makes you think the story is true?"

"I admit it doesn't sound like you. A sordid love affair with a married woman, the wife of your thesis advisor, no less. But they say you left Cornell right after the story broke. And shortly after that, the Marquettes separated. A couple of details that give the story some credence, don't you think?" Sonja smiled slyly. "A person could probably dig up a few more details if she worked at it."

"Why would she do that?"

"I'm guessing this isn't something you're proud of. I'm guessing you wouldn't like people to know. After all, you're the cool-headed professional. Never a hair out of place, right? A

messy sex scandal wouldn't fit that image very well, would it?
You had to leave Cornell because of it. What would it do to your
reputation at Boulder if everybody there knew?"

Jordan choked down the anger welling up in her. "What do
you want?"

Sonja smiled, a look of subdued triumph in her eyes. "I want
to stay. After all, I haven't actually done anything so awful. I
misled you a little bit about Kelly because I wanted you for
myself. But it's not like I did something as reprehensible as,
say, have an affair with a married woman." Sonja lifted her chin
haughtily. "Despite what you may think of me, I'm serious about
my career. So I just want to stay and finish the job. And I want
full credit. An A would be greatly appreciated."

"Anything else? No pile of cash?"

"That's all. I just want what I deserve."

"And if I don't think you deserve an A?"

Sonja smirked. "I think you'll agree that I do."

Jordan noticed Malik standing aside from the others at the
basketball court, watching with concern. Sonja would tell him
regardless, Jordan decided, because of their friendship. She
wouldn't be able to help herself. But would she tell the others?
When they got home, would she start the rumor around campus
and infect Jordan's carefully cultivated reputation? She thought
of her colleagues, her students, of losing their respect, becoming
a laughingstock. If she had to leave Boulder, leave the area, how
would she be able to continue her work at the ice core lab?

Would this old mistake never stop plaguing her?

She stood and faced Sonja. "If I agree?"

"Then I won't tell anybody. Your secret is safe with me,
Jordan." Sonja gazed solemnly into her eyes, implying that they
had a special bond between them now. "It's kind of funny, but
I'm glad to find out you were once capable of losing your head
over love."

Jordan swept past her and walked down to the dock. The
glassy surface of the water reflected the high walls of the fjord
on either side, broken only by a couple of small icebergs below
the tongue of the glacier. It was colder down here than it was in

camp. She stood with her arms wrapped around herself, staring absentmindedly at the water.

She resented Sonja's self-righteous remark about her losing her head over love. At least she had said "love." It wasn't nearly so harsh or cynical as Marquette's "piece of tail." Of course Sonja was glad to know it. It gave her power. But that wasn't what she meant. Jordan knew what she meant. She was glad to know that The Ice Queen was fallible, that she was not a superior being. She was human, like herself. People liked to see the flaws, as Kelly had said. She had loved Jordan because of her imperfections, not in spite of them.

People loved the underdog and the runt. Jordan didn't want love, especially love tinged with pity. She wanted respect. There was no hint of respect left in Sonja. She had defeated her foe, had found her Achilles heel and had brought her down.

Jordan felt weary. She had spent so much time and energy trying to rise above her youthful mistakes. But there were still plenty of people who remembered, like Sonja's friend. The worst thing, though, was that Jordan remembered. No matter what she did, no matter what her accomplishments, she could never escape the reality of her own imperfections. The veneer of control that protected her from the woman who could lose her head over love was thin and brittle, like a shallow sheet of ice on the surface of a lake. It was better not tested; the risk of drowning was too real.

The sound of her students at their game broke into her thoughts. She shivered, realizing she was chilled. She walked back to camp where Sonja stood next to the basketball court watching the others play. Jordan walked up to her and said, clearly and precisely, "I don't accept your terms."

Sonja looked surprised.

The basketball bounced off the edge of the rim and came toward Jordan. She caught it in both hands. "Do whatever you want," she said to Sonja. "I really don't care."

She tossed the ball to Malik, who caught it, looking troubled. All of them stood motionless as Jordan walked to her tent.

She sat at her desk, hearing nothing outside. They had apparently quit playing. Now Sonja was telling them her tale, embellishing it, no doubt, with imagined details.

It wasn't true that Jordan didn't care. She did care. Of course she cared. But she couldn't let herself be blackmailed. Where would it end? What would Sonja want from her next year? And the year after? Besides, Sonja was not someone she could trust.

She knew she wouldn't lose her job over an ancient love affair. Instead, the repercussions would be the whispers, the stares, the way people reevaluated their opinion of her. Nearly twenty years ago, that type of reaction had driven her away. But she wouldn't let it happen again. She would stay at Boulder. She had to stay to continue her work, and her work was all that mattered. She had thicker skin now than she'd had then. And more to lose by walking away. Let them say what they wanted. Let them laugh at her.

She shuddered involuntarily at the idea of people laughing at her.

She had been sitting for several minutes, immobile, when a shadow at the flap of her tent drew her attention.

"Jordan?" It was Malik.

"Come in," she said.

He pushed the flap aside and stepped in, a sober expression on his face.

"What is it?" she asked.

He took a few steps closer. "Can we talk about Sonja?"

She sighed. "I don't feel like…"

"Please."

She relented, gesturing toward the chair beside her.

"Thank you," he said, sitting. "I know she has caused you headaches. But she is good at this work and is a valuable asset to our team."

"I never said she wasn't. It's not her work that causes me… headaches."

"No. She is young and high-spirited. Not always wise. You must have many students who do stupid things."

"Oh, sure. But I've never had one blackmail me before."

He smiled. "She is not very good at that either, is she?"

"What do you mean?"

"She told us about your love affair, when you were in school. The wife of your professor."

"Of course she did," Jordan said with disgust, noting the lingering smile on Malik's face. Even he was laughing at her.

"We all shrugged and said, so what?"

"You did?"

"Of course. What does it matter? We have all had unwise love affairs. Nobody cares about that."

Jordan stared, wondering if this could be true.

"If she apologizes," Malik suggested, "would you let her stay?"

"I would have let her stay before. I overreacted this afternoon. I knew that. But after she tried to blackmail me…"

"She has great admiration for you, Jordan. It hurt her very much that you were angry with her. It made her do something crazy. She seems like she is full of confidence. She is puffed up like a rooster. But she is really not like that underneath. She is scared and unsure of herself. She tries to hide it by being boastful."

Jordan considered his assessment of Sonja. Perhaps he was right. If so, Sonja seemed more worthy of sympathy. Jordan could even recognize something of herself in that show of bravado.

"If she stays," she said, "she doesn't get a guaranteed A. She'll get whatever grade she earns."

"Of course." He smiled. "Thank you! I will tell her." He stood. "She will be so happy. And you will see, she will cause you no more headaches. I will make sure." He turned to leave.

"Malik," she ventured. "Really? Nobody cares about my unwise love affair, as you put it?"

He shook his head, then opened his eyes wide with a thought. "Brian did have something to say about it."

"Oh?"

"He said, 'Go, Jordan!' Then he did the happy dance."

She laughed impulsively as Malik shimmied in imitation of Brian, the Greenland flag on his head wagging.

CHAPTER TWENTY-SEVEN

Pippa steered the boat into the fjord and pushed up toward Camp Tootega at a moderate pace. Along the way she had considered that this trip would have been more fun with Kelly along, if she were speaking to Kelly.

It hadn't been easy avoiding Kelly all week. The town was just not that big. But by Wednesday, the calls had quit coming. Kelly must have finally realized Pippa was not going to call her back. Though she had gotten over being mad after just a couple days, she had other reasons for avoiding Kelly. There were things she needed to think about, seriously think about. It wasn't just about Kelly, although certainly she was the catalyst for all the questions Pippa was asking herself about who she was and what she wanted out of life.

She didn't think Kelly could help her answer these questions. Just the opposite. She was afraid she would be too influenced by her.

If she were being honest with herself, she had to admit her obsession with Kelly didn't seem healthy. Or mature. And then there was that interlude with Sonja. Immaturity of epic proportions! Pippa was still shaking her head over that. She felt like she'd made a narrow escape. She barely knew Sonja. She didn't love her. She loved Kelly. At least she had been sure of that a few days ago, but now she wasn't so sure. Maybe she just wanted so desperately to be in love that she had fixated on the first lesbian who had been kind to her.

Either way, the conclusion seemed to be that Kelly had been right all along. Pippa wasn't mature enough for a real relationship. It was all very embarrassing and she wasn't ready to face Kelly yet. She needed some time to clear her head. The prospect of seeing Sonja again was also making her nervous. She hoped she would be off somewhere working today and they could avoid each other.

Rounding the last bend, she saw the camp up ahead, a cluster of colorful tents tucked into a corner at the head of the fjord. She could see people milling about and two boats at the dock. Dr. Lund must already be here, she surmised.

As she turned toward camp, a series of huge thunderclaps rang out all around her, booming through the fjord like a gigantic drum. Her heart leapt to her throat. At the head of the fjord, a gigantic chunk of the glacier dislodged and crashed into the water, sending up a dramatic wall of water as it plunged in. Pippa was used to calving glaciers, but she wasn't usually this close to them, nor was she used to such an explosive noise, amplified by the narrow gorge. She slowed her approach, waiting for the iceberg to settle.

It bobbed and rolled as it resurfaced, sending moderate waves her way. She turned her bow into them at the precise moment another ear-splitting thunderous crack rang out. Several pieces of ice fell off simultaneously, huge sections of the face of the glacier, crashing into one another as they hit the water. Pippa was riveted by the scene in front of her. She had never seen anything like it. Diverting her attention to land, a boulder on the north cliff came tumbling down the rock wall toward Camp Tootega, bringing a small avalanche of smaller rocks with it.

Someone screamed and the boulder crashed into an aluminum table, taking it and all its contents down in a clattering blur.

The boat bounced wildly as the waves hit. She quickly fastened her life vest tightly across her chest. She held on, her stomach lurching. Ice-cold water splashed over the sides, soaking her legs. The boats at the dock leapt about, banging against the pilings.

The icebergs eventually came to a rest and the water gradually returned to its usual calm. Finally, there was silence except for the voices of the nearby camp dwellers that came to her on the air currents.

* * *

Returning to the boarding house, Kelly ran into Chuck in the entryway wearing his good black shoes and his Panama hat. He was buttoning his coat and clearly preparing to go out.

"Where are you going?" she asked.

"To visit a friend in Aasiaat," he replied.

Kelly noticed how cleanly shaven his chin was, how uncharacteristically neat he looked, and then she smelled his aftershave.

"A friend?"

He grinned. "Yeah. I'm taking the ferry."

"We've got that interview tomorrow," Kelly said, knowing the ferry would take a week to return up the coast. "How will you get back?"

"Don't worry. I'll be back this evening. She'll fly me."

"Will she indeed?"

"She's a bush pilot." He smiled broadly under his carefully trimmed mustache. "She's got a job here tonight."

Kelly shrugged off her coat. "Well, then, happy flying."

"What'll you do while I'm gone?"

"Not sure. I thought I might hang out with Pippa, but she's gone somewhere for the day. I just came from her house. Her brother said she won't be back until afternoon. So I guess I'm stuck here. Maybe I'll organize photos. Or maybe I'll spend some time fantasizing about a lady bush pilot."

"You could do worse." He slapped her heartily on the back and went out.

Kelly went to her room, disappointed with herself for not getting out earlier to catch Pippa. She was sure that if she could speak to her face-to-face she could smooth things over between them. Her brother had reported that she'd taken the day off work, but he didn't know where she was. Maybe she'd found herself a new friend.

As Kelly arrived in her bedroom, she felt an odd sensation as if she were having an attack of vertigo or loss of balance. She stood perfectly still, feeling even more unsteady. Then the floor seemed to roll beneath her feet and objects jumped off the shelves. The light fixture swung acutely and she realized it was an earthquake. From the front of the house, she heard Mrs. Arensen scream, then heard the sound of running footsteps.

She dashed into the doorway, clinging to both sides of its sturdy frame as the rolling sensation subsided and then ceased. Altogether, it had lasted only seconds. There was quiet throughout the house. Only the light hanging from the ceiling still moved, its swinging arc less pronounced with each pass.

Just when she thought it was over, the sound of an explosion rolled over the house and Kelly was sure she felt the door frame vibrate. Was the house blowing up?

She stood frozen in the doorway, waiting and listening, her nerves on edge. When she began to hear the sounds of others stirring, she emerged from her room to find Mrs. Arensen and Jens in the dining room. Several pieces of china had fallen from the cabinet and lay broken on the floor. Mrs. Arensen stood in the midst of the debris looking lost, her hand over her mouth.

"Is everyone okay?" Kelly asked.

Jens nodded. "We're fine. You?"

"Yeah, I'm okay."

"Annalise and Trevor already left for work. Where's Chuck?"

"He's gone out."

Jens bent down to pick up a teacup that had escaped damage. He placed it on the table.

Mrs. Arensen stood mutely in place, staring at the pieces of porcelain on the floor. Then quite suddenly she put her face in both hands and began to sob, alarming Kelly, who had thought her incapable of such behavior. Jens enclosed her in his arms, patting her back. "Ah, mormor," he said in a soothing voice.

Kelly's phone rang and she stepped into the hall to answer.

"Whoo hoo!" Chuck hollered. "I nearly got drowned by a fucking tidal wave here on the dock! You should have seen it. It lifted up one of the icebergs in the harbor and dropped it right on top of some poor sap's boat. Demolished it, just like that. What's going on there?"

"We're okay. Just some broken china. Have you ever been in an earthquake here before?"

"No. Most of Greenland is unfaulted. Earthquakes happen only on the coast and not often. Fortunately, the ferry hasn't arrived yet. It's still out in the bay in open water and appears to be intact. A couple of monster bergs crashed into each other out there and ice went flying everywhere." He sounded excited. "Too bad you weren't out here to film it. Damn! Really something to see. The size of these ice cubes is hard to comprehend, but it looked like two battleships ramming each other head-on."

"That must have been what I heard," Kelly muttered, recalling the explosion. "I wish I'd seen that."

"The ferry's just about here, so I'm gonna go. I just wanted to make sure you were okay back there. Be careful. There could be aftershocks."

After saying goodbye, Kelly considered taking her camera outside and waiting for an aftershock that might give her a taste of the remarkable scenes Chuck had just witnessed. She could be standing around for hours, she knew, waiting for such a thing, and it might never come.

Frustrated, she returned to her room and turned on the radio to see if there was any news about the quake.

* * *

Jordan stood amid scattered debris where the kitchen had been. Still pulsing from the adrenaline rush, she mentally tallied up her students, seeing all of them nearby, all looking unharmed.

Dr. Lund stood off to the side, his hands in his pants pockets, his hat cocked sideways on his hairless head. Malik ran toward the dock with Atka at his heels to greet Pippa as she edged her boat to shore. It looked like she too had escaped injury.

"Wow, that was close!" Julie breathed, walking gingerly around the wreckage on the ground. "This is a mess."

"Aren't we lucky, though?" breathed Jordan.

"Because we're all still alive?"

"Of course that, but that's not what I meant. I meant to have seen that!" She pointed toward the glacier as Brian walked up. "It's not often you get to witness an example of punctuated equilibrium as it's happening. Usually we only observe the results. But right before our eyes, the front of this glacier just receded a good thirty meters. At least!"

In the fjord the hundreds of chunks of ice that had broken off were still bumping into each other, jostling for position. The new front of the glacier was a pristine wall of crystalline white and translucent azure, sheer and dazzling.

Sonja picked up the overturned table and set it upright. It was severely bent in the center. She pushed down on the deformity until she had a semblance of flatness. She carried the table up the slope, setting it down where she could use it to collect the scattered kitchen items. Ever since Jordan had pardoned her, she had been on her best behavior and seemed for once to be truly cowed. Her apology had even sounded sincere and in the end, it seemed there was no harm done.

None of the others treated Jordan any differently since learning of her youthful indiscretion. She realized that it had been a much bigger deal to her than it was to anyone else. It was old news and had no reflection on her present. She really had moved beyond it. It couldn't hurt her anymore and she had Sonja to thank for showing her that. People could overlook the mistakes of the past, especially when a person had learned from them. As long as she didn't allow any future missteps, she would be fine.

"I want all of you up on the glacier," she announced. "Check all the buoys and cameras and see what's happened up there.

Sonja, you can leave that mess. It's more important that we take measurements as soon as possible so we know exactly what effect the quake had. If there are aftershocks, any of those can trigger shifts in the ice. Be careful and stay away from anything unstable."

"Are you coming?" Brian asked.

"I'll stay here a while and clean up. Leave Curly and I'll catch up to you."

As the others began preparations for going out, Jordan introduced Salvatore Lund to Pippa. Whether he expected anything to come of this or not, he graciously listened to her description of the cave and its contents and her mysterious hopes for the discovery of human remains. As before, she did not explain why she expected something so extraordinary to be found.

After they had gone, Jordan picked up the camp stove from the ground and wiped it down, hoping it still worked. A sharp cracking sound drew her attention toward the fjord in time to see a sliver of ice shear away from the face of the glacier and fall into the water like a knife blade, causing almost no splash.

Any photographer, she imagined, would love to catch this action on video. She'd been disappointed to see that Pippa had come alone again. Despite the anxiety Kelly caused her, she had hoped to see her one more time. But when it came to Kelly, she cautioned, it was probably better to leave well enough alone. She had a curious power over Jordan that undermined her senses. Her blowup at Sonja was enough evidence of that. Besides, there was no point in seeing Kelly again.

She lit the stove and turned up the flame, glad to see it still worked.

No, she decided, *I don't need any more turmoil right now. Leave Kelly out of this picture.*

CHAPTER TWENTY-EIGHT

Kelly reviewed her photos on the computer, grouping them by date and subject, deleting some of the inferior ones. Her phone rang and she reached for it, hoping it wasn't Chuck bragging about something else she'd missed. He should take a camera. She would insist on it from now on.

"Hi," she said absentmindedly, scrolling through her thumbnails.

"Kelly, it's Jordan."

She released the mouse and sat back in her chair, giving her full attention to the call. "Jordan, is anything wrong?"

"No. Nothing wrong. The earthquake did a little damage to the camp, but everybody's fine. Pippa had quite a ride in the fjord. She was just coming in when it happened."

"Pippa? She's there?"

"Not now. She's gone off with Dr. Lund to look at the cave. You didn't know?"

"No. I haven't seen Pippa at all this week. So you helped her out and got her an archaeologist?"

"Yes. He's working out here anyway, so it's no big deal to come by and take a look. Pippa happened to arrive at the precise moment the quake hit. She made it safely in, but it's a wonder she didn't capsize with the ice calving off the glacier in masses. That's why I called."

"Because of Pippa?"

"No. Because of the glacier. The whole face of it came tumbling down. Cut it back a hundred feet. It's still calving. You've got some photos from the other day so I thought you might like to take some more now. It's a potentially important documentary of a rare event. Earthquakes in Greenland are fairly uncommon, so this is an excellent opportunity to observe what they can do to the ice."

"You know," Kelly said, "I hadn't thought of that. I'd have before and after shots. Sweet!"

"I thought you'd feel that way. So why don't you come out before all the excitement's over?"

Kelly sprang from her chair. "I will!" She kicked off her slippers, then remembered she was stuck. "Oh, wait. I have no way to get there. Chuck's gone and won't be back until tonight. Even if I had a boat, I'd need a pilot to go with it."

"That's too bad. Maybe you can come tomorrow, but the chance to see calving may be over by then. Still, you can at least get the after shots."

"Yeah," Kelly said, frustrated. "Thank you for calling."

After hanging up, she hit her fist on the desk. "Crap!" Another missed opportunity. There must be some way to get out there. She supposed she could try to rent a boat and a pilot, but had no idea how hard or how expensive that would be. Chuck usually took care of things like that.

Still trying to figure out a plan, she went to the kitchen to get an ice cream bar from the freezer, noting that there was no sign of lunch preparations. Jens was sitting at the table playing a game on his phone. Kelly could hear the beep beep sound effects. He glanced up and acknowledged her with an indifferent smile, then returned to his game. She unwrapped her ice cream and came around to look over his shoulder as he tried to break through a wall of colored bricks with a paddle and ball.

"How's your grandmother?" she asked, biting off a corner of the bar.

The ball missed the paddle and the phone made a mocking wah-wah sound. Jens frowned. "She's kind of upset. The earthquake did a number on her. She'll be okay. But I think we may be on our own for lunch."

"Okay by me. I can always make a sandwich. I mean smørrebrød."

He resumed his game. She ate her ice cream, watching him play absentmindedly. Halfway through the ice cream bar, she asked, "Jens, you're studying to be a doctor, right?"

"Uh-huh," he said, his thumbs working the game.

"So you know something about genetics."

"Uh-huh."

"How would a person get blue eyes if nobody in her family had blue eyes?"

He looked up, quizzically. "Nobody in the entire family tree?"

"Nobody to the knowledge of anyone living."

"There are three ways. Albinos have blue eyes. Light skin, light hair."

"She's not an albino."

"You mean this is somebody you know?"

"It's Pippa."

"Oh. So we're talking about a Greenlander. Another way is a spontaneous mutation. That's how blue eyes came about in the first place. It happens once in a while, but it's rare."

"What's the third way?"

"Through inheritance, but the only way someone can have blue eyes is if both parents carry the blue-eyed gene. It's recessive, so you have to have a mother and a father with both a blue-eyed and a brown-eyed gene. If the two blues get together in the child, you can have a blue-eyed child, even though the parents are both brown-eyed."

"And the grandparents too?"

"Yeah. None of these people would have blue eyes, even if they had the gene, until someone inherited it from both parents."

"And how far back could that go?"

He shrugged. "Back to wherever the blue-eyed gene originated. As long as the carriers kept passing it on, it would still be there, even if it wasn't expressed for several generations. You do see Greenlanders with blue eyes once in a while, like Pippa. The only way to know if it's inherited or not is to have her parents tested to see if they have the gene. But that doesn't solve the mystery of where it came from originally, does it?"

"No, it doesn't."

Jens continued his game and Kelly finished her ice cream, thinking about Pippa's blue eyes, which led her to think about Jordan's blue-gray eyes and how frustrating it was that she was stuck here with no transportation.

"Why aren't you working?" she asked.

"No more tours today. I had a group early this morning and I've got the midnight one. That's it."

Suddenly Kelly had a brainstorm.

"Jens!" she said, clamping a hand on his shoulder.

"Wah-wah," went the phone.

He twisted his head to get a glimpse of her. "What?"

"Your helicopter is available this afternoon?"

"Yeah."

"So you could go out on a little pleasure trip if you wanted to."

"Yeah, if I wanted to, but I don't."

"What I meant was, you could take me for a flight."

He looked suddenly interested. "You want to go out in my chopper?"

"Uh-huh."

"Anywhere in particular?"

"Uh-huh. Can we do it?"

He shrugged. "You pay for gas and buy me a beer."

"I'll buy you a six-pack!"

"Deal!" He reached a fist over his head and she bumped it with her own.

CHAPTER TWENTY-NINE

Dr. Lund relied on his walking stick as they made their way toward the cave coordinates. He wasn't quick or spritely, but he was solid and steady. Pippa guessed him to be about sixty years old, with a tanned, lined face and a slight hunch to his shoulders. She had told him everything she was going to tell him about the cave. She had told him about the rock cairn and about her belief that it marked a grave. He had agreed that if it was a burial marker, it was most likely not Inuit. It had the characteristics of the Norse people, though they didn't normally bury people in caves. It could also just be a pile of rocks somebody built for the heck of it. She understood that, she told him, knowing that the evidence would speak for itself. She was tense with excitement and would have liked to run the entire way, but her companion's pace held her back like taut bridle reins.

"What are you doing on Disko Island?" she asked as they walked.

"We're excavating a Thule summer site."

"That's cool. I know this was a place they came in summer to hunt. Down from the north."

"That's right. Are you interested in anthropology?"

"Yes! Especially Greenland anthropology, but the subject I'm really passionate about is biophysics or phylogenetics, something like that."

He raised one eyebrow, eyeing her with interest. "Is that so? How did you develop an interest in phylogenetics?"

Pippa shrugged. "I've been interested in it ever since I can remember."

He smiled knowingly, showing all his upper teeth. "Let me guess. Eye color?"

She nodded. "I guess my interest in genetics is sort of a vanity thing."

"It's not uncommon for something personal to spark an interest that becomes professional. People become cancer specialists because a loved one has cancer. It's as good a reason as any. Maybe better, because it's not just cold science. It has a real-world relevance for you."

"Exactly. I figure whatever I find out about my eyes, like proof that the Vikings survived by joining up with the Thule, that will contribute a lot to the general knowledge of the history of Greenland."

"That's Greenland's biggest historical mystery. If you solve that, you'll guarantee your legacy."

Pippa smiled at the idea of having a legacy. "I hope this cave will give us some good DNA to work with. Then maybe you'll have a legacy too."

Dr. Lund laughed good-naturedly.

At last they approached the ravine. Unable to restrain herself, Pippa walked rapidly ahead of him to the edge and looked down into it, trying to pick out familiar patterns in the rocks to locate the cave entrance. What had jumped out at her easily the last time she was here was the hole she had fallen through, a dark gaping opening in the plant cover. But today that wasn't evident. Everything looked different. She realized she must not be in the right place, so she turned on her GPS receiver and sat down, cross-legged, waiting for it to get a fix.

Dr. Lund walked up, breathing audibly.

"It's in this ravine," she informed him. "I don't see it, so we'll have to use the GPS."

Dr. Lund nodded and sat on a large boulder, lifting his face to the sky with his eyes closed. He seemed to be enjoying himself on this little hike.

"I've got a fix," Pippa announced, standing. "Let me go down and locate it. You can wait here and I'll call you when I find it. It's a little tricky getting down this slope."

"Okay. Just give a holler."

Pippa descended into the ravine, knocking loose rocks as she went. They clattered down the incline. The coordinates led her to a spot almost directly below where Dr. Lund waited, but she was still not able to see either the opening in the ceiling or the one she had dug to escape. She stood directly on top of the coordinates. According to the receiver, the cave floor was thirty meters below her feet. That made no sense because the cave was only three meters high. The furthest from the cave floor she could be was four meters. So how could she be standing twenty meters above it on solid rock?

She checked to see that the battery was okay and the device had a good signal. It was communicating with five satellites, reporting a solid 3D fix. She decided to walk up and down the ravine a few meters in each direction to see if she could find the cave entrance by sight. She went one direction without success, then went back the other direction, noticing that many of the boulders underfoot were unstable. They rocked and slipped when she stepped on them, something she hadn't noticed before. Everything seemed off today.

When she saw a familiar patch of blooming cottongrass, the very ones she had been picking when she'd fallen through, she dashed toward them. At the edge of the wildflower patch was a pile of rocks that hadn't been there before. She was sure of it. With this landmark to orient herself, she knew where the ceiling collapse should have been. Nothing but boulders. She walked tentatively on top of them and consulted the GPS receiver. Thirty meters below her feet, it again reported.

"Did you find it?" Dr. Lund called down.

Pippa knelt and touched the rocks beneath her, a solid mass of boulders. She climbed down the side of the slope, slipping when one of the boulders broke loose under her foot. Shaken, she stood staring at the mass of rock, gradually realizing what had happened.

A few minutes later she reluctantly climbed out of the ravine and faced Dr. Lund, who gazed at her curiously.

"Something wrong?" he asked.

"I think the cave has been buried," she answered quietly. "The earthquake must have brought down a rock slide and collapsed it. There's no way in. Not that I can find. It's thirty meters under."

Dr. Lund looked disappointed. "Oh, that's too bad." He stood, steadying himself with his stick. "As ye sow, so shall ye reap."

Pippa looked up at him, confused. "What?"

"That cave was probably created by an earthquake in the first place, don't you think? A rock avalanche brought on by a quake. And now it's been destroyed the same way."

Pippa searched his face. "We have to dig it out. To get to the grave."

He pursed his lips, a solemn look on his face. "We don't actually know there was a grave. There was a pile of rocks. Maybe put there by a person. That's all. It was one thing to move a few rocks and take a look, but now you're talking about a major excavation to uncover something that may or may not be there or may have been moved who knows how far downslope by the rock slide. There's no road to bring in heavy equipment. On the strength of no actual evidence, I don't think anybody will go to the lengths required to get in here."

"But they have to," Pippa objected. "This is important. It's the key to everything. It's the missing link that will tell us what happened to the Vikings. It will prove they didn't all die off, that some of them survived by going to live with the native people. And they had children and grandchildren and great grandchildren and I'm a descendant of both Thule and Norse people! To know that, to be able to prove that with hard facts would be huge."

Dr. Lund regarded her for a moment before calmly replying. "Pippa, even if there was a body buried in that cave and we managed to recover it and positively determine that it was indeed a Scandinavian from the Viking era, how would that prove what you're saying? It would say nothing about what happened to the Viking settlers one way or another. It would be one individual who died in a cave and was left there. We wouldn't know why. We wouldn't know by whom. It would be a valuable find, but couldn't possibly lead to the conclusions you're imagining."

"But the DNA," she argued. "It could be analyzed and compared to mine. To prove she was related to me."

"She?" He narrowed his eyes at her.

Pippa stared, then swallowed hard, realizing she had just moved into dangerous territory. There was nothing she could tell him about Asa. Science and scientists like Dr. Lund dealt only with the facts. He was right that the details could never be known from the evidence. Even if Asa's baby was found, it would have nothing to say about Asa and Gudny and their life among the Skrælings. It would only prove a tiny piece of the story. The story that she had experienced wasn't something that could be preserved in bone or hair. As far as she knew, the only place it existed was in her own mind. For science, that was worth nothing. And now the only part that would mean something to science was lost.

Dr. Lund placed a hand on her shoulder and said, "I'm sorry I didn't get to see it. If it had been the remains of a Viking, that would've been something. The bodies we find are almost always Inuit. That's a big reason for the mystery surrounding the Norsemen. We can study the scant remains of their homes, the layout of stones they piled up to make fences, but the people… what happened to them…" He shook his head. "That mystery will not be solved today."

CHAPTER THIRTY

The helicopter circled Camp Tootega once before hovering over the cliff above it. Down below, Kelly saw Jordan standing in the middle of camp and waved to her.

Jens put down as Jordan hurried up the path to meet them. By the time she reached the landing pad, Jens was already lifting off. Against the wind generated by the chopper blades, Kelly held on to her baseball cap with one hand.

Jordan hugged her briskly. "You made it!" she cried over the noise of the chopper.

They carried the camera equipment down to camp as the helicopter receded out of sight on its way back to town.

"Where is everyone?" Kelly asked, glancing around the silent camp.

"They're out working. I stayed here to clean up. We had some damage from the quake."

"And Pippa?"

"They should be back in a while. Will you wait for her?"

"I have to. She doesn't know it, but she's my ride back."

"Frankly, I'm curious to hear how that went. Pippa's been very mysterious about that whole business."

Kelly unzipped her camera case. "I'm afraid Pippa's in for a harsh blow."

"Why's that?"

"She had a dream or hallucination when she was in the cave. She doesn't believe it was a dream. She thinks she was in communication with some ancient ancestor, that she had a vision of the past. It's because of the dream that she thinks there's a body buried there. She'll be horribly disappointed when she finds out there isn't one."

"Are you sure there isn't?"

Kelly glanced up with curiosity. "The only evidence is Pippa's dream. And the runes, but I'm sure they aren't authentic."

"You're a very practical woman, aren't you?"

"Uh-huh."

"You didn't used to be. There was a time you'd have been totally ready to believe in a possibility like channeling an ancient consciousness."

Kelly picked up her tripod in her free hand. "I know. But I was a silly romantic fool back then, wasn't I?"

Jordan raised one eyebrow, looking like she didn't know how to take that remark.

"Pippa's a really smart girl," Kelly stated. "She wants to be a scientist and she could go far. But this tendency to fantasy is…"

"Immature?" suggested Jordan.

Kelly nodded with a smile.

"Isn't that what being young is all about? You have unrealistic dreams and fantasies. It happens to everyone, the dismantling of our utopias bit by bit. That's the definition of life."

"I just don't want to see her hurt."

"But she will be if she does any living at all. In the meantime, I don't see any harm in her believing in this particular dream. There are so many more destructive things to believe in. Many great thinkers have been inspired by dreams. They enable your imagination to burst free of what you think you know."

"I suppose you're right."

If she appeared more cynical to Jordan now than she had as a nineteen-year-old, it was only because she had learned not to voice her more fanciful ideas. That was what was meant by "act your age." It meant to control yourself. To stop yourself from saying and doing things that would embarrass you or your family and friends. That's why she hadn't confessed that night in Jordan's tent that she still loved her. Kelly wanted to show her that she had matured. She wanted Jordan's admiration and respect as much as she had once wanted her love.

Kelly jerked her head toward the glacier. "I saw it as we flew over. Quite a change. I wish I'd been here when it happened. Seems I missed all the action this morning."

"It was scary," Jordan said, "but exciting too. Do you want me to carry something?"

"Yes. Can you bring that bag? That's got my lenses in it."

Jordan followed Kelly down to shore where she selected a spot to start shooting. She set up her tripod and stared at the sheer wall of ice facing them.

"This is such a beautiful place," she said. "Since I've been in Greenland I've noticed how the light seems different. It must be the angle of the sun. It changes the hues. It's very subtle, but definitely there. The light is unusual at night, of course, but even now in the early afternoon, it's like there's a pale gold filter over everything."

"You notice it more than most people, I suppose. You're tuned into it."

"The first night I was here I spent the whole time outside taking pictures. I didn't get to bed until four in the morning. It was so spectacular, light all night long, changing subtly hour by hour."

She screwed the camera down on the tripod and started shooting while Jordan stood nearby, silent, but by no means forgotten.

"It's sort of warm this afternoon," Jordan observed. "Do you want a cold drink?"

"Sure. That would be great."

"We have Coke and lemonade. Or there's some local beer, if you'd prefer."

"Coke would be perfect."

"Okay." Jordan flashed her a warm smile, then walked up to camp while Kelly snapped a few photos, feeling invigorated by both Jordan's invitation to come out and her welcoming demeanor.

This was a Jordan she hadn't seen much of. She'd gotten a glimpse of it that night at the hotel restaurant. Now again today. She could almost imagine Jordan opening her heart. Kelly hoped she wasn't just imagining it. At the very least Jordan was treating her like an equal, not just a troublesome student. If they could develop the beginning of a friendship based on that sort of equality, there was hope that Kelly could build on it back home. The important thing was to do nothing to scare her off. It would take time to attain the kind of trust Jordan required. Kelly was fine with that. As long as things were moving in the right direction, she could be patient.

She walked up to camp, arriving as Jordan poured Coke into two glasses. "Did you get some good shots?" she asked.

"Absolutely. Thank you for inviting me back for this. With all those new icebergs in the fjord, it's a totally different scene."

Jordan pulled a tray of ice cubes from the freezer. "Do you want ice? We've got plenty!" She made a sweeping gesture toward the glacier and laughed lightheartedly.

Kelly laughed too. "Yes, thanks."

Jordan held an ice cube in her open palm, looking at it thoughtfully. "Ice is an interesting mineral," she said. "It's powerful enough to tear down mountains, but if you apply just a little heat, it completely melts away." Water dripped between her fingers as the ice cube started to melt. "It's both strong and weak at the same time."

"A lot of things are," Kelly observed.

Jordan looked up from her hand to catch Kelly's gaze before dropping the ice into her glass.

"When are the others coming back?" Kelly asked.

"They won't be back for hours yet. They have to go all the way up to the furthest of our checkpoints and take readings and download images from the cameras. We can see what the earthquake did right here easily enough, but we also need to know what it did to the entire structure of the glacier, surface and subsurface."

Feeling parched, Kelly took a long swallow of her soda, then said, "Your work is so interesting."

"So is yours! Wasn't it you who rappelled into an ice waterfall? And the other day when you were talking about photography, you seemed utterly enraptured by your subject."

"It's true I like my work. Up till now, it hasn't been this exotic. This place is just magical." She set her glass on the counter. "The other day I took a walk south of town and came to a place where all around me the only color I could see was gray. The sky, the sea and the land—all gray. Even the ice looked gray. But it was still so many different colors, so rich with the differing textures and tones. It was like an artist's study in gray. It was stunningly beautiful and I shot a hundred photos trying to capture that beauty." Kelly sighed. "Frankly, I don't think my camera understands Greenland. I'm still looking for the right settings for the light here."

Jordan watched her closely, seeming to be listening, but she made no comment or gesture to indicate she was. Still, Kelly had the impression she liked listening to her talk about photography, so she continued, turning in a slow circle to take in the scenery.

"It could take a lifetime to capture that gray beauty in pixels. I mean, a photographer could literally work with that one scene for years. Like a paleontologist with a rich fossil bed or an archaeologist with an ancient city." She faced Jordan, who still stared silently, raptly. "Or you with two miles worth of ice, spending your entire career on divining its secrets and never exhausting them. That's how this scene felt to me. I had such a hard time tearing myself away." Kelly shook her head. "There must be millions of scenes like that in Greenland. How many lifetimes would it take to master the entire rainbow of color here, I have to wonder?"

They stood face-to-face, looking into one another's eyes. The depth of feeling between them seemed profound. If Jordan had been almost anyone else, Kelly would have moved into her arms at this moment and kissed her, confident that the gesture would be welcomed. Maybe she would have done it anyway if the sound of a boat engine had not entered her consciousness just then.

"That'll be your ride," Jordan said.

Kelly realized she had only minutes left before she and Jordan parted company for the summer.

"Jordan," she said, gripped with sudden panic. "I hope we can see one another back home. I've been trying to play this so cool, but I'm scared to death I'm going to lose you again."

She saw a flicker of fear in Jordan's eyes, a fleeting look of vulnerability and indecision. She had seen this look before, in the photo she had taken the other day and faintly in the past. But what she had never seen before was that this look was a response to her. *Why?* she wondered. *Why would she be afraid of me?*

"Your being here this summer isn't a coincidence, is it?" Jordan asked.

Kelly shook her head, realizing she had just given everything away. She had just revealed that she was that same lovesick puppy she had always been, chasing the object of her desire to the top of the world for a pat on the head. Jordan would see her as pathetic, just as she had before.

"Not entirely, no. I wanted to see you again. That was part of the reason I decided to take the job."

The sound of the engine came closer, sputtering as it was cut. Their time was up. Kelly heard voices at the dock, but she didn't turn to look. She didn't want to miss her last few seconds alone with Jordan.

"I've enjoyed seeing you again too," Jordan said.

Kelly searched her face, trying to find deeper meaning behind her words, but she was unreadable.

Jordan reached for her and Kelly moved into her embrace. The hug was warm, but not intimate. No kiss this time, Kelly lamented.

"Kelly!" called Pippa. "Kelly!"

She glanced around to see Pippa running toward them. She spun back to Jordan. "Please call me. Let's go to dinner or coffee or whatever you want."

Jordan seemed uneasy. "I'll…yes, of course, I'll call you."

Was that a genuine promise? Would she do it? Or was she just trying to avoid more melodrama?

Any fear that Kelly had had about losing Pippa's friendship was swept away as Pippa plowed into her and wrapped her arms around her. But the look on her face was unexpectedly despairing and her eyes were moist with the onset of tears. So she had already gotten bad news. Kelly glanced over at the elderly man who walked slowly up the slope with a cane. Had it been so obvious to him that the runes were counterfeit?

"I'm so sorry," Kelly said, holding Pippa affectionately. "I know how important this was to you."

Pippa looked puzzled. "How do you know?"

"I just guessed…" Kelly began, reluctant to mention her skepticism again. "Well, why don't you tell me what happened?"

"The earthquake wiped the whole thing out. There was an avalanche. There's nothing left. Dr. Lund never got to see it."

"Oh!" Kelly blurted. "That's horrible. Can they dig it out?"

She shook her head grimly.

Kelly comforted Pippa while Jordan got the archaeologist a Coke and the two of them sat down at the kitchen table. Then Kelly collected her equipment while Pippa said goodbye to Jordan and Dr. Lund. Jordan raised an arm and waved toward Kelly, then turned her attention back to her colleague.

That was it, then, Kelly thought. She was sure she had blown her chance with Jordan with her too-obvious neediness. Why had she not been able to stick to her plan and keep cool? Why did she always have to wear her heart on her sleeve?

CHAPTER THIRTY-ONE

Out of the corner of her eye, Jordan watched Pippa and Kelly speed away, then disappear from view, the sound of the boat motor fading rapidly.

During the moments Kelly had been speaking about her work, Jordan had been battling an overpowering desire to take her in her arms and kiss her. She had barely heard anything Kelly had said. There was no doubt now that Kelly wanted her too. She'd admitted it. She had come here with the purpose of reconnecting and seemed anxious to make sure they would be in touch back home. She seemed almost desperate, in fact. Kelly was still in love with her.

She was filled with happiness to know that, but the idea of Kelly was still so hard to face. The last time she'd given her heart to someone, she'd been destroyed. Kelly had the power to do that to her too. Jordan knew she could feel so much for her... if she let herself. Wasn't it a million times easier to turn away from all that and just go on living her life the way she had been?

Dr. Lund was speaking to her, she realized. She focused on him with difficulty.

"I don't understand," he said, shaking his head, "why Pippa was so convinced there was a body in that cave."

"She had a dream."

"A dream?"

"She believes in her dream."

"Believes it's true, you mean? Why?"

"Because she wants to." Jordan smiled across the table at his perplexed expression. "Sometimes believing is sufficient to make it true."

He opened his mouth to object, then shook his head again. "I'd better get back. It was nice to see you again, Jordan. Come over to the island if you have a chance and take a look at my dig."

"I will." Jordan stood and shook his hand. "Thanks for coming over."

After helping him launch, she walked back to camp. As she approached her tent, she noticed crackling static and indistinct words from inside. She hurried her pace and heard a clear message: "Jordan, come in!"

She dashed inside the tent and over to the radio.

"Jordan!" the tense, male voice repeated. "Jordan, please answer."

She pressed a button on the radio. "What's wrong, Brian?" she asked.

"Oh, thank God! We've had an accident. Sonja's fallen into a fissure. We can't reach her and there's no way she can climb out."

"A fissure? In the glacier?"

"Yeah. The quake broke it up quite a bit and left these huge gaps."

"How far down is she?"

"Sixty, seventy feet. The problem is, the fissure is way deeper than that. We can't see how deep. If she falls, it could be all the way to the bottom. No way to survive that. She's sitting on a narrow ledge. All of our rappelling gear is in Curly. We thought of passing down some picks and crampons and having her try to climb out, but the ice is just too unstable. We can't risk it without a tether."

Jordan took a deep breath. "Is she injured?"

"No. She's not hurt, but she is cold. And scared."

"Where are you?"

"Camera three."

"I'm on my way," Jordan said. "Tell her not to move. Make sure she stays calm."

"Malik's talking to her."

"Good. You call for a rescue team."

"I will, but by the time they get here…"

"I'll be there in a few minutes."

Jordan rapidly loaded equipment into Curly and took off across the rough terrain, paralleling the edge of the ice river, driving as fast as she dared, her nerves raw.

When she arrived at the team's location, she leapt out of the vehicle as it rolled to a stop and ran to the edge of the glacier.

Malik lay on his stomach, his head over a deep, narrow crevasse, his dog standing beside him. The glacier had cracked open, the down side pulling away from the other. The technical term for this feature was *bergschrund*, a German word meaning "mountain cleft." She recited the definition silently to herself. There was a dictionary of geology terms in her head, but as often happened when faced with a real-world example, the definition became superfluous, almost meaningless. It was just a word: *bergschrund*. This thing before her was too big and too awe-inspiring to capture in a word.

She hesitantly peered into the eerie blue depths. Sonja sat looking small and frightened on a shelf of ice four feet wide, huddled over her knees. On her left was a sheer vertical wall. On her right was a menacing chasm that descended steeply, narrowing as it went. Jordan felt dizzy just looking and had to jerk away.

"Did you call for a rescue team?" she asked.

"We did," Julie assured her. "But it's hard to say how long it will take them. She's too cold to stay there much longer."

"Malik tried tossing down his jacket," Brian said, "but it missed."

"How did this happen?" Jordan asked.

"She was trying to rescue one of the cameras," Brian explained. "The quake knocked it into the ice, so she went out to get it. She reminded us, you know, about how you said one of those cameras was worth more than all of us put together."

"We know that was a joke," Julie intervened, frowning at Brian.

"There must have been an aftershock," he said. "This whole section just split off. It knocked her off her feet and she slipped over. The camera fell in too. It's way down there somewhere. Long gone."

Jordan took a deep breath. "I'll go down and get her," she said, steeling herself against the fear she already felt creeping into her throat.

"Jordan," Julie objected, "you can't go down there. Just while we've been waiting for you, it's been shifting and calving."

"What do you suggest?" Jordan asked.

"We should wait for the rescue team. They've got all the right equipment for this situation."

"You just said yourself she can't stay there much longer. Between the cold and the instability of the ice, waiting isn't an option if there's something we can do."

Brian intervened. "Now that we've got the ropes, we can lower one down to her."

Jordan shook her head. "That's too dangerous. If she were directly below us, maybe, but it's not possible to just drop a rope on her. If she has to move around to get to it, the ledge could fail. We can't have her moving until she's got a safety line. Somebody has to go down there and put the rope in her hand."

Malik stepped up to them. "I'll go. I've been climbing ice all my life. I'm the most experienced."

Jordan gazed into his dark eyes, grateful for the offer. Though she knew how to use the equipment and had both experience and training in climbing, she had regularly avoided climbing situations where her fear of heights would kick in. This was one of those situations. She couldn't even look down into that crevasse without getting dizzy. How could she hang over it at the end of a cable? For a second, she considered letting Malik go down. But she knew she couldn't do that. She couldn't let any of them go. It had to be her. If Sonja fell to her death during a rescue attempt, she had to be the one to shoulder that burden.

"No," she said, putting a hand on his shoulder. "I appreciate the offer, but I'll be going."

"Another aftershock and the whole thing could come apart," Brian cautioned. "Or maybe even worse, crash back together. There's no point risking your life too...for her."

Malik stepped in front of Brian. "What the hell does that mean?" he hissed. "Her life is not important? Why? Because she is gay? Is that your point, you bigot?"

Brian shoved him away. "It's nothing to do with that! What do I care about that, you asshole?" He shoved him again, harder, causing Atka to growl menacingly. Brian was unfazed. He took a step closer to Malik, scowling into his face. "My problem with you has nothing to do with that. After all, Jordan's gay too, and she's the one whose life I'm worried about." Brian shook his head in disgust. "God! Is there no end to the ways you think of yourself as special!"

Suddenly Jordan realized what had brought Malik and Sonja together. She was stunned that she hadn't seen it before. Malik tensed, looking like he was about to spring at Brian. She stepped between them.

"Stop it!" she commanded. "We don't have time for this. I'm going down there and you guys need to work as a team. I'm counting on that." She motioned to the group. "Everybody stay off the ice! Brian, you're on the winch. Malik, you stay on the rim and relay instructions to him. Julie, you're in charge of equipment. I'm going to take a safety line down and get that around her first, then we'll get her into a harness and pull her up."

While Jordan got harnessed, she tried not to think about the horrible possibility that Sonja wouldn't make it. That won't happen, she assured herself, remembering what she had recently told Dr. Lund about Pippa's dream. *Sometimes believing is sufficient to make it true.* Jordan had never been good at believing anything that wasn't a proven fact, but this was one of those situations where there was so much at stake she found it nearly impossible not to fall back on a different kind of belief. She closed her eyes and repeated silently: *She'll make it.*

As her harness was cinched tight, she scanned the sky for a sign of a helicopter, but there was nothing. No cavalry coming over the hill.

Malik continued to speak to Sonja in a soothing voice. "Jordan is coming in," he told her. "She is coming to get you. Stay still. Stay quiet."

Jordan was lowered over the edge and slowly began to descend, using an ice ax and the crampons on her boots to stabilize herself. At the sound of creaking in the upper wall, she froze and momentarily held her breath, waiting for the entire thing to collapse. Now inside the glacier, she noticed the air had become noticeably colder and each of her breaths created a small cloud of steam in front of her face. It was like dropping into a freezer. The ice groaned and creaked, each tiny sound rumbling through the fissure.

She looked up at her worried students. She wished Kelly were there among them because Kelly's face would be full of confidence and encouragement and love. Kelly would believe in Jordan and she would be able to see something that none of the others could see, that Jordan was terrified. Because of that, her belief would mean more than anyone else's.

She didn't know if she could keep herself from being overwhelmed by panic. The main thing was not to look down. She would pretend she was climbing down just a few feet, that there was a solid bottom directly below her. She could believe that, she hoped, if she didn't look.

As she descended deeper into the chasm, a part of her, the cool scientific part, took in the blue frozen beauty of the glacier with a sense of wonder. For years she had studied ice, but this was the first time she had been in the heart of a glacier.

Experiencing its power and immensity with such immediacy, she felt a deep sense of awe.

It was only a few minutes, but it was a long, tense few minutes, before she reached Sonja. She slipped the ax into a loop on the harness and let herself hang free a few feet above Sonja. She willed herself not to look past Sonja's perch into the depths of the crevasse below, but to fix her gaze on Sonja, who knelt in a ball, bent over her knees, her teeth visibly chattering.

"Don't stand up," Jordan said quietly. "Don't move anything you don't have to. Any movement could cause a fracture. I'm going to hand you a rope. Put it over your head and around your waist before we go any further."

Jordan gently lifted the looped end of the rope from her shoulder. Just then a section of the wall opposite broke off with a sharp crack and plunged down, crashing and shattering into glassy shards on its way. Taken off guard, Jordan's eyes followed it and she found herself staring down into the black, bottomless depths beyond her feet. She kicked involuntarily, hitting nothing, and her stomach lurched as she imagined herself falling all the way down, hundreds of feet, to the bedrock, her body shattered by the impact and entombed in the ice for all time. Panic tightened her throat. She was unable to look away from the void below. It was like a yawning mouth with ferocious ice teeth waiting to swallow her, its strange, echoing voice, deep and menacing, rising up all around her. Beads of sweat broke out on her forehead as her skin went cold. She thought she heard her name. The chasm was calling to her. "Jordan," it whispered. "Jordan."

"Jordan, are you okay?"

She wrenched her eyes from the pit to see Sonja watching her with concern.

"Take the rope," Jordan instructed. "Don't look down and try to stay calm." She knew she was talking to herself as much as anybody.

Sonja reached one arm above her head and Jordan aimed carefully, tossing the rope into her waiting hand. She slowly slipped it over her body, then cinched it around her waist, all the while keeping her legs and feet still.

Jordan swallowed hard. "Good. You're doing great." She looked up at Malik on the rim. "Take up the slack on her line," she said. "Not too taut."

The situation had just gotten significantly more hopeful, Jordan told herself. As long as there were no aftershocks and no ice came down on their heads, at least the danger of falling had been averted.

"Harness," Jordan called up to the rim.

Julie slipped a second harness over the side and lowered it smoothly down to Jordan's waiting hand.

"Now stand up," she said to Sonja, keeping her voice soft and unruffled. "Keep hold of the safety line with both hands. If anything goes wrong, you'll want to keep control."

Sonja hesitantly got to her feet. When she stood fully upright, she reached one hand out to take hold of the harness, her arm trembling. The harness was just out of her reach.

"You'll have to take a step closer," Jordan urged.

Sonja was clearly afraid to move and Jordan didn't blame her. She took a moment to work up the nerve, then took one tentative step forward. She reached for the harness again, straining to reach it. Her fingers wrapped around one of the straps. As she shifted her weight, the shelf of ice she was standing on split with a loud thunderclap, giving way beneath her. She screamed, the harness tearing from her grasp. Swinging at the end of the safety line, she banged into the wall while ice rained down into the darkness below. Jordan's heart beat wildly, but somehow she managed not to look down.

She quickly anchored her crampons into the wall while Sonja dangled beneath her, gripping the rope to stabilize herself.

"Lower me so I can reach her!" Jordan ordered. She heard the alarm in her voice.

Brian quickly obeyed. As soon as Jordan was parallel with Sonja, she reached out and grabbed her with one arm, pulling her close up against her. Sonja clamped both arms around her in desperation, pulling her off the wall. The cable dug into the ice above them and dropped them several inches with a jerk.

Julie pulled up the useless second harness.

Sonja wrapped herself around Jordan as they twirled slowly in circles.

"I'm so sorry," Sonja cried, her eyes filling with tears. "I'm so sorry for everything."

"Shhh," Jordan said gently, touching their foreheads lightly together. "It's okay. You'll be okay. Now listen to me. I'm going to need my arms for this, so you have to get on my back. Can you do that?"

Sonja nodded tensely, one glistening tear dropping to her cheek.

The maneuver was awkward, but soon accomplished. With Sonja clinging to her from behind, Jordan was able to anchor herself to the ice with ax and crampons.

"Pull us up," she called to Malik.

They ascended smoothly at the end of the cable and when at last they reached the lip of the fissure, Malik grabbed Sonja from Jordan's back and lifted her over the edge to safety. She immediately sat down and started sobbing. Malik knelt beside her and tried to comfort her, wrapping her in a blanket. Brian and Julie each took hold of one of Jordan's arms and helped her out. All of them moved away from the ice onto solid ground.

Jordan lowered herself to a boulder and looked up at the sky, happy just to breathe.

Julie knelt beside her. "Do you want me to help you out of that?" she asked, indicating the harness.

"In a minute."

"You were awesome, Jordan." Julie's expression was full of admiration.

Jordan smiled, then felt tears welling up in her eyes. As the tears fell to her cheeks, all she could do was laugh because Julie's expression was one of complete horror, like, *Jordan's crying! What should I do?* This thought made her laugh even more. Julie patted her shoulder awkwardly, obviously concluding that Jordan, crying and laughing at the same time, had gone berserk.

"Jordan, what's wrong? Are you in shock?"

"No," Jordan managed, wiping her cheeks. "I'm just overwhelmed by the absurdity of life."

"What do you mean?"

"This is the closest I've ever been to looking death in the face," said Jordan. "I was terrified in there. But why should I be afraid of death when I've been afraid of life for so long?"

"Jordan, I don't understand. I think we need to get you back to camp and pour some whiskey in you." Julie unclipped the winch cable from the harness as Jordan sat mutely on her boulder, shaking her head in self-derision.

CHAPTER THIRTY-TWO

Pippa sat cross-legged on Kelly's bed, looking more chipper than she had earlier this afternoon, but still not her cheerful self. Kelly hoped she could fix that.

"I asked you over tonight to talk about Asa," Kelly said.

Pippa frowned. "You're going to tell me it was all a dream and I should forget about it."

Kelly sat beside her on the bed. "Not exactly."

"I know you don't believe it. Nobody does. Dr. Lund didn't believe it. Jordan didn't believe it."

"That's not entirely fair. You didn't give Jordan or Dr. Lund the complete story. Even so, Jordan did make the effort of finding you an archaeologist."

Pippa nodded. "I appreciate that. She's okay." She folded her arms across her chest. "Are you still in love with her?"

Kelly stuttered, eager to avoid any further conflict with Pippa.

"It's okay, you know," Pippa assured her. "I'm not jealous."

"You're not?"

"No. I think it's awesome. You two were made for each other and it's so romantic, your meeting here again after all that time."

"I'm glad to hear you say that, Pippa. Very mature of you."

"So are you still in love with her?" she asked again.

Kelly sighed. "Yes. But I don't think anything's changed. I think Jordan may be beyond my reach."

"If you love her, you shouldn't give up."

"I won't give up. I honestly think she cares for me, but there's something that holds her back."

Pippa looked at the floor and shook her head. "So both of us struck out today."

"Pippa," Kelly said, sympathetically, "Asa's story still lives in your memory."

Pippa nodded fatalistically. "Yes, but I really thought I was going to get some proof."

"Science might still have something to say about it."

"What do you mean?" Pippa asked. "There's no evidence to look at."

"Yes, there is. It's in you. Your DNA. Asa's genes, her children's genes and the genes of any Norse survivor who was assimilated into the native population still exist in contemporary, living Greenlanders. DNA, a wise woman once told me, contains the complete story of evolution. It takes dedicated work by patient scientists to tease out the pieces of the story. I have no doubt you have the patience and dedication to do that."

"Thanks. But a body would have been better."

Kelly laughed. She handed a manila folder to Pippa. "But until a body can be found, I think this may make you feel better."

Pippa opened the folder to see the photo of the cave runes. "This is a nice picture," she said, unmoved. "It's too bad Dr. Lund couldn't have seen the real thing. Thanks."

"I've written the translation on the back."

Pippa turned the photo over and read the transcription that Kelly knew by heart: *For Torben, son of Asa.*

Pippa stared and read it again. Then she looked up with eyes open wide in amazement. "Oh, my God!" she squealed. "Oh, my God! Is this really what it says?"

"Yes. Mrs. Arensen translated it for me. Apparently she's totally reliable on runes."

"I can't believe it!" Pippa looked as if she were going to jump up and down, her face one big joyful smile. "So it's true! It's all true! I knew it!"

Tears appeared in her eyes and she flung herself at Kelly, who accepted her hug.

"I'm so happy," Pippa said, her voice muffled by Kelly's shirt.

When she pulled away, she wiped the tears from her eyes, looked at the photo once again, then closed the folder and wriggled with glee. Kelly was happy to see her rapid change of mood. As Jordan had said, there are a lot more dangerous things to believe in. Let her have her dream. At least somebody should.

"This isn't scientific evidence," Pippa said, "but it's enough for me. And like you said, maybe someday I can prove it." She clutched the folder to her chest.

"I don't think you ever told me the end of Asa's story," Kelly said.

"She went to live with the Thule, she and her daughter and one of the boys from the village. They had a good life there. She survived and she was happy."

"I like that for the ending of a story. It sums up everything that matters in a simple phrase. She survived and she was happy. What more is there?"

"I have to get home," Pippa announced. "Thank you so much for this!"

"You're welcome."

Pippa darted to the open window, slinging one leg over the sill.

"I don't know why you don't use the front door," Kelly said in exasperation.

Pippa grinned and dropped down to the ground outside.

Kelly returned to her computer where she was working on her photo spread of the amazing glacial sinkhole. Chuck thought she could sell it to *National Geographic* or *Nature* or some other magazine and generously wanted her to take the byline. If she could pull it off, that kind of exposure would be quite a boost to her career.

Even though there wouldn't be much writing involved, the project was daunting. It was so hard to pick just three or four photos to include. How did Chuck do it? she wondered, staring at the screen. He could sit down and look at two dozen photos and boom, boom, boom, he'd made his choices. The picture she was viewing was one of those she'd taken from inside the sinkhole. It was gorgeous with its many hues of white and blue and the undulating patterns of the ice, a delicate sparkling sculpture with water pouring through it, drops catching shards of sunlight along the way. No denying this one was incredible. She scrolled to the next one, one of the stills she had captured from the video Chuck had taken. She wanted to use at least one photo that showed her inside the sinkhole. This one was her favorite. She was hanging freely at the end of the rope, her camera in one hand. She zoomed in to look at her face. She wasn't looking directly at the camera. She was looking up at the rim, slightly to the left where she knew Jordan had been standing. Her face was radiant, overwhelmed with all of the wonder of that moment, the exhilaration of this magnificent natural phenomenon and the joy she had felt to be sharing it with Jordan.

She was reminded of that photo from her fourth birthday, of how happy her mother looked in it. This photo was like that, capturing a moment before disillusionment. She shook her head. As she had said to Pippa, she wouldn't give up on Jordan. But she wasn't optimistic. If Greenland couldn't do it, what chance did Denver have?

Hearing a light rap at the door, she turned and was shocked to see Jordan in the doorway, dressed in a long-sleeved shirt and quilted red vest, smiling tentatively.

"Jordan!" She jumped up.

"Hi. Are you busy?"

"No. I mean, yes, but nothing that can't wait. What are you doing in town at this time of night?"

Jordan stepped into the room and shut the door behind her. "I came to see you." She looked nervous.

"Oh?" Kelly was completely taken off guard.

"I think I owe you an apology."

She took a step into the room, glancing at the floor and shuffling her feet.

"For what?" asked Kelly.

"For all the mixed signals I've been giving you. For the way I've manipulated your emotions and taken advantage of you."

Kelly was confused. It sounded like Jordan was talking about something other than the last two weeks.

"The only excuse I have," she continued, "is that you scare the shit out of me. You represent everything I've tried to protect myself from most of my adult life. Loss of control, irrationality, losing my head...over love."

Kelly was shocked by Jordan's sincerity. She knew how hard it was for her to open herself up emotionally. "And now?" she asked, taking a step toward her.

"Now," Jordan replied with a pained smile, "I realize how foolish I've been. I let some ancient mistake rule my life. I mean, what's the worst that can happen if you let yourself feel deeply? A broken heart? But what's the point of keeping it intact if you're never going to use it?" Jordan was emotional, her voice breaking. "I've been so afraid of humiliating myself, of people laughing at me. I was always afraid of losing their respect...like before with Marquette and everybody at Cornell. Like Sonja. She was mocking me. She had me in the palm of her hand. I mean, I thought she did. But, you know, it just doesn't matter anymore. Nobody cares. Nobody has cared for ages. Nobody but me. And the truth is, it didn't even matter to Sonja in the end. It's just as Malik said. She admires me...still. They all do. Me too. I feel so proud of myself. For standing up to her and for going into that pit. I was terrified of both things, but I did it anyway and it felt fantastic!" She gestured with her hands as she spoke, impassioned, but not entirely coherent. "That's why I'm here. Because of all that. Because fear has to be faced or it will strangle you. It will keep you from living your life."

"Jordan, I really don't know what you're talking about."

"I know. I'm rambling. Anyway, I just needed to say I'm sorry. Right away before I chickened out. And..." She averted her gaze and clenched a fist as if steeling herself. "God, Kelly, I've spent a decade bashing your heart and I don't expect it to have come through that without a few scars. But one thing I know about you is how generous and kind you are." She stepped closer and reached for Kelly's hand. "I really want to be with you...if you still want me."

Kelly gripped her hand more tightly, looking into her anxious eyes. She didn't fully understand what had happened to cause this emotional turnaround, but whatever it was, it had brought Jordan here with a sincere apology and a touching vulnerability. Maybe she wasn't expressing herself so well, but it didn't matter. Kelly could see it all in her eyes.

"Yes, Jordan, I do still want you."

She pulled her close and kissed her deeply, feeling the gratifying response of Jordan's eager mouth. When they pulled apart, a smile grew on Jordan's face.

"Thank you," she said quietly. "What a remarkable woman you've turned out to be."

Kelly pulled her in for another kiss, living the fantasy she had dreamed for so long. They stood close, rapturously exploring one another's mouths until Kelly's skin grew hot and desire coursed through her body. They were pressed so tightly against one another that she could no longer sense her boundaries. Jordan's kisses grew rough and desperate, her breath ragged. Kelly backed her against the door, kissing her face and neck.

"I want you so badly," Jordan breathed.

"That makes two of us." Kelly reached between them and fumbled with the button, then the zipper of Jordan's pants, and in a second would have had them over her hips if they hadn't been shot apart by the sound of Mrs. Arensen on the other side of the door, speaking in a startlingly loud and lucid voice.

"Dr. Westgate," she bellowed, "if you are staying at the hotel, the last shuttle will be coming in fifteen minutes."

Jordan rapidly zipped her pants and opened the door. "*Tak*, Elsa," she said, assuming a perfectly composed appearance. "I'll be right there."

Mrs. Arensen gave her a wary look before leaving. She turned back to Kelly guiltily, then stifled a giggle.

"She can't stand a closed door," Kelly said.

"Apparently I have to go. She's not going to leave us alone."

"I can come to the hotel later," Kelly offered.

"Unfortunately the hotel is full tonight. I already checked, figuring I would stay over because it's so late." Jordan shrugged. "Well, at least we had a moment. And I hope I've made it clear where I stand."

"Hmm," Kelly said playfully. "You see, I'm not sure you have. I think I'm still a bit confused about exactly what you're proposing."

"Oh, come on, Kelly!"

"Seriously, you've got fifteen minutes to explain yourself."

"You're a sadist."

Kelly grinned and waited. "Fourteen minutes."

Jordan relented and approached her, taking her loosely by the waist. "I don't need fourteen minutes. One will do. I'm crazy about you. I want you in my life. I think we could work terrific as a couple and I'm ready to try. More than ready. I'm ecstatic. The more I've thought about it, the more excited I am about the idea. I want to share my life with you."

"That'll do," Kelly quipped.

"I know you didn't really need me to say it. You're like a witch with your mind reading. A very lovely and beguiling witch." Jordan took a step closer so their bodies were touching. "Who has me hopelessly under her spell." She leaned in for a kiss just as a loud, warning voice came from somewhere near the front of the house: "Ten minutes!"

"Talk about a witch," Kelly remarked, frustrated. "I can't let you leave now!"

"There's no use," Jordan said, sighing. "I'll try to book a room for tomorrow night at the hotel so I can show you how I really feel about you."

"There may be another way," Kelly whispered. "If she thinks you've left, she won't pay any more attention to me tonight."

"I don't understand."

"There's a little-known back way into this joint."

* * *

A few minutes later, Jordan left the house, saying goodnight to Elsa at the door. She heard the click of the dead bolt as she stepped off the porch. Just like the old sorority house, she thought, walking to the street. And just like during those college days, she felt an air of adventure as she anticipated sneaking into a girl's room. And what a girl!

She couldn't have been happier. It had been so long since she had felt like this, full of hope and overrun with feeling. And more importantly, not resisting. Giving in to it. Welcoming it!

She turned left, taking the long way around to avoid the kitchen and Elsa's sitting room. She made her way along the side of the house, keeping an eye on the windows to make sure nobody was watching. It was nearly ten o'clock, but was still broad daylight outside. People were in the street enjoying the balmy evening. When she reached the back of the house she left the street and ducked behind the house, keeping close to the exterior wall. The other side of the house, the side of Kelly's room, faced the bay. Once she reached that side, she would be completely out of view of passersby.

As she rounded the corner, she stopped short, her nostrils filling with sweet, earthy smelling smoke as she nearly collided with Chuck. He stood leaning against the back of the house, a cigar in his hand, wearing an ancient looking Van Halen T-shirt, a Panama hat shading his eyes. He glanced casually her way, then he took a long puff before saying, "Evening, Jordan."

"What are you doing hiding behind the house?" she demanded in an emphatic whisper.

"This is where I always go to smoke. Can't smoke inside and there's a nice view of the bay from here." He smiled benignly. "Want a cigar? I remember you like this Nicaraguan brand."

"No, thank you." His manner bewildered her, but it wasn't out of character. Chuck was supremely even-keeled. Perhaps even more than she was.

"It's a beautiful night, isn't it?" he said.

"Aren't you going to ask me what I'm doing sneaking around outside your house?"

"Nope." He took another puff. "A nice cigar before bed really hits the spot for me. You know another thing that hits the spot? A shot or two of vodka. Puts me right to sleep."

What the hell? Jordan thought, frustrated. Are we just going to stand here all night chatting about cigars and booze? And how in the world was she going to carry out her plan now? There was no way she could crawl through Kelly's window with Chuck standing here watching.

"Vodka has the same effect on Elsa," he said nonchalantly. "Two shots and she's out for the night. Nope, nothing's going to wake her up when she's had a nip of vodka." He gave Jordan a wry smile. "That's put me in a mind to have a drink. Yep, just the thing." He knocked the ash off his cigar. "I think I'll ask the old gal to join me. Good night, Jordan."

He stepped past her, then paused and said, "By the way, it's the third window down."

CHAPTER THIRTY-THREE

Kelly closed the bedroom door with a barely audible click and shrugged off her robe. She hung it on a hook on the door, then slipped back into bed beside Jordan, who welcomed her with a warm embrace and an eager, lingering kiss.

"I listened at Mrs. Arensen's door," Kelly said quietly. "She's sound asleep, snoring like a bear. Hasn't heard a thing."

"Chuck got her tipsy," Jordan said. "That was decent of him."

"He's a good guy." Kelly pulled herself close up against Jordan's body, enjoying the soft, warm silkiness of her skin.

She was euphoric. It seemed she had waited all her life for this, for Jordan. She had longed for it, dreamed of it, never expecting it to become reality. But here she was, not only occupying her bed, but opening her heart with more honesty than either of them could have predicted. Jordan, too, had waited a lifetime for this, whether she would ever admit it or not. Kelly didn't need any more words to tell her how Jordan felt. She was exuberant and passionate, joyfully unrestrained. It felt so good, she confessed, to trust someone again.

"It's not going to be easy for both of us to sleep in this tiny bed," Kelly noted.

Jordan's open palm slid down the length of her back and across her buttock, halting there to let her nails bite teasingly into the flesh. She took a deep, contented breath before saying, "Then there's no point trying to sleep."

She rolled Kelly onto her back and straddled her, her eyes purposeful, her lean, athletic body hovering as she prepared to take her again. The blackout blinds on the windows created a dimness that colored their bodies a soft blue hue, as romantic as candlelight.

A thin smile appeared on Jordan's lips as her gaze worked its way over Kelly's body, leisurely taking her in. When she had had her fill of looking, she lowered herself and pressed her lips to Kelly's neck, kissing and gently biting. As Jordan's mouth and hands coaxed and caressed her, Kelly felt desire returning. If she wanted to make love all night long, it was okay with her. An entire night, even an entire lifetime, wouldn't be too much of Jordan after all the years she had spent wanting her.

Sucking and biting her nipples, Jordan spread Kelly's legs with her knees, then touched her with her fingers, lightly stroking. Kelly ran her hands across Jordan's back, gripping her skin as she felt the light touch of Jordan's fingers teasing her open. Her breath caught in her throat as she threw her head back on the pillow. Now two fingers, parting her more widely, finding no resistance, sliding with deliberation, up and down. Kelly's legs opened wider and Jordan slipped inside, pushing deep, then again, deeper. Kelly closed her eyes and moaned involuntarily, tense expectancy spreading through her body.

"You're so beautiful," Jordan breathed, her mouth skimming over Kelly's torso. "And so wet." Her teeth closed lightly on the tender skin over her hip bone, then her tongue made a path of cool moisture over her belly.

With each thrust, Kelly moaned deeply, her muscles taut, fully involved with Jordan's possession of her. The trembling waves of pleasure grew more profound and less bearable and Kelly felt she was on the verge of coming, though she had never come through penetration alone. She hung on the precipice in torment and ecstasy until the warm envelope of Jordan's tongue encircled her throbbing clit. A deep, unbidden and ragged moan escaped her lips.

When she went over the edge at last, she went hard with a shuddering cry and a release that took her by surprise. It was bottomless and purifying.

Her breath rapid, her skin hot, Kelly laid her head back on the pillow and quietly said, "Wow."

Jordan murmured contentedly, then released her hold and crawled up to lie face-to-face. "The second one's always best, don't you think?"

Kelly wrapped her arms and legs around Jordan possessively. "I think you're astonishing."

"Astonishing how?"

"Just not how I imagined it. In my youthful fantasies, I mean."

"No? How did you imagine it?" Jordan kissed Kelly's nose playfully.

"Well, mostly I imagined ways I could trick you in to it, since you so obviously weren't willing. Like drugging your coffee. But beyond that, my fantasies didn't go into much detail."

"They were chaste fantasies."

"Not exactly." Kelly laughed. "Let's not talk about my childish fantasies. This is so much better."

Jordan smiled and kissed her. "I guess I made a huge mistake letting you go all those years ago."

"No. You didn't make a mistake. You were right. I was too immature. I was too naïve and needy. My expectations were ridiculously out of bounds regarding love. My first serious relationship was a disaster and I blame myself for most of what went wrong."

"Then I'm lucky you've come back to me now. I get you at your best, when you're ready for the real thing."

Kelly reached for Jordan's hand between them. "Do you believe this is the real thing?" she asked hopefully.

"I do. Do you?"

Kelly squeezed her hand. "Jordan, I never stopped loving you. As far as I'm concerned, this is and always was the real thing."

Emotion softened Jordan's face, then her body relaxed as it molded itself into Kelly's. Her voice was a whisper, like a delicate, caressing breeze, as she said, "I love you too."

CHAPTER THIRTY-FOUR

It was one of those nights when the colors were perfect, the kind of night the midnight tour operators hope for, when the sun is low on the horizon, casting filtered light through a layer of thin clouds. The icebergs glowed pink and orange. Kelly hadn't seen such a beautiful night since her arrival. She sat beside Jordan on the veranda of the Disko Hotel drinking pinot noir. Their view of the bay was classic from this vantage point. Closer in, where the hotel's sled dogs were chained to the rocks, a puppy hopped from one dog to the next, trying to engage the indifferent adults in a game.

"I was hoping to see the northern lights," Kelly complained.

"You're not going to see them in summer with the sun up around the clock."

"How late would you have to stay to see them?"

"As soon as there's an actual night. In the fall. September. I wouldn't mind coming back in the winter someday. I think it would be thrilling." Jordan took a sip from her glass, looking up at the stars. "I've seen the northern lights in Alaska. The Inuit believed that the lights marked the entrance to the next world and that the souls of dead children danced and played there."

"That's a comforting idea."

"Yes. Definitely more poignant than our modern understanding: photons released by the collision of charged particles in the magnetosphere with atoms in the thermosphere." She lowered her gaze from the sky to smile warmly at Kelly.

"Not the same, is it?"

"No. But I think we can still look at it both ways. I think we can choose to interpret with our scientific mind or our romantic heart and experience the same sense of wonder as eons of humans did before us. I mean, look at the stars or the moon any dark night. We know what they are, but you feel awestruck anyway. It's hard-wired into us, to look up there and dream."

"I'm going to miss you," Kelly said sincerely.

"Me too, but it's only for a couple weeks. You'll barely have time to unpack before I show up at your door back home. But I'll miss you too. It's been such a wonderful time."

"To the best summer of my life," Kelly said, lifting her glass.

"And," Jordan proposed, "to all the best yet to come."

They touched glasses.

"Should I leave my window open tonight?" Kelly asked.

Jordan shook her head. "Not tonight."

"Oh," Kelly groaned. "Our last night and there won't be any hanky and panky?"

"Don't worry. There will be hanky and panky, my darling. I booked a room here in the hotel. No sneaking in through windows and struggling to be silent in a squeaky little bed so your landlady won't have a cow. Or sneaking down the hallway at two in the morning to use the bathroom."

"Not to mention how Chuck's turning poor Mrs. Arensen into an alcoholic helping to deflect her attention. She's convinced he's trying to seduce her with those nightly drinks."

Jordan smiled. "Tonight we'll have a comfortable suite with a private bath, a bottle of champagne and a sumptuous feast, just the two of us."

"Then what are we waiting for?"

"We're in no hurry." She waved a hand to indicate the view. "It'll be daylight for hours yet."

Kelly laughed. Jordan couldn't suppress a small snicker of her own.

"But seriously," she said, "we have all night. I'm determined to make it special."

"I don't think there's anything to worry about. Every night with you has been special."

Jordan reached over and took her hand. It was true, Kelly thought. It was like a dream and she was sorry to see it end, but they would begin a new phase back home. Not as exotic as a Greenland summer, but just as special, as long as they were together.

The door behind them flew open and Pippa burst onto the deck, her cheeks flushed.

"Hi, you guys!" she said, squeezing between their two chairs and laying one arm on each of their shoulders. "Don't worry, I'm not going to interrupt your romantic evening, but there's someone I want you to meet before Kelly leaves."

"Who is it?" Kelly asked.

Pippa leaned close to her ear and whispered, "I found her." Then she ran back through the doorway.

Kelly sat up with interest and turned her chair so she was facing the door. "I'm not entirely sure, but I think she's about to introduce us to a woman. As in, a girlfriend-type woman."

Jordan raised her eyebrows, clearly intrigued.

"This should be interesting," Kelly remarked. "Cross your fingers."

When Pippa reappeared, she led another girl by the hand. She was close to if not exactly Pippa's age, had flaming red hair and freckles, pale skin and pretty hazel eyes. She wore loose, faded jeans, and an oversized flannel shirt. She clutched Pippa's hand shyly and averted her eyes. Kelly couldn't suppress a cry of joy at the sight of them, two lovely young women, flush with the happiness of their new discovery: one another.

"This is Charming," Pippa announced. "She's Canadian."

"Charmian!" corrected the redhead indignantly. "You know my name is Charmian, Pippa."

"But Charming is my name for you," Pippa said melodramatically, "because I've waited so long, so very long for my Princess Charming. And now you've come." She held her free hand over her heart for a moment to emphasize the effect of her words, then said, "These are my friends Kelly and Jordan."

Kelly stood up and held out her arms to hug Charmian, who gratefully accepted. Jordan also hugged her, then invited them to sit down.

"We aren't staying," Pippa said. "We're going to the fireworks."

"Are there fireworks tonight?" Jordan asked.

"Yes. Nine o'clock."

"How can you have fireworks with the sun up?" Kelly asked.

"Not much choice," Pippa said matter-of-factly. "Do you want to come?"

"We have other plans," Jordan said with a wry smile.

Pippa's eyes widened briefly, then she turned to her girlfriend with a knowing look. Charmian giggled.

"Nice to meet you," Charmian said as Pippa nudged her toward the door.

They watched the girls duck back inside, but in mere seconds Pippa reappeared, making no attempt to control her glee.

"What do you think?" she asked. "Isn't she cute?"

"She's darling!" Kelly agreed. "Where'd you find her?"

"That's the crazy part. She was here all along. I mean, not all along. They moved here like two years ago. I saw her around but never talked to her. I didn't know she was Canadian. I thought she was Danish. Red hair, freckles." She spoke rapidly and breathlessly. "She's a year behind me. The other day when I went to the library, I saw her sitting between the shelves reading a lesbian romance. In English! I recognized the cover because I'd read it too. I don't think the librarian knows it's a lesbian romance. Or…" She leaned in closer and lowered her voice. "I've had my suspicions about the librarian."

"Well," shrugged Jordan. "A librarian. Of course!"

"Charmian was afraid to check the book out," Pippa continued breathlessly, "so she was reading it right there in the library. It took all my nerve and my heart was pounding, but I walked right up to her and said, 'Hi, Charmian. How's the book?'" Pippa doubled over laughing. "She was freaking out, thinking she'd gotten caught, until I told her about me. I mean about me having read that book too. Then everything changed."

"I'm very happy for you, Pippa," Kelly said sincerely.

"Thanks. Me too. I'll come by in the morning like I said to drive you and Chuck to the airport. Bye." Pippa was gone again in a heartbeat.

Kelly chuckled. "I have to say it makes me really happy to see her with a girlfriend. An appropriate girlfriend."

Jordan smiled her understanding and stood, extending a hand toward Kelly. "Are you ready to retire to our lair?"

Kelly took her hand just as the sound of a loud pop went off, sounding like a gun firing.

"It's the fireworks," Jordan reminded her.

"Oh, right. Fireworks with the sun shining. Seems strange. What are they celebrating, do you think?"

"Maybe they're honoring our rapturous last night together."

Kelly laughed. "Yeah, right. That must be it."

Jordan opened the door and held it for her. "But they needn't have bothered."

"Why not?" Kelly asked, pausing in the doorway.

"Because we'll be making our own fireworks."

Kelly gave Jordan a quick kiss before entering the hotel lobby, happily anticipating their romantic night and all of their blissful days yet to come. They would be fabulous together, Kelly knew, because Jordan had always needed someone to validate her worth, and Kelly had never known anyone more worthy of her love, respect and devotion.